I0684294

PRAISE FOR
J. DANIEL STONE

"Stone knows where your pulse point exists and is relentless in toying with your already fractured nerves!"
—*Hellnotes*

"Wickedly beautiful and poetic prose; nightmarish terror reminiscent of a Clive Barker fever dream. Stone's characters are filled with love and rage, their emotions resonating off the page with the vibe of a heavy metal funeral dirge."
—*This Is Horror*

"I really can't stress enough how much I enjoy Stone's writing. Lush, evocative . . . [he] does an excellent job in transporting readers into his settings."
—*The Horror Bookshelf*

"Stone's ultraviolence and lush writing recall 90's-era horror."
—*Horror News Net*

"Deep, darkly visceral."

—**Dark House Press**

"J. Daniel Stone's *I Can Taste The Blood* is really quite brilliant. A dark, grimy tale that will leave you needing a shower when finished. I have to be honest when I say that [after reading] I couldn't stop thinking about this story. Something about this story just struck a nerve I guess—the sign of a great piece of writing. I'd go as far to say that it is one of the best novellas I have read this year!

—*Ginger Nuts of Horror* (Adrian Shotbolt)

PRAISE FOR *BLOOD KISS*
BY J. DANIEL STONE

"*Blood Kiss* is a powerful book that sticks with you. Raw and subversive, it presents horrific imagery in a stark, unflinching manner that keeps us turning the pages. It's a nihilistic romp through the underground art world [that] captures the outsider energy that attracted so many of us to not just watch and read horror, but make it a lifestyle."

—*Rue Morgue* (Monica S. Kuebler)

"So many fierce images, so immediate and propulsive! There's huge energy in *Blood Kiss*—the energy of a performance, when the audience and the people on stage feed from one another, push each other past all boundaries, together."

**—Kathe Koja, author of *The Cipher*
and *Christopher Wild***

"It's the art-scene, it's the death-scene, the sex-scene . . . the shadows, the madness, the mania. Nightmare, but mostly bone-wide awake. Stone makes it feel like you are the characters . . . in all those scenes. And it's tempting to say, 'Keep an eye on this guy.' Because he's young. Because this is only his second book. But you'd only say something like that to mean one day he's gonna do something great. The thing is, he already has. It's right here. *Blood Kiss* is refreshing as hell. In a field where most are trying to out-thrill one another, Stone is riffing, philosophizing, writing . . . out loud."

**—Josh Malerman, author of *Bird Box*
and *Black Mad Wheel***

"Stone's writing does not skimp on the poetic flourishes, deep philosophical ruminations, or not-so-subtextual subtexts. There is deviance and intoxication and un-shakable imagery and cataclysms and no shortage of haunting moments. A welcome respite from the mania for utilitarianism currently plaguing genre writing. This is challenging work from an author clearly chomping at the bit to screw with convention and preconceptions. Even at it's most brutal—and *Blood Kiss* will goddamn bloody well disturb you at times—it is a paradoxically lovely read."

—*Fangoria*

"Like Poppy Z. Brite, dark and sensuous and filled with artsy characters on the fringes of society. Like Clive Barker, even darker and viscerally sexual, where blood and love come together to paint a disturbing picture. But even more, *entirely* J. Daniel Stone, with a voice like no other new writer I've read. He drips this novel, *Blood Kiss*, with a bleak, disturbing sensuousness that oozes from the pages. Stone makes you feel the pain that goes into art—whether music or painting—and the pain that art causes. He'll make you believe that art has a life of its own—dark and dreadful. And love . . . oh love hurts."

—Bram Stoker nominated author John F.D. Taff

"J. Daniel Stone's *Blood Kiss* is a chilling marriage of Clive Barker's vision and Kathy Acker's style. Stone writes with a wicked carnality that is frightening and frighteningly sensual. *Blood Kiss* will be in your head long after you've finished reading it."

—Bracken MacLeod, author of *Mountain Home* and *Stranded*

"Be warned, J. Daniel Stone writes with a razor blade and he aims to cut you on the very fist page. Stone allows his unleashed id to dance through the pages of *Blood Kiss* as he explores interwoven themes of lust and inspiration in the lives of struggling young artists in New York City. Haunting, visceral and flowing with equal parts poetic prose and madness. A satisfying work from a writer of increasing power."

—John C. Foster, author of *Mister White*

"*Blood Kiss* is a memorable novel bursting with vivid prose, incredible and original characters and enough darkness to cause an eclipse. At times I was unable to put this book down as Stone dragged me deeper and deeper into a New York art scene where the merging of two different art forms creates something totally new, unique, exciting and sexy. It's an immersive reading experience, and one of the most original dark fiction books I have come across in recent time."

—Beavis the BookHead

"*Blood Kiss* is more an experience than a book. By some kind of sleight-of writer's-hand, Stone does more than simply create a world, he leads us from earth to dark "other sides" and back with ease, as if it were all a simple matter of taking the G train between Manhattan and

Brooklyn. And when Stone gets you to the end, well, let me just say that *Blood Kiss* may give you that elusive bookgasm you didn't know was possible."

—Erik T. Johnson, author of *Yes Trespassing*

"Everything J. Daniel Stone publishes breaks new ground, but *Blood Kiss* leaves gigantic furrows of earth in its wake. It would sit comfortably on the shelf between Barker and Kiernan, and it should definitely be on your shelf."

—*Ginger Nuts of Horror* (Shane Douglas Keene)

"J. Daniel Stone's writing possesses a mesmerizing, silken music. He's one of those rare storytellers who can draw you along irresistibly and thrill you with his artistry at the same time. His scrutiny of love and desire is fearless. *Blood Kiss* is a haunting journey through the dark labyrinth of the wounded heart, where obsession can fuel both creativity and destruction. Terrifying, beautiful and utterly unique, it will leave you hungry for more from this brilliant young author."

—Stephen T. Vessels, Thriller Award nominated author of *The Mountain & The Vortex*

Praise for
J. Daniel Stone's
The Absence of Light

"*The Absence of Light* is lush and lyrical . . . a jangled and disturbing book that seeks to transcend through rituals and incantations. This book is highly recommended for anyone who wants dark prose that seeks to transgress boundaries though not designed to appeal to people who want streamlined plots, transparent prose, or simple stories. First novels are often ragbags where writers try to explain life, so Stone has clearly come across more dark wisdom than most people."

—*Hellnotes* (Geoffrey H. Goodwin)

"J. Daniel Stone is a gifted young writer, capable of some of the most beautiful sentences about the most horrid things. [*The Absence of Light*] combines horror, the art world, the music world, the paranormal world, the young, displaced hipster world . . . and combines it all into a heady, trippy story that is sad at times, powerfully dark at others. I didn't just enjoy the book; I enjoyed the act of reading it."

—John F.D. Taff, Bram Stoker nominated author of
The End in All Beginnings

"From the first few pages I was swept into a dark punky world of nightclubs, Jägermeister, craft beer, ghosts, and music. [Stone knows] what it feels like to grow up "different"—different being, queer, goth, fat, loser, outcast, whatever you want to call it. To me [*The Absence of Light*] became instantly important because it represents the power of so-called "outsider" fiction and it is with this power that this book will call its' readers home."

—*Drunk in a Graveyard*

"*The Absence of Light* manages to walk the fine line between the suffocatingly eerie and tear jerking beautiful. J. Daniel Stone gives his characters life in a bleak world resonating with song . . . which you will never want to leave."

—Jonathan Moon, author of *Heinous* and *Stories To Poke Your Eyes Out To*

". . . one part ghost story, one part alternative lifestyle exploration that explores the themes of identity, loss, and the power of art through poetic language."

—Fanboy Comics

Lovebites & Razorlines

Collected Stories

J. Daniel Stone

Lovebites & Razorlines
Copyright © 2017 by J. Daniel Stone

Cover art © 2017 Matt Edginton

Illustrations for "Be Quiet and Drive," "Basement Story 2006," "Lovebites &
Razorlines," "Unveiled," and "Ecdysis" © 2017 Luke Spooner
(carrionHouse.com)

Illustrations for "Metamorphosis," "What Makes a Shadow," "Wormhole,"
and "The Tunnel Record" © 2017 Matt Edginton

Illustrations for "Alternative Muses," "Dark, Fire, Kiss," and "The Long Lost
and Forgotten" © 2017 Matt Andrew (verboten-valley-art.com)

Illustration for "Devil Made of Crystal" © 2017 Chris Taggart

All rights reserved. No part of this publication may be reproduced,
distributed, or transmitted in any form or by any means, including
photocopying, recording, or other electronic or mechanical methods,
without the prior written permission of the publisher, except in the case
of brief quotations embodied in critical reviews and certain other
noncommercial uses permitted by copyright law.

Published by Villipede Publications

Villipede Publications
villipede.com

Special discounts are available on quantity purchases. For details, contact
the publisher.

Printed in the United States of America

ISBN-13: 978-0692980774
ISBN-10: 0692980776

These stories are works of fiction. Names, characters, places, events and
incidents are either the products of the author's imagination or used in a
fictitious manner. Any resemblance to actual persons, living or dead, or
actual events is purely coincidental.

"Metamorphosis" by J. Daniel Stone © 2013 originally appeared in *Ominous Realities* from Grey Matter Press

"Be Quiet and Drive" by J. Daniel Stone © 2013 originally appeared in *Icarus: The Magazine of Gay Speculative Fiction* from Lethe Press

"What Makes a Shadow" by J. Daniel Stone © 2016 originally appeared in *Turn to Ash Volume 1* from Turn to Ash Media

"Alternative Muses" by J. Daniel Stone © 2014 originally appeared in *Tales From The Lake Volume 1* from Crystal Lake Press

"Basement Story 2006" by J. Daniel Stone © 2012 originally appeared in *Monster Notes* from Unspoken Water, reprinted in *Cellar Door* as "The Virtuoso"

"Lovebites & Razorlines" by J. Daniel Stone © 2012 originally appeared in *Queer Fish Volume 2* from Pink Narcissus Press

"Wormhole" by J. Daniel Stone © 2013 originally appeared in *Dark Visions Volume 2* from Grey Matter Press, reprinted in *DREAD (The Best Horror of Grey Matter Press)*

"Unveiled" by J. Daniel Stone © 2014 originally appeared in *Handsome Devil* from Prime Books

"Dark, Fire, Kiss" by J. Daniel Stone © 2017, original to *Lovebites & Razorlines*

"The Long Lost and Forgotten" by J. Daniel Stone © 2017, original to *Lovebites & Razorlines*

"Devil Made of Crystal" by J. Daniel Stone © 2014 originally appeared in *Of Devils and Deviants* from Crowded Quarantine Publications

"The Tunnel Record" by J. Daniel Stone © 2014 originally appeared in *Darkness ad Infinitum* from Villipede Publications

"Ecdysis" by J. Daniel Stone © 2017 original to *Lovebites & Razorlines*

To the memory of suffering,
though you'll always be there . . .

And also to Matt Edginton,
for without his artistic eye and belief in my work,
this collection wouldn't have been possible.

Author Foreword

Foreword by John F.D. Taff

Afterword by Dona Fox

Author Foreword

Like most writers, I'm starting this off with a personal complaint: I need to find the strength, i.e. the right head-space, to get this written. I've always found an "author foreword" to be icky, slightly pretentious, even narcissistic. But they are filled with the fun facts, things that you'd never know, or perhaps, would not want to know. So here's fact # 1: *Lovebites & Razorlines* takes its name from a Glassjaw song, and to state the obvious, they're one of my favorite bands.

So, you ask, what exactly is inside the pages of *Lovebites & Razorlines*? The collected stories are dark, sometimes demented and often twisted, but they all have one thing in common: Love and Hate. Such is why a title like *Lovebites & Razorlines* is more than befitting: it is necessary. Without love—without losing it—we'd never appreciate what we once had; we'd never learn. And hate . . . a strong word as they say . . . hate has everything to do with love. Hate is Love's twin sister, as Death is to Dream, or Desire to Despair, Delirium to Destruction. *The Endless*. Remember them?

I digress.

These stories were written a long time ago (and my opinion of them has varied over the years), but nevertheless they are *part of me*. They are the dissertations and the theses of various phases of my life. They are love letters for the good times and journal entries for the bad. These are the fears that once lived inside my head, mixed with my own personal decadence, philosophies and judgments at a certain age. Time capsules of long dead days.

Friendships dissolved, relationships were ruined and reality was awry during the writing process. But that's what makes these *my stories*. Normally at this point in an "author foreword" I should go into a bit of detail about the art of writing, but I don't think that's necessary. There are plenty of books written about "writing" (not saying I've ever agreed with them, as the process is just too personal to make universal) so the point is moot.

What I will say is that for me a story always starts with an image, an inkblot in my mind just waiting for me to discover it. From that point I just take off. No plotting (how boring), no character outlines (do these even work?), no goals (pity the writer who is in this business for a "goal"). Once the pen hits papers, and especially when fingers tap the keyboard, there's no going back.

I must also add, as even though it's blatantly obvious, that every story in this collection is set inside New York City (the place I was born and raised) except one story that takes place in San Francisco (inspired after I spent 5 days there for my 26th birthday) and another that takes place in a fictional town I created in my first novel *The Absence of Light*.

If it's not already obvious, I'm truly, unrepentantly in love with my city. From Brooklyn, to Queens, Manhattan to The Bronx. Yes, I'll reluctantly even say Staten Island. For me, New York City is endless potential for stories. Even though the landscape has changed dramatically during the most impressionable years of my life, it still is the city of art and soul, despite its current corporate appearance. No matter where I go, I still feel the familiar electric . . . tiny sparks of inspiration. No other city except Madrid has done that to me.

As you go through each story, I provided a brief reason as to why I wrote it, or what was going on in my life at the time (which is much better than stuffing it into an "author foreword"). You should also note that the stories collected here were written, in most cases, long before they were sold. I don't know if that means they weren't any good, or if that means my brand of fiction is just unpopular. Probably a bit of both. And I'm even more tempted to believe that these are just crappy stories in general as I feel that I'm a different writer today. I see so many flaws . . . flaws of youth, of fiery passion, of spontaneity. You won't really find any discipline in these pages. But I think that explains something important about me as a person, as a writer, and about the kind of things I was going through at that time in my life. I write the kinds of stories I want to read. Always.

These tales can't be separated from my eternal being— even though the parts of my soul from which they were born are long gone—as they are/were important for my growth not just as a writer, but as a human being. Today, I'm writing to you as a freshly turned 30-year-old man, but you will find in these pages the teenage me, the me of my early twenties, the me of my mid-twenties. Maybe you can spot the shift, maybe not. Doesn't matter.

Peace in Rage,
J. Daniel Stone

New York City
April 2017

Foreword

So let's talk first about *passion*, shall we?

I'm not talking about how you pine over *that* boy in Civics class or conjure lewd (and perhaps physically impossible) carnal scenarios featuring Dolores in accounting or maybe even your spouse, although those are the types of things you undoubtedly think of when you're confronted with the word *passion*. No, I'm talking about the things that drive your life, the things that make you want to get up in the morning, shit, shower and shave (or whatever ablutions you make to begin your day), and slog through the various mundanities of your life. Whether it's your kids or money or selling stock or collecting stamps or watching birds—or, yes, even sex—there's something that moves your gears, gets your heart beating, gets you fired up.

That's the *passion* I'm referring to.

That's the *passion* Dan writes about.

Oh, there's plenty of sex, to be sure. For what's passion without a little sex?

For J. Daniel Stone (or his *real* name, which, if you know him even a little bit, if you've ever heard his speaking voice, suits him *perfectly*), it's art. Specifically, writing. I think that, if you don't know this now, you'll definitely feel it by the time you're finished with the thirteen passionate stories in this, Dan's first collection.

Peace in Rage is Dan's signature line, much as mine is *King of Pain*. I'm sure Dan looks at *Peace in Rage* sometimes and shakes his head, much as I sometimes do with my *name de marketing*. A little pretentious, eh? Sure, but also, very, very fitting, for just as Dan is filled with passion, some of that is enmired in rage. Rage boils over through the pages of his stories, draws blood in many cases. Art, says Dan, should inspire passion and passion often breeds rage. Sometimes, the heat generated by whatever it is that grinds your gears has to go *somewhere*. Here, in this collection, plenty of characters find out that *somewhere* involves blood and darkness and death.

For Dan, it goes into his stories.

There are a lot of comparisons made about Dan. "He's the next Clive Barker" or "He's sort of like Poppy Z. Brite." Sorry to say, I've made some of these myself. It's annoying, for sure, especially for the author. But, hell, that's what people do with anything new. It's a way to describe something indescribable, by tying it to something known. I understand that, and I'm sure Dan does, too, even as he rolls his eyes. So, I won't try to describe Dan in this way . . . *again*.

Instead, I will tell you that there's a freshness in Dan's writing that I find just as appealing today as I did when I came across his first novel, *The Absence of Light,* nearly five years ago now. An immediacy, a visceralness that makes his words leap from the page and bitch-slap you. One of the qualities of Dan's writing that appeals to me most is his poetic use of language, the lushness of his sentences, the attention to word choice and how it sounds in a line.

This appeals to me because it's what I aspire to, as well. Even in today's world (Ugh. Hate to bring that up.), words *mean* something. They say things. They paint pictures. And Dan knows how to do this. His words are evocative when they need to be; soothing when they need to be. Filled with rage when they need to be.

They draw blood when they need to.

So, here's what we're *not* going to do here. We're not going to talk about the stories individually. You're going to read them, just as I have. You're going to be swept up in them, as I was. You're going to be disturbed by them, as I was. You're going to not just read Dan's *Peace in Rage*, you're going to *feel* it. Whether it's in the interplay between Rez and Delilah in the haunting "Metamorphosis" or the two pain junkies in "Alternative Muses," or the . . .

Well, there, you almost had me talking about the stories!

Read them already, and get a taste of how Dan sees the world around us, the decaying, decadent, sensual, terrifying, beautiful world. See how it fills him with passion. Experience Dan's rage.

Then, well . . . go make some art yourself! Dan has . . . and will continue to, I expect.

And hope.

John F.D. Taff
August 2017

"Metamorphosis," written in 2011, came to me while riding the 7 train late at night on my way back from seeing A Perfect Circle two different nights during a very humid July. It's one of those stories that began with an image and took control from that point on. The impetus was that rainy ride where, half-asleep, I gazed as a punky kid drew in permanent marker on the seat what looked like to me a skeleton with wings, or the mythical Mothman.

This is an adjunct tale to my first novel *The Absence of Light*.

METAMORPHOSIS

Two a.m. on the Number Seven train, flickering fluorescence, ghouls of the city tucked into bed, and Delilah felt like a little girl again. Her mind and body were lost within the sights of New York, a concrete jungle of no redemption, no sorrow. Everything was so new, so *surreal*.

The train hummed on, soulless. It passed dark and dirty towns where the seldom person walked, where graffiti and blood was still wet as orgasm and drug dealing had a half-life. Neon puttered poorly on every corner; blackouts marked the poorest areas. The smell of fire was the universal sign that you've slipped into a place too many levels below the poverty line.

"How about a tune?"

"Not now, Rez. I'm watching the towns come alive and die . . ."

"I'm sick of New York. Nothing excites me anymore."

"Oh, no you don't. Please don't start that 'I'm bored of everything crap.' I have a head—"

Too late. Rez vice-gripped the Warlock and polluted the airwaves. Sweaty dark hair mangled his sharp face and fluorescent light skidded across his multicolored nails as the rhythm of a city boy inspired by night spit melodies like stones. Long pale fingers raped the guitar for power chords and pinch harmonics. Rez had only been playing guitar for a month, so his riffs were rusty. But if he played any longer Delilah thought she might shove him onto the unforgiving tracks.

"Come on, Rez, you're butchering my music," Delilah pleaded.

"Are you going to beat me toothless?"

"Not the brother I love. Never that."

"So you'll listen to another?"

"No. But I'll show you how it's done."

If Delilah thought about her one central passion, it lay within the mayhem inspired by music. If she thought about Rez's best suit, his most natural ability, it lay within the written word: short stories and vignettes. But he was always open to trying a new artistic medium to extinguish whatever demon polluted his head at the moment. Because of this, Delilah knew that his guitar playing would never be truly sharpened; his laughable riffs and choking scales would forever haunt her. With that thought, Delilah prepared to remedy his poor playing, bring soul back into it. And so she let her voice fly like a phantom, like a silver river.

> *I've seen pleasure and felt sound*
> *They say darkness is the absence of light*
> *But without the light everything is alright*
> *The twin stars will shine bright*
> *They still believe in me tonight*

Delilah was the lead singer of Electric Orchid, a band whose underground sound ravaged airwaves as if it were the illegitimate child of Black Sabbath and Nine Inch Nails. She knew that if the rest of Electric Orchid were here now to witness how Rez brutalized their music, they would've spit beer in his face and forfeited the glittery darkness of the stage, the golden crescendo of keyboard and guitar.

"Good show," Rez said, sipping a local pumpkin ale as he put away the Warlock. "Ah . . . the spirit of the season."

"Season or not, this falafel tastes like fried chick pea ass."

"Better for the ride into Manhattan."

"Yeah . . . I've had enough of Queens," Delilah whispered.

Just before Forty-Second Street and Grand Central Terminal there came the sound of electric snapping and metal crunching. The train came to a grueling halt, throwing Delilah to the other side of her seat. Rez spilled his beer and dropped the Warlock. The conductor's robotic voice complained of technical difficulties, that it could be an hour or so before the train began to move again.

Delilah stared out one of the windows to see what had gone wrong, her reflection the ghost-glow of deep-sea lanterns, her lipstick too dark on a young face, eyes so bleak they clouded the windows to her soul. *GrAnDmA DEATH WUZ HeRe!* was scratched into the plate glass, but Delilah looked past it, through the dark jungle of her dangling dreadlocks, and let her mind travel the indeterminable dark.

She saw wet eyes stir beneath pink lids, pale scales pulse incandescently, and the flutter of ghostly wings. Despite the warning signs about the electrically charged tracks, Delilah was already opening the back door. Before her nothing but darkness, stretched and dense as tar, pricked by pitiful underground light bulbs, but it seemed safe to go exploring.

"There's a small gap between the train and the tunnel walls. We could follow it out," she said to Rez.

"We could get fried by the third rail," Rez retorted with a sly smile.

"Just follow my lead."

The air inside the station was hot and thick as syrup. It made the tiles shimmer, clogged the pores of your skin and ran dirty sweat into your eyes. Pitiful fans failed to cool you down. Sweat was part of life this far into the terminal, as were the rats grown to the size of no return. Always something in New York. Always a show to catch.

A photographer was taking photos of the empty train station just as the two kids were regurgitated from the darkness of the tunnel. Hot waves of light glinted; a pirouette of rainbow energy formed a patina across the dilapidated station. Pictures were how he catalogued the world, its maledictions and misfortunes, the only way he could test reality and try to break through it with his own eyes. For what you see is what you get as they say, but in his mind fact and fiction were one.

What if there *was* more than just the now? What about the auras, the unlimited or ultimate reality? Photography was about letting the senses take control, to be patient as Buddha and watch sound metamorphose into color and ride it into oblivion, to taste the lushest sights, to feel all of the damp and wretched smells of the world.

But chatter filled the quiet station now: two souls bent upon the conversation of trains and music and debauchery. He saw the boy's tight black clothes that made him blend in with the tunnel, saw the girl's pale flesh swathed in fishnet and her snaky hair. The way his thin body jittered, the boy looked drained of energy, in need of delicious sleep. But sleep was for the weak, he presumed, by the way they carried on arguing and drinking beer from paper bags like vagabonds, like drifters, like soul-suckers. They were both covered in a thick, black dust. Train dust. Maybe insects. It was plausible, but they could've given a fuck.

"Help me up," the boy said. "I'm your passenger."

The pale, snake-haired girl was already on the platform, rolling over onto her knees and out of breath as she hauled up the guitar case. What manner of things had diseased the platform was of no matter to her. She would lick the ground and not be remorseful, would taste the piss and dirt of the rats, the countless toxicities that have marked the ground here. This girl was tough inside and out. He could feel it.

It's like you never had wings, two small voices whispered.

"Hey, Delilah! You gonna help or are you waiting for the Seven to squash me?"

"Always gotta bail you out, Rez. When you gonna learn to take care of yourself?"

With the last of her strength, Delilah pulled Rez up to the platform. Her black tattoos bulged—bats flying over a dastardly moon and some kind of squiggly roadmap. Beneath lay a tracery of raw, pink flesh. Razor scars. Delilah lit a Camel and smoked it without a care in the world. Rez sat against the guitar case and pulled out a tiny flask, curling up with a beat-up copy of a biography about a notorious beat poet.

"Now what?" Delilah asked him.

"We wait. Or we keep walking."

"Hope there's enough in that flask for me. Good for energy," Delilah cracked a nefarious smile.

"Jäger. Your fave."

Delilah took a long swig and then cocked her ears to the sibilant silence. "Hear anything, Rez? Anything at all?"

"I hear nothing but sweet music," Rez said, kissing the air like a drunkard.

"Yes you can. You always do."

Rez could hear things others could not, no matter how much he wanted to ignore that talent. His mind could ride the same pathways that dead souls traversed while searching for salvation or damnation. *Hear them. Hear them.* Does he taste the colors, feel the smells?

Feel so alive . . .

But it was Delilah's presence that put the photographer's curiosity on edge. Soon after she took her swig from the flask, Delilah began to sing a maddening tune. It was intimacy wrapped in lunacy and tied with a bow of blood. It was Heaven and Hell teasing the rotted sex of purgatory. The pressure was on now; his finger just couldn't hold it. A momentous nightmare spun the world.

Everything was focused on Delilah and her singing. One moment she was an a cappella songstress, the next she became shrouded by a matrix of opaque light. Glittering tendrils slimed her body like invertebrates made from bits of dream; starlight broke the jagged laws of the universe. He wanted to grab the light and take the ride of his life into the chamber of her mind.

Then he saw her memories, the butterfly blade gleaming, the teardrop cascading upon the sharp tip as it descended. Blood slithered angrily, a crimson trail of redemption across her forearm, glowing black beneath a cold, mountainous sun. In his mind he heard sweet, heavy music. Behind her a curlicue of smoke rose and a scarecrow hand bolted like a thunderclap, controlling her arm to cut herself again and again until there was no more pain, no more pain . . .

This was it.

The camera flashed and a tidal wave of light coursed through the station. That's when Delilah turned her head rapidly, angrily, protectively. He saw her hair snap, saw her mouth open. Then her pale hands were reaching for his throat, voice shrieking the most effervescently painful sound he'd ever had the pleasure of hearing.

Rez caught the flash of the camera and was reminded of a past that he was much better off forgetting. *I knew that kind of light once. I knew a photographer once.* But then it was all about Delilah, as always, and her short temper. She'd already begun to scream before Rez saw the bony form she was grinding into the candy stand. The Pakistani man behind the counter yelled, but when Delilah flicked her butterfly blade to life via a neat hand trick, the man shut up.

"They heard you!"

"Who? There's nobody here!" Delilah growled.

That was when she lifted the kid so high his dirty sneakers were dangling an inch above the floor; the camera looped around his neck was near to choking him. She had ripped the collar of his Radiohead t-shirt and her nails left a couple of raw scratch marks from his collar bone to his chin. One of them was beginning to puff and bleed and bruise.

But suddenly his attention was stolen away by what the kid was holding in his other hand—a tiny jar with two skeletons cradling one another in a protective embrace. There was residue smeared across one side of the jar, like they'd tried to climb out, or as though someone had shoved them in with too much force. But deep within the glass prison Rez heard a small conversation, a poem, a harmony as if a haiku.

You and us, just like we are . . .

Little ghosts in mason jars . . .

And then Rez was no longer in the train station, no longer listening to Delilah scream and no longer watching her choke the kid. He saw the skeletons rise on broomstick legs, supporting each other's feathery weight while they held hands. Rez heard the gentle crack of arthritic bones, heard the clatter of decayed teeth starting a conversation. Their bony fingers tapped the glass, a gobbet of blood winked across their backs.

Feral voices filled his ears.

I watched you change . . .

To feel alive . . .

"I'm a photographer!" the kid said. "I photograph auras, and yours is fantastic. Your voice . . ."

"Fucking pervert! I oughta throw you on the tracks."

"Yeah . . . see your *brains* go splat and shit," Rez said.

Delilah turned her head. "You're not helping, smart ass."

Rez looked at the jar again and then back at the kid who was now blabbing about strange angels, music and Delilah's spirant voice. Rez thought that if Delilah held him any tighter, she might kill him by asphyxiation. And now that Rez had gotten a good look at him, the kid seemed harmless. Those two dark eyes spoke only of loneliness, the talent of precision, and the ring of kohl liner around them was the mark of disdain. Curiosity burned within him; Rez could sense it. The rest of his face was covered by a long horsetail of hair, jet black at the ends. A misfit art-fag whose life was ruled by insomnia, creation and the need to find a gentle balance between the two.

"Snap out of it Rez!" Delilah demanded. "What do we do with him?"

"Toss him," Rez joked.

Now you feel alive, the skeletons whispered.

"No, don't!" the kid shrieked. "They're talking. They're finally talking, and it's all because of your bond . . . your music. You two are twins, aren't you?"

"How in the hell could you have guessed?" Rez smirked. "Don't I look just like my ghoulish sister here?"

"Rez, shut it. What do you mean *talking*?" Delilah asked. "Who's talking?"

The boy was sweating now; the air in the station became suddenly too hot to handle.

"I pulled off their wings, and set them in the glass. They're fallen angels. *Twins.*"

Wake up, Delilah. We've been watching you.

She was on the floor of the Number Seven train, starfish missing a limb, and staring at graffiti again. *GrAnDmA DEATH WUZ HeRe! GrAnDmA DEATH WUZ HeRe! GrAnDmA DEATH WUZ HeRe!* The strange kid and the hot platform were gone; the train's air conditioner was refreshing. There was nothing to fear, everything in this moment was safe. Not like she ever felt fear to begin with. Delilah very much liked to stand up to a challenge, unlike Rez, whose anxiety ruled all feelings that guided him.

In this moment they decided to stay in the train for fear the third rail would give them the shock of a lifetime. They sat back and drank their beers while the lights flickered and the drone of elevator music forced them into insanity. Delilah thought about that kid, thought about the jar he held with the twin skeletons.

Do you feel alive?

We don't.

There went the voices again.

"Gotta wait until we slide into the station like that snake from Anaconda," Rez said.

"Monkey blood!" Delilah quoted the movie's most famous line.

Suddenly the back door slammed. A coal-faced hobo came skidding into their car, begging for chump change and crying about his doomed life of bedsores eating away the skin of his ass from being wheelchair bound.

"Just one dollah' would set me straight," he said, rolling the chair across the train. "You got any money, little strange girl?"

"No."

A begging hand outstretched toward her; a squiggle of blood daubed his chin, but he licked it off in a flash. Delilah knew that he'd put himself in that chair with the bottle and needle. She could see the mosquito-bite track marks running up his trembling arm, and so her empathy ended. But then she saw a great, winged creature tattooed on his other arm, and that his solid white eye gleamed upon her with disdain as he spit a green gob of phlegm onto the floor.

"You mother fuck—"

"Delilah! Be nice," Rez said.

Just as he was wheeling himself away, Rez flicked a nickel to the bum.

"You can have one of these, boy, for your kindness," the man said.

There in his lap, after removing a very smelly blanket, was an array of jars. They glowed like mystery incarnate, like journeys yet to be had. What fermented disaster lay inside them, what the beggars of the city collected to make these strange concoctions flabbergasted her: a dollop of molten incandescence, blood exploding like liquid fire. But what she found was much more surreal.

Alien limbs twisted in torturous positions; there were finger bones, mammalian tongues, rabid tarantulas and a billion silverfish. Delilah saw taste buds swollen like pimples ready to be popped; the delineated flesh of eyeballs peeled back like the skin of an onion. The finger bone was jellied in formaldehyde, and she could smell the horrible scent of a morgue. The appendages were pale and gleaming; the florescent light chinked off their scaly surfaces.

"I want them all," Rez said, eyes wide.

"Only one. Pick one."

"Alright," and Rez rolled his finger in the air. "This one."

"Aha! That's the one for you," the man said, rushing away.

It was the very last and most loathsome jar, so old and delicate it looked as if it was worth nothing, but it fingered Delilah's attention gently. Dust hit the air as Rez popped the top. They both gave the other the look of complete assurance that Rez's nickel was well worth giving up even if it could've paid into their beer fund. Inside was a murky suspension of moonlight and sound, membranous append-ages slicked with clotted blood as if they were ripped right off a great, winged insect.

Two pairs.

I pulled off their wings and set them in the glass.

"Did you hear that Rez?"

Twins.

"Nope."

"Liar." Delilah gritted her teeth.

She bolted for the man in the wheelchair but slipped mid-stride on his spit-wad, bashing her head against the seat. There was a soft cracking and a clash of her teeth as her jaw locked shut for a moment; blood ringed her lips like candy apple syrup. Rez lifted Delilah to her feet and sat her on a seat.

"This'll make you feel better."

Rez sparked the joint to life with his green jet-flame lighter. The spicy cloud shrouded his face, his soft features twisting into pleasure. It was time to go, time to get the fuck out of this claustrophobic space. Delilah was beyond restless. She kicked the train doors until they opened like silver lips, jumped out and was soon engulfed by the dimly lit station.

It's like you never had wings . . .

"I don't believe one word this hack says, Rez."

"You haven't even given him a chance."

Delilah unwillingly let go; the kid coughed and wheezed before he was able to stand straight.

Now that Rez got a good look at him, he didn't seem so strange. The prototype of himself, a ten-year-old body stuffed into a young adult's soul. But it was the jar in his hand on which Rez couldn't stop focusing. The twin skeletons were writhing; he felt their tiny hearts spring to life, felt their formaldehyde lungs take in air again.

Embryos.

Delilah and I.

"The shadow is an unconscious complex. It's the repressed and suppressed aspects of the conscious self."

Delilah's head bobbled. "What the hell are you talking about?"

"Your shadow . . . it's old and numb and shedding skin."

Delilah looked down and saw an opaque form behind her. It was the same shadow she'd seen her whole life, the same shadow she'd been forced to become friends and fight with—like Peter Pan—to ultimately accept her insomnia.

"Change is coming, Delilah. I saw it in your aura. I heard it in your voice. You can wake them . . . you can make them fly again. You and Rez. Together . . . with music."

"You don't even know us."

"In New York, everybody is one in the same at some point. We're all family."

"Well I've lived here my whole life and I don't agree," Rez said.

"The bond you two have is eternal. Just like the bond I've collected in this jar."

And then the kid started to walk away. Rez could not bear to see him go, could not bear the thought of *not* reuniting those twin skeletons with their wings. Delilah didn't even take a second to think. She was already following him as Rez pulled out the jar that the bum had given him, opened the top to look at the wings. They were still alive, flapping laboriously and oozing hellacious, black blood. Then he ran after the photographer.

"Did you do this to them? Did you?"

"They sleep too deep for me to wake them up."

"Why? Because you killed them?"

He didn't answer, but the jar shook violently in his grip; tiny dark eyes lit, minuscule nostrils fogged the glass and four tiny hands begged for freedom. That's when Rez heard the whisper of reptiles—small, undeveloped voices, the kind that you hear between the walls at night, the kind that keeps you awake until you cry yourself to sleep.

It was their voices, the things trapped in the jar.

Screaming.

Aching.

Agony.

"Sing for them. Let them get back to the sky."

"But why did you do it to them?"

"I once thought love could never die. So I captured it . . . but soon realized that love takes work to keep alive, that it can't be just kept on display."

"Love?"

"Yes, like how you two love one another. You fight big, but you make up big. It's a wonderful bond."

They followed the boy to the far end of the terminal, and he opened a door that looked like it belonged to a garbage shoot. Down the stairs, no turns, just steep stairs. Above, the moonlight was feathered through a manhole cover, reflecting wanly back into the open sky. Finally, they landed in a room that looked like it might've been ripped out of a crocodile's daydream.

"They came to stop our wasteful existences. Look at all those people above us. Decadence, greed, delirium and ignorance. Not caring about the next generation is the biggest trend."

"But we're born to die . . ."

"It doesn't have to be that simple. It can be so much more. We're not just meat puppets."

"Sucks to be informed," Delilah said, her eyes wandering around the space.

"And as you can see, I'm a bit of a hoarder."

A cascade of rot ringed the spanning walls, ripped books bulged within wilting cases and a shelf of tin cans collected water drippings from the street above. Tiny aquariums filled with cephalopods, all coiled and slimy and presumably unhappy. The smell down here was not of death or grime, but of ancient civilizations. Rez imagined dinosaur bombarding through here. But then something did, in a squeaky, old wheelchair.

"You!" Delilah screamed.

It was the homeless man from the train, and this time the tattoo on his arm was fiercely swollen.

"You gave us this!" Delilah pointed to the jar.

"I did, for your kindness. But kindness always meets a mission. And you have one now."

The photographer held up the jar. "We've tried to set them free—"

"You trapped them!"

"We only wanted to see what would happen if we were able to keep them with us. But we were wrong, so wrong. They wilted and died like flowers."

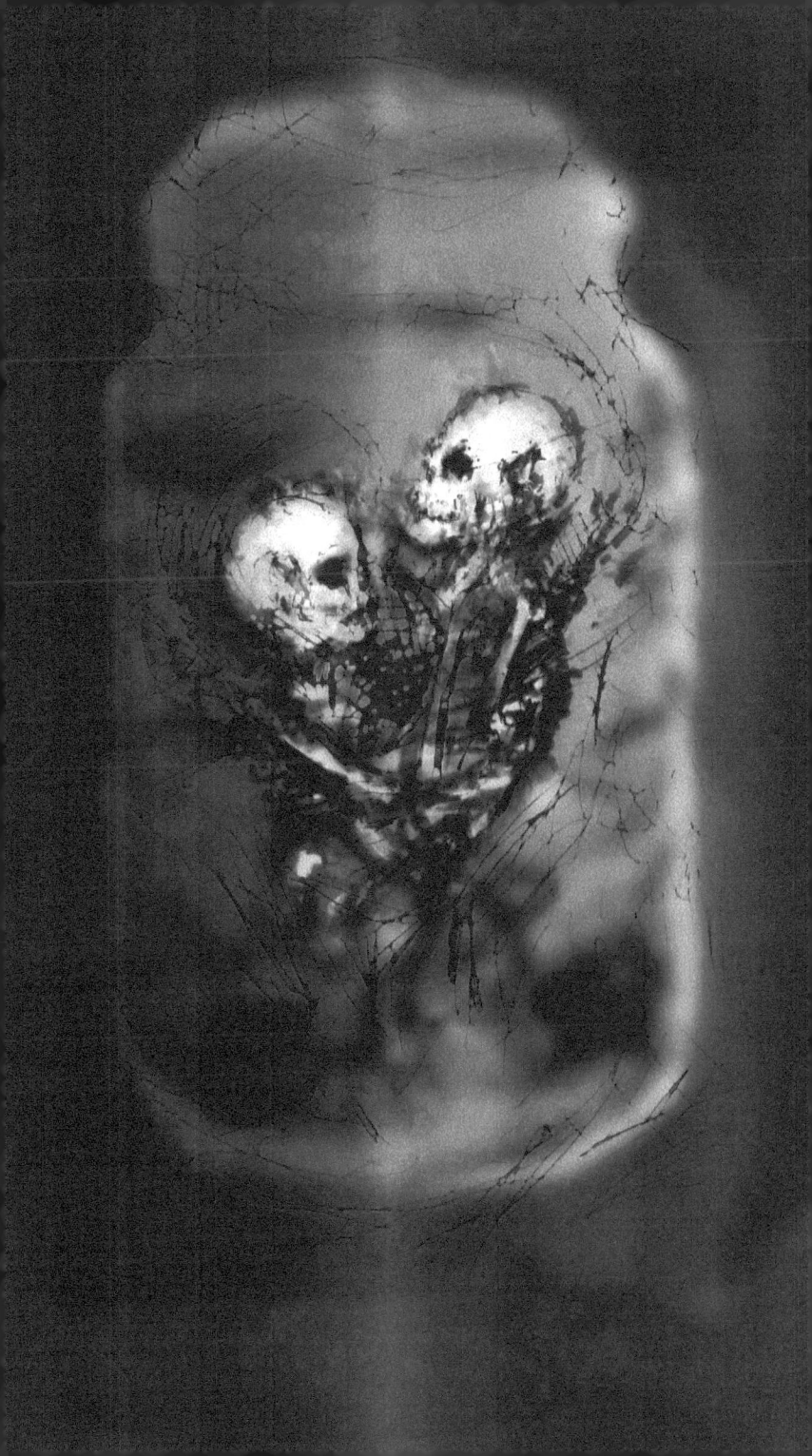

"Died like we do," the kid said.

"Are they Angels?"

"Not sure."

The boy snapped one last photo of the jar. "Their aura was once unmatched, but you Delilah have matched it a hundred fold. You and Rez, together!"

In New York, everybody is one in the same at some point. We're all family.

"What are you?" Delilah asked.

Rez felt a shiver run up his spine and into his head. The little skeletons were talking again; the jar with the wings was bouncing in his hand. All of a sudden he gripped Delilah's arm as his head filled with catastrophic images, with glittering black light. A nightmare stole his vision with a hand made of plasma, of fever. He was hearing something, feeling something, *seeing* something.

They were younger than Rez expected, little feral people with no sex or gender. Behind them a spider-shadow swirled beneath the moon, but not a light, nor the shadow of something angelic. Two blue tongues lolled from singing mouths, stained red and furious from the pain; four wings clamped to a cutting board and picked off angrily, one scaly appendage at a time from tiny spines, like peeling the skin off a rich fruit until they are greased in purple blood.

"I know what you mean now. I know it," Rez said.

"They're eternal."

Rez opened the guitar case. Custom Warlock from strings to knobs; it glowed when he plugged the chords into the portable amp and distortion pedal. He sat back against a metal side rail scrawled with cryptic graffiti, swirling shapes that began as words he knew, but ended as meanings he was better off not knowing. He could stretch his mind and dig his hand into a part of the conscience he could never unravel without this absolute quiet. The grit and grime inspired him; the vision of the torn wings led him in the right direction.

Something came to life.

It was music.

"Yes! Play!"

Tonight Rez would shape himself into a well-rounded artist, not just one of the written word, no matter what Delilah said. Tonight he was going to set them free. With his skate shoes anchored to the metal rail, and with the glow of the distant skeleton moon above, he played. From his book of pitiful poetry and badly drawn scales, he began a few songs he knew, and then ripped into a jam set. Rez pulled off the rhythm surprisingly well, his body rising and falling as if he was writing a musical scale in midair. Each chord was a rocket ship; every strum was an angel dropping glass tears from the sky.

Delilah's silvery voice flew out of her mouth, complimenting Rez's rookie chords. He knew Delilah's music had a strange, hallucinatory power that could wake the dead, but he never truly fathomed that he could do it together with her. He never truly expected to see the miracle.

Both jars exploded.

The room became maddened with stroboscopic light. It was a slow, rhythmic swing to the song of solitude, the whisper of faded time and shredded dreams. Bloodied appendages became air born and the tiny skeletons bowed to accept them. Rez saw flesh meld together, saw old wounds heal like scabs. The twin skeletons took one last look around, their deep eyes wide, thankful, endless. Their wings buzzed and their hands rose to the heavens as they squeezed through the metal grate in the ceiling to become lost between the moonlight and electric sky.

2011

"Be Quiet and Drive" was written in 2013, birthed out of a trip I took to San Francisco for my 26th birthday. San Francisco was a city that I had always wanted to see. I always imagined it to be New York's seedy sister. But upon arrival, I became immediately horrified at the massive amount of homeless on the street, and the surprisingly huge of amount of graffiti on everything from exposed brick walls to cable cars. As a New Yorker born and raised, I was convinced my city was king when it came to bums and graffiti. Man, was I culture shocked. And so I got to thinking about graffiti, and love, and bums. This is the result.

Chi Cheng died that same year.

BE QUIET AND DRIVE

For Chi, who left us too soon.

Love is an arrow that propels through the dark.

What a feeling to be able to stand on top of the world and not notice the blue-green sphere from which you came, to not worry for air or breeding disease beneath your skin as you fall prisoner to the radiating landscape of stars and spiraling galaxies.

To hope for a cure is to betray yourself.

Yet we do it with such conviction.

Love is both bitter and sweet, but which flavor lasts longer, the bitterness or the sweetness? They say it's better to have loved and lost then never to have loved at all. It's how you come to understand pain, forsaken and ashamed, each day as a part of you withers away, suffocating in suffering.

Love, from what I've come to learn, is a virus.

San Francisco, you could say, is a place that doesn't feel right. What a city to arrive in to forget that you were ever a dreamer, a thinker, a lover. It's a dreadful dot on the world map permeated with an arrogant West Coast attitude and an existential fakeness. It's a place that wants everything from you: your soul, your livelihood, your pride and your pain. I'd never stumbled upon a city so cruel, so ripe with poverty and yet so sumptuous with promise!

I arrived just after dark via the haggard BART transit system. Bums swelled in the streets, teeth-by-jowl, as if a little piece of New York had followed me here. Warm mountainous moonshine filled their glassy eyes; dirt-ringed hands shivered, begged. I pitied the genetic selfishness that possessed them to constantly implore, sucking whatever they could out of any passerby: coins, food, a cup of warm whiskey to scramble their hopeless dreams. Bums are the living, breathing result of what a corrupt city can do to its people.

I grabbed a road map, gave up two measly bucks and caught the notorious F trolley on a road to nowhere. San Francisco brooded and throbbed; its streets were rank with filth and flotsam. It's an old city, much like New York, and so its sidewalks are cracked and its citizens are naturally hostile. It's a city that's very much alive and in charge of its people, making decisions for them and not giving a fuck about it.

New York became a pale memory; the five fuck-up boroughs that twist between one another like roping limbs after a good night's fuck was a layman's paradise in comparison. I wondered what happened to the hippies, to John Lennon's mantra of "All You Need is Love." And then I remembered the bums, and looked out into the night again, realizing that what I was witnessing was no longer a city of peace, love and understanding. All I saw was shame, and rage.

Another selfish city.

Something about Joey was very unordinary, much like San Francisco. I didn't know where he was from or where he was raised because he had no accent. I could not tap into my born and bred street smarts to place him. I soon learned that much like New York most of the people of San Francisco come from somewhere else.

He met me atop Lombard Street in his usual cool-cat California get-up: tight band t-shirt and black jeans marked up in serious aerosol paint, a backwards punky hat covering the coarse black hair; half-hopeful gleam in his smoky eyes. Lombard is a notorious maze-like road in San Francisco where the hills gyrate and where Chinese luxury is safe-guarded by filthy Filipino migrant workers.

We found a seat atop a sun-worn wall and took in the briny Pacific winds, marveling the sounds of the ever-churning city below us. Twilight was hot and alive, brushing across Twin Peaks, the skeleton trees and two bony lovers like deep purple shadows.

"I don't care where, just far . . ."

Wavy California voice, sun-kissed skin so gold against my New York pallor. Joey talked and talked as usual, about uneasy things like sexual deviances, bathhouses, street art and how he was going to one day leave a melodramatic stamp on San Francisco. I always knew this to be true in one way or another; his talents far exceeded his age, twenty to my twenty-four, but he was just as clever, just as street savvy.

"This city . . . it's alive. It's vengeful . . . ruins everyone," Joey said with a hand rolled cigarette lolling between his lips.

"A glass coffin; a shopping district atop a growing graveyard. I know."

"I hate how it's gotten into me."

"I ran from New York and you want to run from San Francisco."

"Don't say it like that!"

My little Joey . . . the sensitive dreamer, forever young. How could I be so rude? I was to always take care of him, because I'd promised, of course. If he wanted to go somewhere far, why should I not follow? I wrapped my arm around his tiny shoulders, sunk my nose into his hair and took in a great breath. He still smelled the same as the first day we met: sweaty sun block mixed with a dash of liquor. Suddenly, he began to shiver; the Pacific winds proved too cold.

"It's not that, Tony. I went to the clinic you know . . . finally got tested."

For him to tell me that out he'd gone to the clinic alone—to bear the shame of a needle stick by a rude technician—that hurt the most. While I was curled up in bed, dreading the day's loathsome comic book patrons, Joey was traversing the bowels of the city. My heart sank imagining him scared and alone at the clinic, exploding inside from grief, from a fear he'd kept dormant for too long.

He wasn't outwardly sick, had a great appetite, but somehow he just knew it to be true. As long as I've known him he talked about it, but I always put it off, told him he didn't need any status as long as we had each other.

"And?" the frog in my throat barely let me speak.

"I'm positive," words echoing straight into the pits of San Francisco hell.

I all of a sudden smelled latex, imagined Joey's lonely little body curled into itself as some rude nurse read the report to him. The unusual twist of his frown was sweet and infectious as the virus running through him.

"Which means you are too. I guess you're going to leave me now."

Joey stopped the drag on his cigarette. His tears soaked the collar of my t-shirt. I kissed him, but he wouldn't kiss back. I didn't know why he took the news so hard. He knew that I was all too familiar with the replicating, debilitating, bloodsucking virus, and that I wouldn't allow it to kill him as quick as it did my friends back home. But then a thought hit me: even though San Francisco is the center for this kind of disease support, you can't help to just feel so alone.

As long as the sickness is not inside you, everything is okay.

For that I pitied Joey, wiped his tear-snot on my shirt. I wanted to cry myself, but couldn't allow myself to break into pieces no matter how easy it would be. I had to be the strong one, always. Joey was extremely passive in nature and would crumble at the mere sight of me being weak. But I was very weak, for him I was the weakest wimp in the whole fucking universe.

Not that he knew it.

"Do you think this heartbeat's just a lie . . . to fool the sky? Did the clinic lie?"

There came the poetic drawl that made me fall in love, his inspirations born and bred by the dark days he spent in the streets peddling money with the bums who touched him in the wrong places . . . the diaphanous swirl of blood and junk in the hypodermic still a harsh memory. It was no secret Joey had been a junkie and was supported by an ephemeral family of gutterpunks who shared needles and bottles because they could not afford anything new.

But this was the only way (from what he told me) for Joey to explore his imagination; to shed skin, to feel the meat of his soul tenderize into something greater than this simple reality. *We humans are all energy beings*, he would say, *forever transcending, changing, and mutating*. It's what possessed him to become a master explorer of flesh, arranging many tricks a night to test the limits of his sexuality. The needles were merely a test to see how many times he could poke his vein before it blew and spread ghostflowers beneath his skin.

It was a heavy way of life.

Now we both were scarred.

I forgave him. It was all I could do. Why fight? Why bother? I was a willing participant, positive or not. We decided to leave Lombard Street, craving cheap beer and a calm atmosphere to clear our heads. We might've gone to an art gallery, or watched a movie, but hell, I knew exactly what we were going to do: put on a show. We wanted to get far away from reality, and that only happened when Joey created dark and emotional aerosol portraits for the public.

Downhill we went. Our high top sneakers left rubber skid marks across the asphalt as our eyes became affixed to the bright colored housing, the strange outlining moldings of ornate flora and destitute art-deco. The walk was hellacious but the night-wind guided us on our tiny journey back to downtown San Francisco. Joey fixed his face before a scrappy store window and I kept a look out for the city and its selfish snake-like hands, making sure it would not try to coerce Joey into something dangerous. It had done enough of that already.

"James is talking about a cure-all. A miracle drug, Anthony. He can hook me up."

I hated when Joey used my full name. It meant he was upset.

"No such thing as a cure-all. And James is a fair-weather friend. You know that already."

"You can come with me; we can get cured together. Please Anthony. I'll make the money. I'll hustle. I'll paint all day. You can work doubles, right?"

His eyes were bright hollows, but filled with limitless potential. I thought about that cure-all, the scam it was, how lovely it sounded but how too good to be true it was. For some reason I knew that the city itself was planning this . . . planning to steal Joey from me in some morbid fashion. But then again, nothing was as bad as the thought of dying quicker than we're meant to. The clock is ticking.

"Doubles at the comic shop? No one in the Castro is interested in comics anymore."

It took me a second before I realized we were in front of our apartment. Now Joey was wracked with the familiar madness that first attracted me to him: he was going to get rid of some of his feelings through art. The bag on his back was full of spray paint cans, plates and various dark objects he used to create perfect shapes and various effects on the canvas; the speakers in his hand would be used as a backdrop for his creations.

We set up shop at Spear Tower, a small park within the ass crack of Market Street, the only part of San Francisco that is of no interest to frazzled tourists lost and crying for their hostel. At this end of town there is no lush shopping or creamy clam chowder steaming from sourdough bread bowls, no gaudy ghosts of the tourist trap known as the Fisherman's Wharf, or the blubbery growls of sun bathing sea lions. This makes it one of the few places known to be filled with natives: the aerosol artists born and raised on the old flower power streets, the holiest skateboarders clattering along concrete benches with their oily hair, their young skin winking with sweat.

"Only asking ten dollars, folks."

Joey began his usual street peddling and I simply gazed in awe at how much money was about to be made. Music tore into the square from Joey's iPod connected to cheap boom box speakers: Deftones, "Be Quiet and Drive." My favorite band. People cluttered around us. The art crowds in San Francisco are plentiful; their long faces are sun-kissed and their minds wholly pickled from the latent heat, and so they can easily be assuaged by a street artist with a quick and careful smile such as Joey's.

I opened my hands, collecting money as the smell of his spray paint wafted. It reminded me of the familiar smoggy odor of the city I had left . . . a city addicted to graffiti culture, yet one that had also alienated it. But like most things in the world, the more you try to fight it the more pollen it spreads. Street art might have been turned into an illegal form of expression in New York City, but in San Francisco it was a thriving underground practice.

"Support the show. Sit back and relax."

That slow rhythmic voice soothed me, a full body massage. I forgave him for all that clinic business right then and there, for poisoning me in more ways than one. I looked at the twiggy skaters and thought about their youth, their liveliness. How free they must feel, how feral they are with no lover to worry about, no disease slowly killing them. When I turned back to Joey he'd just finished two pieces using a bowl and fishnet leggings as templates to spray the colors across.

A galactic candyscape; a form of infinity.

Eternal Energy.

Once again money was quickly planted into my hands. I nearly tripped over my shoelaces when I saw the next few pieces Joey was creating. Jagged skies, iridescent moons, crooked Phoenix trees, globules of stars dripping and shooting over a mossy Golden Gate Bridge where a tiny figure had hanged himself off the edge. I imagined all of those kids who had literally thrown themselves off the bridge, sick of life, sick of the virus.

Joey's work was full subtle messages that I barely understood: suicide, a city brimming and alive. To say he was a mad genius with something serious to say, is to fall short of him. And so I grabbed the cityscape portrait for myself, the slime-green of it draping like ectoplasm across an endless San Francisco sky. It would shimmer beneath the sun and become shadowed under a gibbous moon. It was the most interesting piece of his I'd ever seen, like the picture itself could come alive and infect me, eat me.

And hell knows that Joey did just that.

We shared a place downtown, Taylor Street, the ratty district. Here the bodies of bums lay around, cold and creepy, cradling beer in brown paper bags, sucking on the bones of fried chicken and whatever vermin they could catch. Half of them lived like the living dead, the other half were literally dead. Their piss and shit mark the street as do the fiercest canines to fire hydrants; their language is unstable and insulting. But Joey loved this part of town because it reminded him of how he'd left this circle of demise, how he evolved to survive off his street art and not his body.

It's what turned him on the most.

Joey was the kind of bottom that demanded my full superiority. It was part of his nature. If I asked him what he liked, what he wanted out of me, he'd get soft and leave the room. He needed a man to control him so he wouldn't have to think about anything, so he could just let go. I'd always been a purveyor of control, and so our sex life was nothing less than carnal. Two feral bodies and eight limbs tied into a wet fleshy knot can't describe it any better. Sex was the one thing we both had in common, the one way we both felt the freest.

I took advantage of the dominance he craved, which slowly grew into my natural comfort zone. Sometimes Joey's necessities often made me question our relationship;

I remembered those nights he'd come home stinking of some dark part of the city, catatonic as he sat on the edge of our bed, not wanting to wake me as he confessed what had gone on at whatever party he attended, whatever trick he met up with. He was always honest about cheating, about shooting up between his toes so I'd not notice. My ridiculous love for him always let his infidelities slide since he often wept in my arms, the man who he truly loved. The only man he could trust.

Joey was a hundred pounds soaking wet, so he'd be an easy prey to stalk, use and abuse by the untamed people of this city. The worst part of it all, the part I had to accept in order to be with him, was that he believed that sex should be shared between multiple partners, to never be contained. Nonetheless our nights together were bright with lust and natural attraction.

He submitted to me as always, face down with his limbs spread in all the deviant positions of the clock, little tongue darting across his lips. But tonight an image betrayed me, one I always had a hard time getting used to, though in this moment it was all too perfect. I thought about other men bare-backing him, clutching the sharp handles of his hipbones, their seed wetting that swollen pink asshole as they shot the virus straight into him. I became inversely aroused when I should've been screaming. Yet, to see Joey's face alight with pleasure and pain, to know his fetishes were fully exorcised, turned me on more.

Some nights it made me secretly masturbate.

He loved foreplay. For now the world didn't exist; the virus didn't exist. The feral game of breeding guided us. I ran my tongue down his flower stem spine and kissed the smooth juncture of his ass. I'm a certified butt and thigh man, and so it was no sadistic chore of mine to wedge my face—then my cock—between the secret compartment of Joey; legs like fairy wings, the strong muscle between his balls and ass a slippery slide to infection. Happiness stretched madly across his face; his back arched rhythmically as I entered. His heat enveloped me. I could not stop fucking him, could not stop the passion. I would not cry, would not break.

Somehow I knew something was not right.

Though our bodies were swathed in one another's sweat, lips sticky with spit and craft beer (all the things that livened our love making), Joey began to scramble, to shift uneasily beneath me. He was *resisting* me, something that I knew his passive nature did not allow. Guilt, or excessive thinking, it did not matter. He would not take this moment from me as he took everything else. I was born to do this; sex was my escape art. And so in this moment I was a nervy medical practitioner, a daring proctologist. I gripped Joey's arms and flattened them to the bed, ramming him harder, a punishment for bringing us one step closer to death and departure than we should have been. Life already has this in mind the second you escape the jellied birth canal. Why did Joey have to fuck this all up?

Our dresser shook and incense fell to the floor. He begged that I stop mid-stride, that I was hurting him. But this sudden masochistic pleasure forced me to ignore him. I wanted to be the fucking cure-all; in this moment my sperm was made of a billion virus warriors that would slime Joey's intestine and eradicate that killing disease. And so I finished inside him. I felt my penis swell more than ever; a hard throbbing squirt pushed deep inside the endless pipelines of his intestine. I thought of my millions of children, my warriors sliding into his gut, invading his bloodstream and then sliding out victorious.

Nothing happened but the sticky aftermath of a good fuck, my slime crawling out of his sphincter and across his smooth inner thighs. After, Joey would not let me spoon him like we usually did; rather, he wanted that I cradle him, and sing a lullaby as he cried. It was the most depressing moment of my life to understand that I'd given all of my heart, my very blood and living soul to this boy, but that all of it was a waste.

I managed to fall asleep, and dream, no less. An hour or so, I don't remember. We were exchanging bodily fluids as usual, and I thought not of contracting a disease, but rather, our genealogy became connected far beyond the laws of biology. Our DNA twisted into one devilish strand; our blood was shared, as was our thoughts. We were one. We could give back love and addiction. We didn't have to be co-dependent because were a single being! Like a computer whiz I was able to pinpoint the tumor-like virus and eradicate it, and at last we both were vindicated, happy.

What a tease when I woke to the shaky voice.

"If I don't get this bug out of me, Anthony—"

Full name. Upset. All downhill from here.

"How long was I asleep?"

"I'll go myself if you won't go. I have enough money. And look!"

He was motionless at first, his hand cradling my head, his breath tainted with cigarettes and rum, before he grabbed something from the nightstand drawer and a plethora of pencils clicked against the floor. One bare leg crossed my torso and I watched the fruit of his loom hang ripe and sweet in the moonlight as I rubbed my hand along his toned thigh muscle.

He showed me a chiaroscuro sketch, one of the industrial district of San Francisco where electric lines still powered a ghost trolley, where the buildings swarmed around its seldom visitors like a great black trench coat. At the end, the far end, a phantom rendition of The Golden Gate Bridge haunted me. It could've come to life, that picture, eat me with no remorse, it was that creepy. At the bottom was Joey's street art signature. An uppercase J that swooped like bat's wings.

"When did you draw that?"

"While you were asleep. I dreamed it would look this way. The final destination at the end of a long, exhausting road," and Joey was all smiles again.

I grew reluctant and annoyed at his indifference to the actual facts at hand. This wasn't the Joey I came to know, not the thinker, the artist. We both knew there was nothing at the foot of that bridge, nothing but scarce housing, patchy fields of grass and the Pacific Ocean spreading itself like a most unfortunate lover. But it was what he had to do, and if he needed that much attention, I'd oblige him. Joey always made me do the things I never wanted to do anyway.

"If only I was as smart as you, Tony. My life wouldn't be so fucking *wrong*."

His eyes were dark pieces of stone. There lay no more life in them. Had the virus finally burrowed into that soft cushiony brain? He was using my wits against me, the fact that I'd been a prude my whole life, that I thought things out before I acted upon them. I guess he misunderstood our sex life, the fact that I'd acted before wondering what disease lay beneath the catacombs of his skin, like it did my friends back in New York. But if he needed to use that against me (a bad characteristic that happens to most couples when they get to know one another so well; you say things you don't mean; you hit them and then become insanely guilty about it), I'd let him. He was foul enough as it was.

Back on the not-so-right streets we were just about to catch the F when he decided he wanted to bike it instead.

Night was crisp as always, the hills were still sloping evilly, and the city blossomed with its amalgamation of emotions. I knew this feeling of mine would get us nowhere other than in the throes of love-hell. My love for Joey was susceptible; his youth was impenetrable.

All of a sudden I was reminded why I never wanted to love, or grow old. I wanted to find Neverland. Oh, the thought of growing old, to see the skin upon my face sag slightly more each day before the mirror, to see the kid I am today fall prey to the deceptive noose of age is an undesirable tomorrow. I never wanted to wilt like a flower, or be scattered ash in the loneliest oceans. To wilt is nothing but a shame, nothing but a mockery of the man or woman you once were, now bound to a wheelchair or stuck in bed all day, with nothing but your own thoughts to torture you, shame you, break you.

For this I seldom looked in the mirror. I'd already seen what age and one simple human error had done to my friends back at home. I've seen their immune systems fail and the virus chew them from the inside, smelled the open and wet sores like bottled death. It had killed many I knew and loved, boys who once could put Johnny Depp's *Nightmare on Elm Street* looks to shame, boys who suddenly metamorphosed into crooked old men with stumps for arms, eyes like dried grapes, slowly folding back into the fetal position.

You come into this world curled and leave it that way as well.

You think I'd have learned my lesson.

I let Joey do the guiding. He knew the ins and outs of San Francisco, its trashed alleyways and sub-basement meth parties, all the places I could never even dream of. He painted these scenes, the emptiness, the abuse. I just never caught onto them. We sped like demons through the fanatical, luxurious streets of Union Square.

Joey looked awesome riding that bike, a boy with no worries other than art and breathing as he yelled out the directions, his hand darting left, then right, commanding like nothing I'd have ever seen before. Not like our sex, not like the life-sucking microorganism inside him. I wondered if this moment was sort of an escape art for him knowing that soon he'd be leaving his melodramatic mark upon the city.

"Tony! This is it!"

Finally we slid into the industrial section and stopped to read the sign, SOUTH CITY, and such a strangeness it exuded. The street itself was clotted with ash and muck, the collected pollution of greed. I could feel the weary eyes of detachment, hate and hunger watching me. A numbing coat of despair laved my body and it made me instinctively put my arm around Joey, protecting him. But he wanted none of it as he took off his hat and sniffed the air. I saw his nostrils flair and the slats in his face become alight with curiosity and deviance. The smell of spray paint and tobacco smoke was choking, but it only seemed right within the effervescent presence of Joey.

"This?" I asked.

"No time to get cocky," he spit back. "Beggars can't be choosers."

I rested my body against a brick wall, too dark to have noticed that it was freshly painted. There might lay a cryptic message in blood (now smeared on my back), or a violent screaming tag of graffiti from an aerosol urchin looking for a way out of this city. But then Joey's misted lips met mine, his tongue familiar, warm and searching, his hands controlling! I resisted him, but he wouldn't have it. His elbow cocked upward and he pinned my neck; his teeth tore into my lower lip as he unzipped my pants and jerked me off until I came. Only when I managed to pull myself away from the wall did I notice the smudge of words: *LoVe YoUr CiTy*

"Don't you love me anymore?"

Yes, I wanted to say, but didn't.

Joey guided us through the weird town, and only if I could do a mere justice to describe the decay, the shame and the malice. The destitute blocks were absolutely alive; its seldom citizen seemed a morbid lot. We were very much alone, and yet I'd never felt more claustrophobic in my life. The moonlit streets wavered like aching blood vessels; the spangled windows remained dark and mysterious. The buildings clustered together uneven and malcontent. They did not ascend like the skyscraper demons of New York, but rather it seemed they that they rubbed dry and angry against one another, embracing preemptively for an enormous earthquake.

I could not imagine what souls lived inside those buildings, what dredge ripe with filth and disease sputtered bad tasting lyrics about his sad life, the regret he had for just trying to have some fun. He would cry about having no job to feed his family or his bad habits. Perhaps this part of town once boomed, now overshadowed by badly painted edifices and fallen storefronts. But I wasn't scared. Not even as the shadows imbued us as real as spider webs, not even as the streets themselves looked like a river of black.

"It'd be much easier to track the place down if I could find someone to talk to."

"You mean you dragged us here on a whim? Don't you think this is just a tad ridiculous?" I couldn't stop myself from being so impatient. I was scared.

"Of course you'd say that. You're the careful planner as I'm just a fucking pup. Isn't that right, Anthony?"

"I didn't mean it like that."

The sky changed, as did Joey's temper. Part kaleidoscope, part hallucination . . . creepy guide into oblivion. I saw the alleyways unravel like black tongues; the sidewalks stretch into crazy frowns with glittering trails of broken glass for teeth, stained by liquor and marijuana smoke. The Golden Gate Bridge was a rusted husk in the distance. I was witnessing the living portraits Joey had already painted, the ones that hanged like a lynching in my apartment all wet and stinking of this wretched part of the city.

"If you can't do this with me, just go. Fucking go, Tony."

Before I could get a word in, before I could take his hand and beg him not to be mad at me, that it was just his nerves talking, he was already gone. Running like he never knew who I was—like we hadn't shared two years together—running into the great black gullet of this stinking city! *I don't care where, just far*, I thought. And yes, I wanted to choke him, beat him even, anything to knock sense into that cute little head of his. But I could not. And so here I stood, cold and alone, in a place I knew nothing about, a place that could have eaten me as much as taken advantage of me.

Eventually, I came to the conclusion that the earth could rot away and I'd not give a fuck. Perhaps Joey thought the same. Perhaps this notion guided him to become a man that I did not know, guided by the frivolous sex we had last night. Or maybe this city was already inside of him, (if we could just forget the rationale) that he in fact had shot up his last dose of liquid fun and now it was time to flush it all out one way or another. I had a spreading fire of worry inside me now; I could stand around like a stupid straggler no more.

The sound of a spray paint can guided me; the scrape of sneakers echoed in the maze of streets. The scream of hypodermics plunging into veins was clear, a virus spreading wild. I turned a few vacant corners and saw nothing. It wasn't until I reached a dead end did I figure that I was lost.

I'd die here, become one of these south-side dwellers until the sun stopped its forever burn.

Somewhere, I heard the echo of Joey's toneless voice. Somehow I could taste his blood beading from a new vacant hole in his vein. Desperate . . . alone. He needed me! I followed his voice down an empty block and pushed past a heavy door that led into some sort of a warehouse. Beams crisscrossed overhead like a serious construction violation. Young families of bums were possessed by a heavy drugged sleep; a few starry eyed kids were painting and drinking beer. I could read their graffiti upon the beams, *KoLd HeArTeD YoUtH* and *No ChUrCh iN tHe WiLd*.

My foot punched through something wasted, rusted, crunching to a fine red dust beneath me: a dome of needles as old as time itself. These might have been used by the kids as young and free as Joey; these might have been the needles that held the cure-all. My feelings swam through a juxtaposition of terror and empathy. What might posses them to believe that they could rid their bodies of a three-decade plague that has yet to find an official cure? What might possess a youngling to venture on the edge of humanity for a chance of survival?

Hope?

And then I witnessed the most illogical sight my eyes had ever seen. If for one second I thought reality was playing a trick on me, I knew I'd be lying to myself.

I saw a body. I knew those bones, those masterful hands. Joey was just wrapping up a crazed portrait, one of gloomy streets and a shimmering cityscape. He was using his own blood. I called his name but he did not hear me. My body refused to move; my central nervous system and skeletal muscles were in an all out war!

When Joey finally turned his head, even within the murky light, I knew he was only looking through me, his eyes like hollows, his skin still sun-kissed and the backward hat upon his head ringed with sweat. He did not blink when he pushed the needle in one last time. He wasted not one drop.

And then he walked right into the painting.

I've tried to put the pieces together, tried to find the clues in the studded aerosol sketches, the smelly oils and chunky acrylics . . . but failed. Perhaps it was my own dismay since I could not follow him into the great dark landscape myself. I'll always remember that look of glee: he was finally free from the virus, as were countless other young kids who had created their own portraits, never to return.

And so I take myself to Twin Peaks, to Lombard Street, wondering how long it will be until the virus chews me from the inside out, if I'll ever see the skin of my face grow old, my hands wrinkle. Perhaps it'll be a blessing to die young, to enter the state of perpetual energy without losing every ounce of my dignity.

Never has a city seemed so alive, so eternal. San Francisco is indeed a shopping district atop a graveyard, and it will always recycle its people as each decade some-one grows old, someone dies, someone is born, and someone falls prey to disease.

2013

"What Makes a Shadow," to me, is a sort of appendage. A necessary addition to my second novel *Blood Kiss*. Written in 2014, this story grew out of a song, "Sisters of the Moon" by Fleetwood Mac. Something about that song inspires me. Be it the mysticism, the seductiveness of Stevie's voice, or her haunting lyrics. At the same time, I needed to get the mania of performance art out of my head, looking for an answer about what cannot be answered. Shadows, magick and paint. Somehow, it made sense.

WHAT MAKES A SHADOW

" 'Come with me if you want to live,' " Dorian quoted.

Above Tyria his magnificent countenance; teeth big and bright, eyes so dark she considered them a wrong thing. Clutching his paintbrush like a heart, they both faced the store window—Brooklyn's only esoterica—Dorian's reflection brilliant as hers was dark.

"You chase the impossible," Tyria said.

Dorian smirked. "But that's not what it should look like."

"What do you mean?"

"Don't you see it?" Dorian pointing nervous.

Tyria licked her labret piercing and looked deeply into the abyss. Jade eyes and white-blonde hair glowed like deep fish scales, but the light was unable to reach its depth. To her left in the reflection Dorian's face changed, the streetlights forming fiery arcs. And when she looked at herself she was certain that the darkness was looking through her.

Intense. Silence.

"I can't accept this," Tyria said. "It's taunting me."

Dorian clicked his gum. "Thought I was the only one."

Tyria turned her gaze away from the dark spot and looked at the shelf of candles and herbs. Books were opened like lazy mouths, the words indecipherable because the dust was so thick. But that did not stop her from imagining the marveling prose. She lit a cigarette and licked her lips again, so dry they could crack, and before she could even think about moistening them with a drink—because drinking always put her in a safe place—Dorian was already putting the flask in her hand.

"Vodka," Dorian said.

Tyria took a generous gulp. The liquor exploded over her tongue sweetly, but sent a spike up her nostrils. Pain reawakened in the back of her throat—she had been screaming in her sleep—which made her think that she might be bleeding, as if the dripping ghost of cocaine.

"Peek-a-boo!"

Dorian tapped the window. Tyria saw her shadow tremble like a puddle does to an oncoming truck, impossibly changing. On the third rap his hand broke through the glass as if it was dark quicksand, and it made Tyria think of Alice falling down the hole. Dorian's eyes rolled back as the shadow's maw swallowed his hand, but Tyria pulled him free before the nightmare could suck him in.

"Let the madness begin."

Inspiration came to Dorian at the strangest moments. Tyria watched him assemble the easel, lay out his bulging tubes of paint that dripped and stained the pavement. In his hand a pencil and the waxy lead on the canvas formed a blueprint monster heart. He argued with himself, pulled at his oil-dark hair as if deciding if he was crazy or not, but Tyria knew that this was the work of a genius; this was how Dorian created painterly moods of transgression and obsession.

"I need to find it."

Dorian dipped his paint brush into the darkness, then slashed his canvas in malachite green and a swooping black; in the center pale flower petals raged in red circles, forming a freakish ribbon. Werewolf teeth and a staircase of tongues unraveled into an endless throat that dared the viewer to descend. Tyria did not know where he was going with it, what the hidden message was, but it was entrancing. She lost herself in his art. It ached with a mad fervor as the red depths jiggled like the jellies beneath one's skin.

"If I keep drawing I know it'll reveal itself," Dorian said.

"And what if it's greater than you or I?"

"Nothing is scarier than real life. Think about it."

Then black, spilling silent as a spider. It imbued the steel toe of Dorian's vintage boots, twisted up his leg. When he grabbed it his arms flooded with void, became lost within the dark. The shadow wanted to be known. Give it a bit of finger, and it will come crawling, hungry, seething.

And then, without pretense, Dorian pushed his hand in.

Tyria felt a mute sensation ricochet inside her chest. She fell back in agony, smacked her head against the concrete. On the floor, dizzy, she saw Dorian's physiognomy become possessed with pleasure and pain. He screamed, he cried, he touched himself sexually. Tyria felt her heart stammer, her legs go numb; every tattoo she had grew wings and talons, lifting her by the outer layer of thin pale skin as if nailing her to a cross. Dorian took note of this and removed his hand.

"It's a like a fever dream you can taste, touch . . . hold."

Two weeks later, little blue pills for sleeping, bags of powder for waking, and Tyria was still trying to make sense of everything. Not that there was anything to make sense of, not that there was any way to change what she had seen. For now, there was just the notion that something had come to her and Dorian, something that wasn't constricted to the laws of science.

Three days flew by without a single word written. The sun glowered and the moon sizzled. There was no sign of the muse; it was as if it had been swallowed by her own dark thoughts, then locked in the center of her brain's maze and kept hostage by the Minotaur. She hadn't the strength to croon over any lines of poetry, could not bring herself to open the wounds even if Dorian depended on them for the next performance.

The shows were now at their height of intensity; every date sold out as Brooklyn was hungry for a spooky time. Tyria headed the stage each night with a story to tell, a cigarette between her lips and a silver ohm necklace gleaming between her breasts. Dorian remained secure in shadow, his canvas wet with blood and spit and paint. The images he produced were derived from the energy in the room. Each show unique to its audience; each image their hologram.

Somehow, spoken word poetry mashed up to live art attracted people. It was always a queer sight to see Dorian and Tyria perform together, and the alchemy they built was damn near explosive. The words that fell out of Tyria's mouth coiled like smoke and collected in the minds of its listeners as condensation does.

This was always Dorian's cue to grab them mid-flight and rub them raw against his canvas. The spectacle confirmed. In turn, this gave the audience the chance to wander inside the head of a painter, but vicariously through the sound of Tyria's deep voice. Audience participation was the most treasured part of their shows—they were not merely spectators, but fleshy appendages.

And the crowds loved it.

They always wanted more.

Tyria plucked a children's book from her shelf called *What Makes a Shadow?* and leafed through it lightly. When you run, your shadow runs, but you can never catch it! In that moment she realized that everything has a shadow. The sun, the moon, the stars and even the tallest trees. But no shadow could move so lithe and dark as her own. Sometimes it tugged against her mortal flesh, yearning for freedom. As each show played on it became aware of the world and its endless possibilities.

What would it do if it escaped?

It made Tyria give up on mirrors, even though vanity was a word missing from her vocabulary to begin with. Life was much simpler when you woke up without fear or conviction of narcissistic social circles. Why not dress in the first rags you found, eat the first thing in sight or start the day off with a beer?

Her reflection had become a mocking ghost, and its shadow was long and sinuous as a throbbing highway road. It often amazed Tyria how many mirrors she had now that the look of her basement apartment had taken on that of a funeral parlor. Heavy black veils and red velvet blankets kept everything hidden in the dark.

But it was rather lonely. Just her, the drip of the leaky faucets, the daddy long legs prancing across the tile and the soft sound of pages turning in a book. Adelaide had asked for the needle's hand back after a sixteen-month divorce and Tyria could not stop her, though she loved her more than life itself, Adelaide was an adult who made her own choices, thus, her own messes.

Sometimes, she wondered if Adelaide was even alive.

Tyria lit a cigarette and sat at the table. Art 'zines and paperbacks brought about the smell of old libraries; cigarette ash swirled in the air. She knocked the books to the floor and set her bare feet atop them to think about her next move in life. That was when she noticed all her tattoos had changed.

Googly eyes filled with moonlight; cephalopods moved in time with her sore muscles. The scars she bore—ones that had already healed in ornate patterns—were slowly opening, painless marvel at how flesh parts without touch. It reminded her of holding a rotten fruit, and then squeezing softly to see the pulp dribble.

Her cell phone buzzed, Dorian's name in capital letters, but she let it ring out. She didn't feel like recalling how he was elbow deep in her personal abyss, or that scheme of pain spreading across his face. It had changed the ink on her skin, so it could definitely change someone's way of thinking. But, oh, how he manipulated her organs, cradled the very beat of her heart. Had Dorian pulled out a piece of that darkness and used it on his canvas?

"My paintings are alive as you are," he had said

When she finally fell asleep she was assaulted by cold nightmares and broken record dreams. There came introspection and depression. This was not the first time she had seen her shadow take flight, seen it so alive. Might it be the night she became a woman and received her monthly blood—when every girl loses the innocence she never had—or might it be the night daddy touched her in the strange alien loam between her legs? Imagination of escape set off the alarm in her bones; light became the enemy as the dark twin wanted to be noticed.

She woke up spitting ash; the cigarette had burned her forearm. In the ghost-gloom Tyria found that the muse had come back to play. She opened the spiral bound notebook, pale-arm-cradle like Cthulu's phallus, rolling her inky words on paper to get all the insecurities out of her head she began to write. The La Kaligrafica pen moved in stark rhythm to her mind's music, filling up three pages before she had to force herself to stop.

In the tiny crook next to the stairs she heard someone dealing tarot. Above, the sounds of metaphysical cere-monies and esoterica came to life. The pagan dance to Tehuti, Odin, Hecate and Kali made dust fall lightly upon everything. Down the wall came herbal streams of hyssop water, warping her posters and making her clothes smell like a séance. Tyria took a broom and hit the ceiling but wound up punching a hole through it, allowing tiny clouds of benzoin powder to fog up the room. A regular person might run from this brand of squalor, but the rent was dirt-cheap.

Tyria ignored the ritual drumming above her head and thought about poetry. Hers was built from an abusive childhood and it might have been what saved her, but these days it was in a sad state. Poetry lay in the gutters of creative failure, somewhere between the lost art of reading and the act of loving books. Dorian would agree, but the rest of the world found her to be overzealous when she talked about art.

The stereo turned itself on, Fleetwood Mac's "Sisters of the Moon," and so Tyria began a sage and sweet grass smudge to clear the pathways. The smoke was as dark as the woman at the top of the stairs; the melodies brought out the worst of her thoughts.

And then a metamorphosis in the candlelight.

It detached from her body and almost took the wind from her. On the wall it left behind a glittering slime, inexorable. It was a selfish thing, always there so long as there was light. But if shadows are the dark twin to your bones, why was Tyria's trying to get away? Shadows are muscle memory, the body's black appendage. They crawl when you run; they know all the things that you hide and are always one step ahead of you in this skin game we call life. Shadows are the oldest living ghost of its kind, following you from birth and all the way to your inevitable death.

Tyria closed her eyes and willed it away. When her phone buzzed again she decided to listen to the voicemails. Dorian's usual ramblings. *Come out, come out, wherever you are.* His words slurred, but the inflection clear. Tonight he was going out and her company was expected. There were shows to be had and money to be made. The advertisements were getting around faster than expected. Dorian was drawing them himself, each one sharper, wetter, and infinitely more disturbing than the previous.

The walls of the esoteric store were blood red, the floor an old oak that moaned to the weight of passing bodies. Dorian had never seen a color so close to that which lives in the marrow of our bones, and so it pained him to look at it. But Dorian knew that blood spoils once exposed outside the body; the cells oxidize and rot almost immediately, a sight and smell familiar to him as he used his own blood in his paintings, forming spirals of bright oxygen-rich red to the deep color of rust.

"It's not blood," Tyria said.

Dorian smiled. "Mind reading?"

Her deep voice crawled across the table that separated them and ran up Dorian's body like a windy rat. He shook it off, slowly realizing that the store wasn't big enough for him to flail his arms: one room taken over by the mingled fragrance of herbs, spice and incense. The shelves were lined with various hoodoo icons, grimoires and skulls; Egyptian gold, a rainbow hue of candles and bowls for smudges. A hand-painted portrait of Ohm lay relaxed in its throne of leaves and salt.

"There's got to be something here about things that exist beyond our knowledge of planes and dimensions," Dorian said, tucking his long hair behind his ears.

"We know it's there. We just don't know what it is," Tyria said.

"But that's the part I don't like. I'm a man who needs to know."

"So let's keep looking."

Dorian fixed his eyes on the statues and hoodoo herbs. A small scarlet altar was encased within a crystal cabinet that held bits of bone, teeth and a fossil that looked like a Velociraptor talon. It was all of no interest; he wanted only to get back to the stage and meet the shadow again. But when he turned he saw Tyria fiddling with an array of jars, her finger dipping into one labeled BASIL, and then another called ANISE.

"Ingredients to tonight's dish?" Dorian joked.

Tyria flipped him off. "These aren't for cooking."

She exchanged the jars in her hand for one labeled SWEET GRASS. Tyria twisted open the top, stuck her fingers in so that Dorian heard the gentle crush of leaves and seeds, smelled the ancient recipes of heaven and hell. Tyria's eyes were closed, pious; her hair fell like corn silk across her brow. Then she showed Dorian a yellow stoppered bottle labeled ASAFOETIDA.

"Devil's Dung," Tyria said.

"What?"

"Putrid stuff."

Dorian could not wrap his head around what she just said, and even though Tyria warned him against it, he uncorked the top of the bottle and took a whiff. The odor climbed into his eyes and made them water, hit his nose like a fist. He almost dropped the bottle as he gagged for fresh air; it was the most awful thing he'd ever smelled, so unlike the welcoming odors in the other jars.

"Told you," she said.

"Fucking reeks."

"In magick it's used for protection and exorcisms. In science it's used for clearing the airways."

"Smelling salts?"

"No, totally different."

"What don't you know about aberrations?" Dorian said.

"I only know what interests me. And things that—"

But then Dorian's ears perked up; a sly shape became his face. Something was pressing against the small of his back, slithering up his spine. He dropped the stoppered bottle and it exploded into a million yellow shards. Herbs and seeds scattered and the room began to stink of fetid waste. Then Dorian's suspicions came true; the fear in Tyria's eyes instilled fear in him.

"You felt that?"

"Please . . . not here," Tyria said.

Something small and dark trickled from her mouth. Dorian stared in awe as the insubstantiality began to stretch and grow. Tendrils and vines; an unholy nightmare of giant jellyfish tentacles seized Dorian's vision.

I see you

And it reached for him, cold and slimy as oil dripping off an iceberg. Tyria's eyes became vessels of hate and decay as it rose out of her skin to embrace him like a hand. But it could not be a hand, could it? Dorian did not know what makes a shadow—or what could make it want to separate from its fleshy symbiot—but whatever it was, it had to be brought to the stage.

"I don't care how, I want it now," Dorian said.

Tyria was silent as a spider. But then she found her will, her breath, and let out the scariest sound in the world: an eruption from the back of her throat, blood staining her tongue red. The thing was above them now, tarantula dance, and the few people in the store took notice of the strange feeling growing in the room. They dropped their trinkets and took cover as Dorian reached into the void, pulled it down and over him as if he was ripping the wings from an angel, ripping to see the glory of holy silver ichor.

"STOP NOW!" Tyria yelled. "Goddess! Have you come?"

And then everyone fell to their knees, hands in the position of prayer; a small copper bowl filled with offerings was slid toward Tyria. Dorian lit the herbs of sage and sweet grass to cleanse the room, a trick he had learned a long time ago. *We brought the show here*, he said. But Tyria was holding her chest; the way he hugged the dark was as if he was choking her.

"You can't do that," Tyria said. "It hurts me."

"I have to feel it."

Dorian's smile went horribly bright as Tyria's stitched into something evil. A girl lost her balance during the ritual dance, falling into a votive candle that lit her hair on fire, filling the room with hot orange light, leaving no trace of darkness behind its luminescence. As smoke enveloped the shelves and the people the shadow crawled toward the door.

"Oh no you don't."

Dorian emptied a stoppered bottle, held it in his right hand and began shoving some of the shadow into it. Tyria fell to her knees and waited for it to end.

"Now I have it." The bottle glowing, and inside it a dark downward spiral. "To the stage!"

The moon glowed red as blood. The stars were teeth in the propitious sky.

On street level Brooklyn was alive with hipsters and stragglers, winos and yuppies. The fashion of poverty and bourgeoisie could be seen; the greasy white stench of pizza cheese and the verdant spices of slow roasting lamb mixed inexcusably.

"It doesn't happen too often," Dorian said, his hair covering his dark eyes.

"It's gorgeous."

"The way the moonlight touches you makes the shadows find their place."

"How do you know so much about these things . . . the moons and stars and astrology?" Tyria close her spiral bound book.

"I read a lot."

"Sometimes when I look in to the sky I taste darkness and light. Sometimes, when I look at you, I smell danger."

"And you're just beginning to scratch the surface of your gift. Soon your talents will far exceed anything a regular person could ever fathom."

As they approached the warehouse Dorian lit a cigarette for Tyria and himself. Its façade was cryptic and the door prison-esque. The windows were shadowed in scarlet and carved into the mortar was a square and compass insignia. Above them a lugubrious gargoyle clawed its way into the bleak horizon.

"We're performing here?" Tyria said

"Why not?"

"It looks like a satanic church."

Dorian laughed. "It's actually a gallery."

And then from behind someone standing in line said, "You seek trouble."

"What?" Dorian said.

"Saw you in Catland," another said. "Will it come to life again tonight?"

Dorian rubbed the neck of the stoppered bottle, showed them the swirling dark matter. Before they could ask questions the crowd tripled in number, art-types looking more than appropriate beneath the cHilDrEn Of ThE mOoN banner hanging above their heads. Dorian rubbed his finger across it and breathed in deep; Tyria garnished the walkway with the herbs of sweet grass and asafoetida.

"What're you here for?" Tyria said to the crowd.

"To understand."

"There isn't anything to understand," Dorian said. "It's about believing."

"This is not *The X-Files*," they said in unison. "We want to spread the gospel."

"The gospel?" Dorian said.

And then the crowed moved forward. Tyria thought about what they said, that their shows were gospel, that they had a story to tell. Maybe the story was not as lucid as she wanted it to be, but it was there. Stories come in all shapes and sizes; they are not all linear and easy to follow. Sometimes one has to work hard to understand them.

Inside she stepped upon the stage; a warm gush of light spread below her. Black pillar candles formed a small maze as if leading to the center of the universe. Behind her, something like a shadow poked its head out from the light, but Tyria lifted her foot and it ran into the dark spaces of the room.

"This is the beginning of the lunar tetrad," Tyria said to the crowd. "We pray to the Goddess for her protection."

A few kids responded blandly.

"The earth's shadow is cast across the moon tonight, and we will see it in red."

Heads turned, hair shot up like sparks; arms draped in moth eaten clothing raised up. Cigarettes filled the air with pale smoke that matched the night's strange demeanor. Tarot cards hit the air like bats. The Moon and The Hanged Man, The Star and The Ace of Pentacles. Their meanings escaped her, but she recalled once being told about benevolence turning malignant, and the loss of the path to enlightenment.

The cheap PA system began a steady tempo of calm drumbeats. Tyria fastened her hands to mic, swung it from side to side to see the chains and black velvet glide in the air like gargoyles. She felt like a goddess. Dorian brought out a paintbrush, dipped it in his palette, then proceeded to draw wild arcs of white bleeding into red and red bleeding into white.

Blood Moons.

And so she took a deep breath, the kind that could stop the world in its twist, to begin with a vignette, story of lonely times and drug parties, drinking and ghosts. The meaningless ways to hide the hurt that you no longer wish to feel as poetry ripped itself from her tongue.

> *He came to me when the moon was red*
> *Hell amounted in my bed*
> *Black beauty lithe and mean*
> *To uncover the darkness that's inside of me*

Her voice was a curlicue of sound and body, falling hard as a star. Tyria shined brilliantly; the eyes of the crowd filled with tears, hoping to see something escape into the atmosphere, but be as real as a belief, as our own consciousness.

And thus it came.

No way to stop it. Female in shape, a deep-sea creature dried upon land. Light fusing with dark so that everyone could now see it take over the room like an alien skin.

To her right Dorian kept painting.

Black rainbows and terrifying prophecies, great winged things soaring through fiery skies; fossils long thought extinct were turning back to flesh. He opened the stoppered bottle and poured out the liquid shadow. She saw the crowd gazing into the painting, pirate ships sailing across waves of blood; girls with jellyfish hair screamed with pain and violence running in their veins.

Tyria threw a handful of asafoetida leaves over her body. It drove her insane.

And the crowd incanted.

It's there!

The black thing rose to the fluttering crescendo of her words. Dorian's face flushed colorless as it touched him with scaly appendages. But he did not let fear stop the mission. Rather, he rubbed it against his canvas, which put fear into Tyria, fear that he might actually kill her.

Dorian stabbed the painting. It bit his hand.

Tyria growled into the microphone. Sparks filled her mouth.

There came a popping sound as the electric cut out and the light bulbs exploded. Dorian ran to the door, pushing it open with all his might to let light of the blood moon rush in. And that's when Tyria felt her shadow pull itself free of her skin. Her head hit the floor as soon as the last patron exited.

"I remember it just like that," Tyria said out of breath, sweaty and tired.

"And now it wants us to put on a show again."

"No," Tyria said. "It wants to hurt me."

"But we're in control now," Dorian said.

Tyria took a long pull of her Camel. "Are we really ever in control?"

Nothing left to do now but think about the ways in which she can make things move with her words. Dorian was still drawing, a hundred different sketches of that night, tawdry angles and impossible nightmares. She can stare at his art all day, anything better than dreaming.

Anything other than falling prey to a ray of light, to look
behind her and see a shadow cast.

2014

"Alternative Muses" won 2nd place in the first ever writing competition held by Crystal Lake Publishing. But anyone who has ever read the story usually lets me know that it should've won first place. Then again, when do we ever get what we want? Written in 2013, I don't really remember how or why this came to be. I think it burst out of me after reading Harlan Ellison's *Deathbird Stories*, a remarkable collection that everybody needs to read. Also, pain and pleasure come into play, a Clive Barker staple.

ALTERNATIVE MUSES

I dream of needles curved into claws, epidural baths and ice crystals incinerating my guts. Legs open, wishbone pale and ready to snap . . . but who would get the bigger half?

Me riding Peter in a drug-blazed sexcapade, my tits hanging like strange fruit and his big hands cupping them as if to pluck. His bottle-blonde hair coarse as matted fur, mine a finer velvet dyed darker than black. The heat of him violates my warm wet core, and then he drops his seed in a sticky tangle, smearing thick between my thighs.

He is running away.

Then the shark hook plunged, unzipping the wrinkled flesh between my legs, the result of it scattering darkly on the apex tip, rising toxic fragrance like carrion. My screaming became the agony of ecstasy; I wanted no part of the gestating glob of meat inside me, no part of birthing innocence and raising it corrupt.

I only wanted Peter's mouth on my pussy, fat lips on lips. I wanted him to drown in the menstrual blood he stole, to excavate that life-sucking liability he left behind like a dark treasure. Men have it so easy: spill their love in a few liquid pumps and then move on. It's the woman who has to deal with the consequences.

Why do we dream of such abandon? Why do we long for sudden death when we're all on borrowed time? Though I deserved no redemption—pain transcending pleasure— the idea of my body bursting at the heat of passionate contact with sharp metal vexed me. Why let this thing take over my body, deplete me, erase me? Mammalian procreation is as supernatural as the storybooks tell it: a creature growing within, thus which lives off your blood.

And then I remembered the invitation.

Human Suspension.

Celebrate the darkness.

No drug can take you higher.

Filthy excuse for a club in the Meatpacking District, sideswiped by a lowly alleyway where the rats fucked on display and the Hudson stretched like skin about to tear. A few raucous stops on the L train from Brooklyn—loud Puerto Ricans cracked out of their minds, book-worm hipsters trying to hide their vulnerability—and we arrived, living in-real-time the dissonances, disconnections and debaucheries wrought within the city's last subculture of self-mutilation.

The human body is the final canvas, our ultimate escape. We've used up all of our other artistic resources— pen to paper, pencil to sketchbook, acrylic and oils, dance and music.

But art is a bottom dweller: it always finds a way to survive.

The patrons careening outside were all young and vicious, a crowd I knew well: the darklings, funzies, the furiously bored and lost. Kids out of work, kids who had too much time on their hands to paint their faces white with arsenic, kids who dyed their hair like a Mardis Gras stew; kids with too many emotions to control and too many family members telling them how ugly and stupid they are. If there was a chance for any of them to feel normal, it was within a place where metal fixed into flesh suspends you high above any reality, a place no drug could ever transport you to.

Peter and I only wanted to scope out the joint. On the ride over I explained to him what the Superman and Suicide pose was, how one can look like they're flying or hanging from a noose, depending on the area in which your body receives the hooks. *Receive*, not pierce. Peter put his arm around my shoulders hesitantly (he just didn't want to hear about that stuff), and then his hand touched my stomach, which was already starting to protrude through my PANTERA t-shirt. His reminder that I was knocked up, that I had to resist the temptation of serious fun.

"It's a primitive practice," Peter said to me in passing. "You can't be serious."

"I'm *dead* serious."

"Don't talk like that, Mom."

I stopped, my heels clicked abruptly. "Take this damn thing out of me. I don't want it."

He pulled me into the subway. We argued recklessly, oblivious to how loud we were, the passengers looking at us with disdain, the rats and the roaches scurrying away. Peter didn't like the club, in fact he wasn't the kid I'd met last year, that lost soul who wanted nothing more than to drift like ash across the scariest seas, to live life like there was no tomorrow. Had he forgotten he was the one who showed me the invitation?

Haunting words splattered like a crushed blood orange, concealed in plastic like something dangerous, or ancient. I dangled it between my middle and pointer finger while smoking a hand rolled cigarette. I was skilled in this fashion, could manipulate any of my limbs to catch a drag off the joint while snorting a bump of coke sprawled on a mirror; a tab of acid would easily melt over my tongue.

I inhaled deeply. The tobacco was Peter's, cheap as the parchment rolling paper. We lived cheap, ate less than modest but didn't consider ourselves dirt poor. We hardly worked. Peter sold whatever he didn't snort and I had a gig at a sad titty bar in Williamsburg. A lot of guys called me Lydia or Marilyn (fuck if I know if they ever found out my real name) but I liked to refer to myself as a young Dita Von Tees.

Now the crappy attempt I'd made to roll a homemade cigarette left me in a battle against gravity, trying to not let it fall apart. Peter was best at rolling cigarettes . . . the best junkie, the best lover, the best purveyor of pain. He was the best at everything that is deemed terrible. So naturally that attracted me to him.

We met at a metal dive bar and upon first kiss he sliced my finger with his pocketknife because he said he wanted to make sure my blood was red, and that I must like pain given all the gauges and studs of surgical steel running through my lips, my nose and both ears.

We've not been able to take our tongues out of one another's mouths since. He was the answer to my fucked-up prayers; I'd been craving a man who could keep up with my love for pain before pleasure, ridicule before compliment and self-mutilation. What a joy it is to fondle your first world problems, swallow it like the best pill in the world, then cut it away at the command of your own hand.

"I'll just leave," he said angrily.

Never settling down lived within the blood of the Gypsies. Peter was no different: thin scruffy face, lanky bones, big brown eyes and long matted hair that twisted out of control. His clothes revolved around a single pair of ripped jeans, filthy Converses and a leather vest that hung off his shoulders like an old skin. He'd come to New York for the sights, and so what better in-the-flesh sight was there than myself, a girl born and raised in the city that never sleeps, the kingdom of horror and glum.

While everyone else fools themselves thinking New York is the capital of fashion and glamour, I remain busy looking for its deepest, darkest, baddest places. I yearn for the smell of gunpowder, the clicking fingers of corner gangsters and the taste of blood. Have you ever looked beyond Fifth Avenue, ever gone into the deepest parts of the subways, the whorled expanses of tunnels and dipped your head over the side? Afraid of what you might see?

A dark mirror to reflect your pathetic life.

"I love you, Trigger. But I won't watch you kill yourself . . . and the baby."

That's my name, like the finger's final destination before the bullet plows through someone's head. He said it sweetly, of course, a way that made him irresistible. Arguing caused him to give into temptation. In no time he was strung-out on poppers, staring at me with fully dilated pupils and claiming that I was polluting his thoughts and depleting his self-esteem. The truth was that he corrupted me by giving me this living, growing disease.

In my eyes I hadn't corrupted him *enough*.

"I just wanna stay fucked-up forever. Keeps me grounded."

Peter was what you'd call an old-school junkie, the kind who worshipped the psychedelic swirl of lava lamps, the kind that enjoyed being strung-out over black light posters. He rejected conventional cigarettes, drank liquor from the bottle while challenging the radical views of our ever-shrinking world. Aliens and the Madonna's nipples tipped with blood (the Holy Mother, not the singer) and neon Rage zombies tumbling out of a 3D poster. He could babble for hours about the eerie similarities and radical differences between Pollock, Dali and Bacon, or Burroughs, Kerouac and Corse.

I didn't care for any writers or painters. I focused my attention on testing the limits of my own flesh, marking myself up with piercings like fine beadwork and tattoos as if I was a living canvas: The Illustrated Woman. Our stark differences made our relationship all the more interesting. We abused one another, we abused together, we loved to hate each other's vices, but still made time to celebrate life as if tomorrow the world would end.

Peter's philosophy was that humans are all doomed anyway, to be placed into a wall, six feet under or sent to the incinerator. Running from this future or into it? The ice caps are gone, the carbon dioxide levels in the air are at its highest. Extinction is near. So why not live it up? Why not fall headlong into your own destiny?

That's half the reason he did not believe in rubbers and more of the reason why I kept drinking when I noticed that my menstrual blood had stopped and my belly started to swell. I skipped the doctor—couldn't afford that shit—and managed to get my hands on a home pregnancy test via five-finger discount. That night my brain was swirling on craft beer and salvia smoke; I peed madly, missed half the bowl, but managed to get enough on the stick. I waited in angst, and fuck my life, it was true: pregnant.

The thought of my and Peter's DNA being passed down to a little son of a bitch at first was enlightening. We could start a new breed of people, the type that are not born prude and uninspired, the kind that celebrate creativity. We could make a billion children that would do something to help save this fucked-up world. And then I was struck with an image: a selfish infant begging for my tit milk. It freaked me the fuck out.

"I'll drink until I puke out my uterus," I said.

"Or we can just hang you upside down and beat you with a stick," Peter joked. "Piñata style."

"Might as well shove your hand up my cunt and rip the damn thing out. It is a *damned* thing."

Peter went eerily silent.

"Or we could actually, you know, pretend to be normal. Young parents are everywhere in the boroughs."

"But don't you see all those advertisements in the train stations against people like us? The crying baby faces . . . and all those confused, unhappy parents. *Honestly, Mom, chances are he won't stay with you. I'm twice as likely not to graduate high school because you had me as a teen.*"

"Since when do we listen to advertisements?"

"Just making you aware."

"That creature inside you is special. It's made of what we're made of."

. . . he won't stay with you . . .

Six weeks passed. Time was running out. A woman knows she only has a limited amount of time before she can get rid of it cleanly. It had already started feeding from me. I guess no matter what a woman does, the fetus will find a way to survive, find a way to adapt even if the environment it's provided is toxic. Peter tried to make me feel better, tried to convince me that us becoming a family was special. I somehow knew he was lying. I'd already dreamed of him leaving me, dreamed of the utmost gruesome abortion: my own body rejecting the fetus; a claw raking me clean from the inside out.

"Trig, baby, I'm just as scared as you. But curious at the same time. Don't you wanna know at least what it *looks* like?"

"I'm not curious," smoke looping around me. "I'm still deciding what to do with it."

"Keep it, baby. Keep it."

Peter's deep eyes locked onto mine; I couldn't see the shady grey irises that I fell in love with. But I was so hormonal Peter no longer had any power over me. He could not fuck me with his mind games, could not make me think any differently. I stood around playing with my hair before the mirror, attacking myself at the weight I was gaining; my heels didn't fit right anymore, my fishnet stockings were all torn now.

My face looked bloated, my piercings painful and choking. I was forced to take out the black jewel in my navel because the skin was beginning to thin around it like parchment. I hated myself. I wanted a change. No one should tell me what I can and cannot do with my body. It's my world, my universe, and my temple. This thing inside is not part of me. I reject it like an intestine does feces.

I'd rather experience a thousand half-loves well worth leaving than take your madness home and watch you dance inside my uterus . . . where no one sees you but me.

4 a.m. and Peter asleep; me pacing our studio like a fucking lunatic, the call of the club chewing me inside. That or the fetus? A wire hangar stared at me, home-made weapon fit for abortion. It would indeed be bloody. So I ran out the door, mouse quiet, and headed for the Meatpacking District. The L train was full of latent lunacies, solitary bastards, muttering crack heads and an overwhelming sense of hostility. The conductors weren't even human. I wondered if real people drove the trains anymore.

I walked the triptych streets and paid no attention to my grumbling stomach, or my aching pussy. I wanted metal, no doubt. I wanted the ultimate sodomy. Nothing in the world could have satiated me; not Peter's touch, not conversations with a highly trained psychiatrist, not even a fucking a drink. The call of human suspension was too strong.

The club was smoky and cryptic, marked up with hundreds of band insignias like charcoal art. Freakishly young faces were smeared in what seemed to be blood but could have easily been lipstick. I didn't get close enough to find out. You would think at this harsh hour, where dawn is about to break over the sharp city skyline, that the dark little clubs and bars would be emptying. They should have been raided by police for illegal drug recreation and underage drinking.

Not here.

Bodies folded into one another, zombie-slouched and slow; hands crawled like white spiders across flesh, wet and pleasing. Leather covered limbs locked into one another; chaps clasped tight against pale spongy asses. Sweat and sex and death shot into my nose; pain and curiosity and glum raced within me. This club bred folly and brutality. It seemed whatever decency people were taught was left at the door before entering.

And then she arose on stage left.

Dark princess: tentacle hair, strong limbs and black eyes. She saw me; I saw her. We made love through the electric air without an iota of physical touch. Angel. Devil. Sorceress. But then the selfish thing inside me kicked, breaking our telepathic fuck session. The pain shot down to my legs, numbing them, then to my head where fireworks dripped before my eyes. I stumbled; a fat metal head caught me and balanced me back into reality.

The show began.

"WHO WANTS BLOOD?" she screamed.

Her arms spread wide and her head lolled, gyrated. The music was a loud soundtrack of screaming guitars and raging dark techno. I watched her feet leave the stage, watched her soar high above the surprised faces. Her tits hung flaccid, nipples like the stems of old mushrooms. She was in no pain other than the ecstasy of transformation in her self-mutation. *Suicide Pose*. She was a solo vignette. She gave poetic reason to hang from hooks, gave purpose to it. I thought how freeing it must feel, how beautiful it is to choose your own destiny . . . even if it's for just a little while.

I wanted that freedom as well.

"Where the fuck were you?" Peter's early morning voice stroke-like.

"At the club," my voice tainted with satisfaction.

"You're knocked up, did you forget?"

"Don't remind me."

Spilling sun yellow warm as egg yolk, and Peter sitting Indian style with a pipe to his lips that smelled of berry tobacco. He wasn't mad at me of course, that wasn't in his nature. I could do no wrong in his eyes. But I will say that for every passing day with this growing child inside me, Peter was starting to become more and more obsessed with the idea that he had to take on some kind of responsibility.

But if I asked him to get a reputable job, like working the kiosk at the mall and make some real money, he'd laugh and continue smoking his strange and colorful Gypsy leaves.

"I thought we had a deal to never go to that club."

"I had to find out."

I was before the mirror again, undressing slowly, the spot between my angel wings tender. *Suicide Pose*. As soon as my shirt hit the floor I saw the spot where she had hooked me, saw Peter's eyes widen in the mirror's reflection. No blood, just a set of welts. Peter knew exactly what it was, and he jumped to his feet and began the strangest tirade in the world. He pulled at his hair and raked his scruff with the nails he didn't have. Not angry, not concerned, just appalled.

"You used to be so into this," I snapped.

"Only before I knew I was going to be a father!"

"I told you, I'm not keeping this thing. I'm going to drop it off in a dump—"

He forced his hand over my mouth hard enough that my teeth to sank into cheekflesh, much like the fish hook did to my back. Spit and blood and lipstick were all I could taste. In all the years I'd known him he'd never showed any signs of physical abuse. But everything changed at that moment. He was now the Peter I'd already dreamed of, full of confusion and ready to run. I half hoped he'd punch me in the stomach, self-abort this thing. But he didn't.

Peter's grip on me was strengthening, but his confused face showed that he had no idea what he was doing. We were both in an awkward position. And so that's when I felt the bitch inside me take over. I clocked his nose with my elbow; the cartilage crushed warmly, but the bone cracked horribly. He shrieked, but I was on a killing path, using all of my baby weight to pull him down by his dirty cardigan to punch and spit on him.

All of a sudden it was over.

He gave up.

"Goddamn it, Trigger!" A shimmering worm of blood crawled down his chin.

"Don't ever touch me like that again," I said. "I'm in a *delicate* condition."

"Why . . . why are you doing this? Trying to get me to HATE YOU! Trying to tear us apart?"

"It's in your pathetic nature to do such . . . Gypsy scum!"

"I love you, Trigger . . . LOVE YOU! Why did you do that to yourself?"

"I'm my own person, Peter."

And just like that he was running away. Didn't grab anything, not his pipe, his records, his books or even his clothes. He didn't even look. Out the door he went. Out of my life he was, forever.

Alone.

With this thing—his thing—still well and alive inside me.

I dreamed of clawed hooks and sexual abandon. Faces covered in leather masks and eyeliner so dark I could only see black. Here the monsters would come alive, but not the kind you have come to expect. I watched myself as if I was outside my own flesh, free from the imprisonment of bone and conscience. Swollen belly stretch-marked and ugly; my hair tethered and my skin vulnerable. Earthquake beats blared from the DJ booth as terrible looking bodies thrashed, moshed and convulsed.

Alone, so alone.

No more tears left but the ones that were to come from agony. She was above me again, Dark Princess, raging beauty queen, and I was hers to control. The ultimate succession into human suspension. Like I'd already learned: the body is the final canvas. *There is no difference between love and pain. They are the same hopeless obsession.* The hooks dived, my legs opened and my back arched. Blood misted my face; pussy juice slicked my inner thigh as my water suddenly broke.

The next night I had to get to the club.

4 a.m. is a time that never lets me down; it knows why I have nightmares, and why I want to suspend myself above them. L train lunacies berated me once again, but this time I noticed the people as if under a different light. They were all rather sad, gaunt and bleary. Their faces were to be pitied and their hands kept shaking, their legs jittering for another quick fix. No matter how much New York City has cleaned up the boroughs, they can't rid us of our flavor.

The Meatpacking District was so alive. Darkness laced with sizzling urban neon. Regret stitched up in the night like a black silk blanket. The High Line Park gloomed above me with trespassers and graffiti maestros. I was envious of their creative freedom, their passion, and their drive. They had to do what they were doing, had to create. There was just no other acceptable life than that.

I was inside fast, my memories of Peter fleeting and the ache within me about to be cast off. Stage left, stage right, it didn't matter. I passed the first checkpoint with ease, as if they already knew the click of my heels, the way my pro-truding stomach curved through my lace cardigan. She found me, or I found her, and we didn't exchange any words, any warnings.

It was time.

Face up, legs open, and this time I'd be flying like an inverted Superman. There were many hands, many faces, but no towels to wipe up the blood. A skilled piercer draws no blood to begin with. The first hook rushed through the clamped flesh of my vulva. The pain was sharp, blasting me with heat all the way up to my womb. The next few hooks dived into the muscles between my breast and armpits, my upper thighs and finally my nipples and navel. I was a canvas of red, black and blue.

Fly.

They began the hoist. Each tug on the rope was a war of my body against the universe, against gravity's pull. My skin clutched hard to my bones, unwilling to let go; my muscles turned to liquid and my nervous system exploded. I was creating my own story high above the human landscape below me. I was the new reigning queen of body modification vignettes. The Dark Princess was me.

And then I saw Peter. He was crying, appalled and angry. His hair was frayed and his mouth was bleeding from biting his bottom lip. But I turned away from him. Physical pain is just a sensation, fleeting. It passes, even as your skin separates from your body, even as you fly high above the shimmering candyscape of strobe lights and swirling smoke.

I knew so much about pain then. It hurt the most to see him sad, but I could not and would not know the pain of childbirth. I'll remain in this anti-hero pose forever, like meat hanging and waiting to dry, or until the hooks rip into my uterine cavity and carve it hollow.

2013

.

Written in 2010, "Basement Story 2006" is still a personal favorite of mine. Delilah and Alex have been with me for many years, long before I even wrote *The Absence of Light*. They are the avatars of myself and a childhood friend. This story was born out of my own fear of basements, how dark they can get, how the mind can play the worst tricks. No movie, no book, no campfire tale, can scare me more than my own mind.

Delilah and Alex are both featured in my first novel *The Absence of Light*.

BASEMENT STORY 2006

Venturing into the basement that rebellious day, sixteen-years-old and your best friend is a year younger, tagging along like the brother you never had. Your best friend means everything to you, and he feels the same: two unhappy hearts living an unhappy life, but together you find a spark of light at the end of a boring tunnel.

Flasks in hand, black leather trim, and a shot of stinging Jägermeister every time you say you're scared to go in the basement . . . too weary of that treacherous, damp dark that could swallow you whole. Nothing stands in the way but you and the door, tall rectangle of ancient wood, knob like the golden eye of a cyclops marking your every step. Turning back is out of the question.

"Open it," Delilah said.

"No."

Delilah had been curious as a cat since the day Alex met her, dark haired androgyne, tough as nails and always grinding her teeth. She listened to heavy metal while napping, industrial while showering; shrieking guitars and sibilant vocal melodies soothed her soul. But as much as Alex loved her, and would abide by her wishes for they always promised adventure, he just couldn't do what she said, not right now. He'd heard too many noises down there.

"It's just a basement," and Delilah swung her lengthy hair over her shoulder, smelling of licorice and apples and sweet clove smoke. "What about your flowers, your precious orchids? They need water."

Delilah just wouldn't let it go.

"They don't need that much care, you know that already."

Her face took on a fascinating glow tonight, even as one hand slithered out of her pocket and tugged Alex's freshly pierced ear. It hurt. It was annoying. Alex took a step back, pressed himself against the door and shook his head, but Delilah pulled his ear again. The pain sent a hot bolt down his legs and his feet did a marvelous dance; wavy black hair spun out of control; a sketchy blur of pink and yellow converses slashed the tiled floor.

But no matter what he couldn't let her do it; he didn't want *it* to get out. Still, Delilah was serious; her teeth were bared now and her shoulders scrunched like a football player. She was drenched in so much sweat that her Nine Inch Nails shirt stuck to her skin like a condom on a limp dick. Her face met his again; sapphire eyes meaning business, innocently brutal. Within them were an eon's worth of dreams and nightmares.

"*Do it*," she hissed.

The finality in her voice was all it took. He bowed like a crane in front of the door, feeling a slight breeze, cold and ugly, then put his eyes to the brass key hole, wondering if *it* was looking back at him, wondering if some tongue would slip through to take out his eye. But nothing stared back at him, too dark to see this October night. Then Alex remembered that only music called it out.

"See anything?" Delilah said.

"Nope."

"Well then we've gotta go down there."

"Delilah . . . please," lips tight over his small teeth, ghost of lipstick smeared across. "It only happens when I play the piano. Don't you remember?"

"Remember what?"

"You were here with me. You saw it!"

"I didn't see shit," Delilah snarled, evil smile like a bird. "Get to playing. I'll wait *here for it.*"

". . . I don't know, my grandparents—"

"Grandparents, schmandparents. Where did you hide the skeleton key?" Delilah asked with an upturned hand, pale palm like a small monkey.

"On the key ring . . . by the front door."

Delilah flew out of the kitchen, leaving Alex alone for the longest two seconds of his life. *Can't do this, she's wrong. We mustn't mess around with the thing in the basement. My parents are dead, been dead, and there's no such thing as ghosts or the boogeyman.*

"Got it!"

Delilah slid the key in, clicking lock sound like the end of days, and the door creaked open. Four feet took baby steps; four hands shivered, and two hearts began to beat faster than they ever expected.

Winter when it first happened, when fingers manipulated piano keys and called out the thing from the basement. Alex and Delilah had cut class that day because they didn't like to be stuck in the prison known as High School. They much preferred to learn by their own vices, their own adventures, rather than being cooped up in a classroom headed by someone force-feeding you things you'd be better off not knowing.

This day they hid away from the world inside a dumpster on the edge of the school's property that they called The Hut. No one remembered where it was, and thus no garbage was ever put inside. It was the place Alex could rest in before class, before the big mother fuckers decided to steal his lunch money because they had nothing better to do but fight in packs, before kids and teachers would stare Alex down wondering if he was a boy or a girl being that he wore tight jeans and band t-shirts.

Alex had been born with the gift of androgyny, and it was no mistake that some days he was called a lesbian, and others days a twink. And it was no secret that this didn't bother him. Alex loathed being labeled *boy* or *girl*, and so he left people to their judgments, but the lunch money monkeys never stopped.

Lucky for Alex the past few weeks saw a dissipation of bullies; Delilah had shown all the boys how sharp her butterfly blade was, cutting herself in front of them, her forearm marked up like a sopping blue print of flesh. Nothing more frightening than the sideshow freaks at your door.

In The Hut Alex had an electric heater, two small lava lamps and a velvet blanket for comfort. Delilah's hands cupped one of the lamps, throwing soft colored shadows in the near reflection. Alex was outwardly freaked out; he hated snow, hated to wear heavy clothes because he was so skinny and all they did was weigh him down.

The snow was getting thicker, huge flakes came down like ice chips flying off an Edward Scissorhands sculpture. But this kind of weather is normal when one lives in a patch town deep within the coal region of Pennsylvania; best to dress up warm because once winter came, it never stopped. Snow in October? Thank you, global warming.

But Alex had also dreamed of his mother again.

She was locked in *that* closet in the basement.

"She died giving birth to me. Not murder or anything," Alex said.

"So then why are you scared?"

"I don't know. I just am."

"It's a classic horror tale, *The Thing in the Basement*. And we're living, breathing characters."

"I guess so."

"You look tired, Alex."

"I didn't sleep a wink last night, too worried . . ."

"I bet it's only a fucking rat, maybe even a bat."

"You and your damn bats. You need to just go out and get one. There are so many in these Pennsylvania forests."

The snow was piling up now, and a line of water was squiggling down the inside, small glittering river. Delilah lit a black votive and put it between their shivering bodies, soothing pinpoint flame yellow as a dandelion, adding more heat to The Hut like blood to the brain for conversation.

"I've been having fucked-up dreams, real fucked-up dreams, Alex," Delilah said with her finger in her mouth, chipped maroon nail polish like the missing pieces to her soul.

"Still like—"

"Yes, like I leave my physical body and can walk in the land of the dead."

"Like a shaman?"

"No, I don't believe in any religion, not even mystical ones."

"Black Sabbath talked about out-of-body experiences in 'Behind the Wall of Sleep.' Did you know that?"

"You've told me a hundred times," Delilah lit a cigarette and let the smoke form around her like an embrace.

"I like when you do that trick with the smoke, it's funny."

Delilah rolled her eyes. "*Anyway*, I'm thinking we should—"

"No."

"But you can play the piano while I—"

"NO!"

Delilah's face soured in shock.

"Why must you fuck with the dead? Haven't you learned your lesson?"

"Yeah, spare me, I already know . . . since the graveyard incident. I got drunk and fell in a ditch . . . couldn't get out until you and Jimmy pulled me up."

"They *pushed* you into that ditch, Delilah; you didn't get drunk and fall."

"So what? I read in *The Wild Boys* that with certain drugs you can create your own near-death visions."

Alex nodded. What else could he do? When Delilah got into one of her famous moods, when her mind was set on something—a simple task, a fucking plate of macaroni and cheese—it had to be seen through to the end. If she didn't, she might throw a fit, and Alex hated seeing Delilah cut herself. She told him once that she'd stopped, but at times those suicide ghosts come back to haunt old territory.

"I'm not kidding anymore. I'm scared."

"You don't have to be scared, I'm here with you. Your parents are dead, but if they're walking around your basement like Captain fucking Howdy, we should get involved," cigarette smoke whirling now, trickle of cold coming into The Hut.

"When does it happen . . . your out-of-body experiences?" Alex asked curiously.

"Like I said . . . when I sleep. And when did these dreams start for you?"

"I think I've had them all my life, but now, well, since puberty they've been getting worse."

"Let's start with this."

Delilah pulled a dimebag out of her back pocket, opened the seal and filled The Hut with the sharp verdant smell of an open field. She broke it up and quickly rolled two joints and passed one to Alex, masterpiece in white. Alex lit the joint and took a hit; spicy green smoke suffused his mouth, his throat. His head began to spin almost instantly; the effect smashed him like a sock full of pennies, and as Delilah was talking, the world he knew clicked out.

When Alex woke he was in his living room with Delilah, dreaming of the grand piano, dream as cold as fever sweat as he stared down the basement door, waiting for it to open to his wicked tune. But the thing only woke at night, insomniac phantom much like Delilah and Alex. It was always better to play in the dark anyway, by candles, because not even a sliver of moonlight made it through the trees in this part of town.

Face forward before the grand piano, each key like polished slivers of bone. Alex pressed his bony fingers against the piano keys. The notes climbed free from the air, swirled above them like shooting stars, *Moonlight Sonata*. Delilah was all of a sudden next to him, her face vacuous, her eyes blue diamonds in the soft dark, eyes that sensed oncoming danger.

And then Alex saw why. The basement door was slowly *moving*; pearl-colored fingers wrapped around the edge, sliming their way to freedom. Suddenly Alex's vision whirled as if inside a funnel. Then Delilah was pulling him as she ran toward some kind of light at the end of the tunnel: fetus breaking free of the placenta, exiting a blood-slicked womb.

And he woke up.

"Grandpa's asleep, Alex. What's it you want to tell him?"

In this memory it's nighttime, and the moon was full, huge beach ball like an omniscient god staring down into

Alex. Its light slid off of the windowpane, gliding across the wood island where Grandmother's kitchen knife lay as if ready to spring to life and turn flesh into a red ruined mess. Grandmother, veined arms like small purple serpents twisting beneath thin skin.

Alex saw every stress line, every bruise she had endured in that kitchen, every knife scar like a mark of relief. She was a marvelous cook, and a marvelous talker. Grandmother: the treasure chest of advice, of solace and care. The stove was hot with some kind of loaf, and Alex smelled ketchup and the sizzling red juice of butcher meat. She was taller than he remembered, gaunter.

Back at the cutting board, Grandmother worked her magic with the knife; onion sliced in half and carrots chopped. Alex watched her, young boy not yet fifteen, but with a face so childish one could mistake him for five years younger. His hair was growing out of control and his features were so smooth one could not tell if he was a boy or a girl.

His eyes were locked onto Grandmother, long hair scaling down her crooked spine, and the twist-tie of her pink apron. She almost looked like the woman he saw the other night, the one at the foot of his bed with the deep set eyes and pin straight hair. But it was a dream he remembered, nothing his own mind couldn't have made up before he went to bed. He knew dreams were how the body filtered the stressors and sensory stimulation of the day out of one's mind, and he'd been thinking of her heavily.

"It's my mother. She came to visit me."

Grandmother slammed the knife down. "Don't say that, Alex."

"She comes when I play the piano."

"Your mother was our daughter," wet hands on Alex's face now, sharp onion stench and carrot smear across his cheek. "We loved her, and you would have too, but she died giving birth to you."

Grandmother's eyes were spider-webbed red and the palest green in the center, soul of a jewel: the badge of making it past sixty years of age. She was going to cry, so Alex let the conversation go. He wouldn't think of her anymore, her body shaking and cold. It was like a bad memory waiting to be let out of purgatory. For a young kid with nobody to talk to, no parents to tell him how to go about these kinds of problems, he had to suck it up, and wouldn't tell Grandpa either. It was best not to wake him until past ten at night anyway.

"Your grandfather works too hard at the Gheligg factory for you to be making up these tales. He needs his rest and his sanity. Please . . . for the sake of this house, speak of this never again."

". . . never again, I won't. But I know from the pictures in the closet down there."

"You've been snooping?" Grandmother shook her head. "You know, sometimes, when your mother went snooping we made her stay in that closet . . . with all the lights out!"

"Are you serious?"

"And she would complain about a . . . presence in there. But you know us Pennsylvania folk, we don't believe in that kind of junk."

"Why that closet though?"

"We didn't believe in hitting. Now let me finish cooking," and Grandmother winked as Alex stepped away. "Oh, Alex?"

"Yeah?"

"She used to love to play . . . that same piano."

Kitchen behind him now, bright square in the dark living room, his back to the wall so to not see the door on his way out, the formation, the chiaroscuro illusion, and Alex sat at the grand piano. Black lacquered surface, tooth-white keys ready for him to play. One finger at a time, knuckles moving in symphony with the tortured music in his head, and Alex played until the house swelled with scales and notes, until they tore away from the piano and sifted through the senses.

Then the old brass knob turned and the basement door creaked open. But Alex ignored it and continued to play, moving his limbs in tempo with the brand new song he'd written last week, a blend of rock ballad and orchestra. He didn't see the warbling fingers clutching the edge of the door, the nails rimmed in black blood, and the wretched face behind the curtain of hair; not until he heard Grandmother screech, dropping her knife to the floor, spill of carrot and onion slivers, and the basement door slamming shut as his fingers moved off the piano.

A few weeks later, Alex lay wasted in his own dark thoughts, still dreaming of the woman. He and Delilah had broken into the local morgue and accessed some records, looked up names and tried to pair them with faces, but no luck. Alex couldn't even remember the face too well, and Delilah had yet to admit that she'd even seen it. His grandparents were of no help either, and Grandmother would not speak of her daughter, not of anything.

Alex knew that old people were to be respected, so he left them alone, and stopped burdening them with the talk of his sleepless nights, of his worsening dreams. Plus, Grandmother was an academic and academics do not believe in life after death. In death there is just blackness, but trouble is that no one has risen from the dead to prove this . . . not yet anyhow.

So Alex cut class with Delilah more than usual. He wrote his troubles in notebooks, filled three a week, and this showed no signs of stopping. His words evolved into lyrics, ones that Delilah fine-tweaked. But words never suited him well. Alex was suited best in writing out his fear in music, in the piano. So he replaced his prose notebook and began to learn the mysteries of musical scales. He drew wiry looking notes with ugly faces, C major, D harmonic minor, and raging chords.

Delilah showed him her notebooks too, words she'd scribbled when drunk, when feeling like life was worth less than what a pig could spit, when wishing of a better life. They became attached at the hip, weaving together the strings of music like a tight piece of clothing. These songs were the demons Alex held deep inside his soul, the fright he felt living within his own home, the one place he should've felt *safe*.

The music books piled high; the sessions grew longer and their songs tighter. Delilah's voice changed; her poetry buzzed over Alex's scales as she fused harmonics and a capella, the sultry sounds of industrial and heavy metal. Alex's fingers were strengthening too; his knowledge of chords, scales and time signatures were limitless.

They were music's children—bent backs, slouched jaws and growing brains—daubing poetry on loose leaf, musical notes on ruled paper to materialize them into songs: self-taught musicians practicing loud and hard as maestros. Even Alex's grandparents said that they were onto something good, and Delilah's conservative adopted parents approved dismally of her celestial voice, her stinging lyrics.

Their music was inspired by and dedicated to the macabre. It raged with unpolished talent as much as it was loathsome and dark. It calmed their nightmares, their hummingbird hearts, and one day they would start a band, but when that day was both of them didn't know. But their music didn't stop Delilah's need to see what Alex was so afraid of, even though he'd forced their practices to daylight hours because he knew night is when it came alive and crawling for fresh air from the dirty basement.

"I want to see it!" Delilah demanded.

"No! It's a demon . . . a mermaid . . ."

"Mermaids aren't evil."

"That's like saying there aren't any *good* witches. Are you that naïve?"

Delilah snatched a handful of Alex's hair and made her butterfly blade flutter open; she traced the hollow of Alex's pale neck softly, coming around to his sharp nose and thin lips. She always had trouble controlling her anger.

"I'll gut you like a fish, Alex. Isn't that what they said in the movie?"

"I'm not scared. Go ahead. It'll stop my dreams."

"Forget it. Let's play . . . now!"

"It won't come."

"Because all we've done is practice . . . we've never really *played*. We've never really put on a show."

"A show?" Alex twirled his dark hair in his thin white fingers, wormy things in a forest of black.

"Yes, let's put one on. Now."

Nothing could stop the moment. Delilah began the song, voice like ground diamonds sprinkled over a decadent cocktail, a song she called "My Personal Hell." Part love story of the dream world, part mystery of her missing past. Alex put his fingers to the keys, creeping slow as death into Delilah's silvery voice.

From the window yellow spirals of sunshine dripped and streaked across Delilah's face. Alex noticed there was not a cloud in sky; only a fine vapor was at the window. Some kind of watcher? A soul? But once the graceful twirl of music hit its crescendo it was gone. Their first show came with no audience to applaud but it felt so right, so feral. They paid attention to nothing but the sounds.

But then the basement door opened slowly, hooked finger sliming the knob.

Down cement stairs untouched in weeks, and Grandmother avoiding the basement now too. Delilah first, brave girl with nothing to fear for she'd been more curious than ever. Alex behind her, gripping tight, best buds, and Delilah squeezed him back tight. *I'm here to protect you*, he thought he heard her say.

Dropped down the last step and nothing out of the ordinary, wide square space, a single pool table scrawled with Alex's pre-pubescent poetry, stacks of newspapers, dust bunnies and landmines of mouse shit.

The darkest part swarmed with orchids; long green stems stabbed the air, petals swirled white and red opened their eyes. A rare carrion species from South Africa looked like a vile head of cabbage and stunk like evil. Alex loved orchids; he'd been growing them since he was a kid and had mastered their intricate care. Orchids are some of the most fastidious flowers in the world; too much or too little water, light, and air could kill them.

"I don't see what you mean," Delilah said, small joint between pursed lips colored in pale red.

"It's empty, I know. But it's down here. I'm scared out of my wits. I wanna go upstairs."

"*Not yet*," Delilah scowled, gritting her teeth so hard she drew blood.

"It's like a whole new world. I don't know my own home."

Alex was half right. Delilah could feel the strangeness down here, could smell it in the musty air: Hell, the devil's lounge, whatever you'd call it. A room that collected sadness like flies on a glue trap, a jar full of rage spilled from the shelf of madness. Bad room, indeed, but what made it this way? What was the secret?

They both walked further in; Delilah noticed daylight was nowhere to be found, blocked by piles of newspapers lying against the only window. Their grasp was broken by the pool table—bad luck to separate. Like lovers on a romantic stroll, who let go at the sight of an oncoming pole and then break up a month later. Delilah ventured to the closet, black boots moving across the basement floor like an ice skating rink made of gravel and mist.

She thought about the only television to ever set foot in this house, that it was locked in that closet because reading is fundamental: the television only brainwashes. Alex planted himself by the orchids, eyes closed, face covered by vampiric hands, black nail polish resembling beetles.

"I don't want to see what you're going to do," Alex said, putting a joint in his mouth and lighting too fast so that cinders billowed down to his lap.

Soon the basement was filled with smoke, swamp fog thickness. Delilah cackled because she was always the tough girl. Nothing scared her; she didn't believe in ghosts.

And then she heard a faint scratching noise.

Captain Howdy wants attention.

"I'm going upstairs. I don't give a fuck anymore!"

Alex scrammed, broomstick legs running so fast Delilah barely had enough time to scream for him to stop, to stay with her in this cavernous hole, Bat Cave's evil sister. Fuck it. Delilah's hand found the doorknob and she opened it so fast something came tumbling down toward her: dirty ragged hair, faint white hue of pissed-off eyes in its face. Delilah did a pratfall as she stepped backward, but saw that it was only a mop. Simple mop, and embarrassed, Delilah kicked the floor, hurting her ankle.

Then another *scritch-scritch-scritch*. Flies buzzing inside her head, keys slammed to the counter.

In a fit of rage she rushed into the closet, pulling out the television by its chord; blankets as old as Alex's grandparents full of wasted smells came out too, and old photographs scattered everywhere. Ancient family portraits of ancestors long dead, the women of the first settling family dressed in sober black lace, fresh as pilgrims marching off the *Mayflower*.

Then there were other photos too, from the early Seventies: tie-dye patterns, swirly bell bottoms and long hair knotted down the entire length of a girl's back. The woman resembles her puritan ancestors; Alex too. She's in all the photos, ones taken in the very living room above Delilah at the same grand piano, same fingers as Alex, playing and smiling. Delilah knows that this is Alex's mother by the signature sharp features and long black hair delicate as rain. There are hand-written piano scales, lyrics too, and notes about strange things happening when she played her music.

Scritch-scritch-scritch.

Delilah heard enough. She gripped the hang bar, pulled her legs to her chest and plowed them through the wall. An explosion of sheetrock and old spider webs blasted her, and below the pile a small rodent stirred, afraid of the big monster in front of it with the painted nails and lips pulled tight over teeth.

Delilah cupped the mouse in her hands, laughing at herself for being so jumpy. It was proof that Alex was wrong, that dead mothers can't rise from the grave and come back to haunt their offspring. Ghosts are not real. Reality itself is what we should be afraid of.

But then Delilah hears the piano take charge.

Notes drummed above her head; deep, dark chords weeding their way through the thin floor boards as if some vicious plant. The song is well practiced, dreamy, can put a motion movie soundtrack to shame, can make the symphonies of Beethoven and Mozart sound amateur. Delilah sits by the photos, smoking the last of her joint, watching the room grow smaller around her, darkening like that tunnel she seems to always walk through in the slippery void between sleep and dream. Each note is quick and haunting as chamber music in a seventeenth century play.

Then the photos next to Delilah begin to stir. Not just stir, but come together, paper and ink globs melding into one entire being. And then it happened. First it was the hair, then the whispering, and then Delilah sees its eyes: careless and lost, palest green like a lucky charm, deep-sea gem brought up by a brash fisherman. The hand comes up from the floor first, slimed in plasma, reeking of death and confusion and brine. Delilah dropped the rodent and bolted for the top of the stairs, just in time to see Alex waiting for her with his foot stamping the floorboards.

She was a believer now.

2010

As a native New Yorker, born and raised in Queens, I can safely say that Manhattan is the capital of superficiality. A band that I love, Glassjaw, touches upon this subject a lot, and they're from my own backyard, Long Island. Makes me proud to say that. Superficiality has always been something that annoyed me. It can do some real damage to the ego of even the strongest people. But . . . what can it do to the weakest of us? That's where this story came from. The title is aptly taken from a Glassjaw song of the same name. This was written in 2011.

LOVEBITES & RAZORLINES

It's said that adventure is born from the fire of monotony spreading inside a person's brain. I sort of felt the same way, and that made me want to go out on an adventure of my own. Last month when the trees' leaves fell from the branches like droplets of blood, and the city skyline became the color of pumpkins during twilight, I felt my life come to a screaming halt.

I ventured out by foot and loaded up my metro card, touring the city streets by bus and the dark wet underground by train. I had no intent of sleeping or eating: it was time to dream. I thinned myself until my arms looked like prison bars and my face a living skull. I never had a good appetite anyway (I saved most of it for cheap beer and an embalming bottle of 151). I was forcing my palate into panic mode, so much so that it took anything that I put into my mouth: mince meat, a festered pack of chicken, pork chops cut straight from the swine. Raw meat, not the delicacy of the western world.

I was always meant to be different.

Then I remembered why I did all of this: I was alone, yet again. Alone, so alone. Hellos and goodbyes ringed the mouths of temporary flimsies like sweat waiting to be wiped clean; ephemeral bodies polluted my bed just long enough to leave behind the ghost of their sweet scent. I should've been used to this as I'd shared my life with solitude for a long time—in dive bars where boys never welcomed me as their nightly companion, or in the back room of the porn shops still straggling across 8th Avenue—because the boys that accompanied me never wanted so much as to stay the next day. They were only in it for the quick fix while I clung to them for a conversation; a cup of fucking coffee in the evening hours.

Sick with the love-bug I was.

This was, of course, my own fault. I had a taste for the degenerates of the city, boys considered out of my league, to be frank. Mainstream culture teaches you to want them, would have anyone begging for crumbs at the feet of these A-listers, and I fell right into the trap. Turn the television on and BAM! there's a lithe beauty slammed into your face, telling you that's how you should look if you want a love life. I, of course, thought I was stronger than this, that I could resist such simple temptation.

I wasn't.

My part of town is littered with fashionistas and super-ficial superheroes. They're the type of people too stuck in the latest wave of fashion to care about anything else, anyone else. They don't have the time or patience to deal with someone outside their social circle (namely me). But I made it my business to force myself in.

Intoxication is the perfect weapon. I can get whatever bitching boy I need by way of a promised drink, smoke and a comfy bed. They just never want to stay past that first night, and I always wanted to keep them so bad. They didn't think I was worth it, and some boys would even demand payment, forgetting that I'd housed them for the night. But I'd give it up with an invisible fist thrusting into their vacant faces.

And then once the anger faded, the love bug would bite me again. Sepulchral poison thundering into my head like possession! I had to have love, what else was there to do in life? Didn't humans evolve from raging monkeys into a species that depended on a partner for more than mating? Why did I have to be so rudely thrown out of the equation? Life is about relationships and how you build them. Love is the fuel for it all.

I had to have it, simply put. It would be a cure for my sickness.

So much of that sickness made me question my own sanity. I never knew I had it in me (though I must've, for I'd been nibbling raw meat), but when I grabbed the handle of the hammer it spilled to me all of its sinister secrets. Concealed under piles of paper scrawled with the terrible poetry that I hadn't published yet, the hammer said that everything would be alright, that the music I was blasting would mix thrashing bass and vocals with nascent shrieking terror. Glassjaw is so great that way.

The hammer plummeted without him expecting it.

I felt the metal chink into bone, split his skull. The blood engulfed me like a tidal wave and warmed my shuddering body. So I plunged again, and again, until his shiny yellow hairline started pulling away from his skin with a red-wet suck, until it was shot through with gore. That rendered him unconscious, and it was then I realized that I had a taste for blood: a mouthful of salty heaven.

Naturally, right? I'd already been eating offal butcher meat, training myself to become some kind of carnivore. His blood soon clotted along the edge of my bed, twisting out of his head like a water fountain gone awry. That meant his precious little heart was still beating, and that he could hear me. I could've ripped into him at that moment and fed from his viscera, but I was barely able to catch my breath because I had found a penchant for murder. I was going to be in love, for real this time.

"You should never trust a man who offers you a warm bed and drink for one night only," I said to the barely breathing beauty.

I moved the little fucker into my bathroom, a place swarming with insects and moldy tiles. I could give a fuck about cleaning; there was too much dreaming to do. And now that I was living my fantasy, there was no time to waste! I had packs of ice in my freezer and I dumped them all in the tub, watching the skin on his face go gray and eyes stare blankly into me.

I spent the rest of the night watching cheap B movies that only a nerd could love, surrounded by books and a comic collection so huge and overzealous it's too embarrassing to speak of. The characters in movies and books never left. By the power of the pause button or a bookmarker I could revisit who and what I wanted and not be judged. I watched the screen for four hours straight, unshowered and sticky with blood, already smelling the faint gaseous threat of decomposition. I'd been watching an old television show called *The Hunger*: suspense and sex mixed into one dangerous vial, and it made me think of my own life.

On the nights when I was alone, when I could not find anyone to suit my vicious desire, I lay in waste dreaming. I wrote in a scrappy notebook and dabbed the pages with bloodied fingerprints; I read books of the macabre, the darkly fantastic and of outer worlds to steal my soul. Who needed a soul on this evil earth if one had to be alone? I could survive just fine as an unholy ghost, I knew, and perhaps that's exactly what I was going to do.

Poetic justice? Perhaps.

Books sailed my mind out of this world and dipped it into the brains of many others. I could read the same novel in spring and smile, but read it again in the following winter and I'd be a wreck. My moods were worsening. What lie beneath the tattered covers might turn a pauper into a prince, might turn a boy into an artist, but I'd learned morality is only skin deep and that it couldn't be trusted. *Books are tiny universes concealed within ink and paper. Art is the rocket ship.*

When I read *Frankenstein* by Mary Shelley I realized that I hadn't become sick, hadn't felt a searing anger that winter. A roaring seed of lust exploded in my gut. I had found an answer. Not so much a zombie novel—but in a sense it could be—as it is a novel of struggle and necessity for life. A novel where the point of view came from the monster himself! I was this sympathetic monster, and this understanding clutched my heart with a cold dead hand, just like the hand sitting in my own bathtub.

Frankenstein was the key to my locked life. Like the mad doctor in the book, I was going to make my own lover. But not in the way that crazy Victor did it. I'd not collect bones from charnel houses, nor utilize the limbs of animals from the local butcher. I'd simply build it from my interim lovers. I imagined the eyes I wanted to look into, and the hands I wanted to hold, formulating a plan while I basted my own organs in vodka. I'd yet to shower either because I still had a boy on ice in my bathroom; and so it was time to release him from his hell. I recalled Mary Shelley's madness, her empathy for the monster, and suddenly everything was right, justified.

The memories of those pages spoke in tongues: forever, eternal, perpetual.

I could be pitied if people heard my story.

It was time.

In the tub he sat erect. His arms were pale and limp as death allows. The color had drained out of his face, shimmering faintly in the dim bathroom light. The back of his head was a swamp; there was a sticky smear of gore along the place where I'd slid his body into the tub. I rubbed my finger into the cold mush, bringing the blood to my tongue. It was like wine gone to vinegar.

I liked nothing on his body but his hands. They were soft and lovely. His face had lost the youth I'd been so attracted to at first; his eyes were dried glumes within hollowed sockets. I wanted no part of them. But his hands had stood the test of time, hadn't yet curled into a rigor mortis ball, and so I was able to hold them for a moment and stare into those depthless eyes, wondering if he hated me for stealing his life. But he only had his hormones to blame.

For the incision I drew a small line across his wrists like a surgeon preparing his patient. I'd forgotten how long his fingers were. These were the hands that had grabbed my hair as we thrust into one another; these were the nails that had dug furrows into my chest during indulgent orgasm, the hands that had begged me to stop as I rained the hook of the hammer into his head.

I faintly remembered that he'd learned to play piano as a young boy, such is why those fingers were so strong! I imagined his flowing blond hair behind a grand orchestra, thin white fingers stretching to reach every key on the piano, his head bobbling to the music. But then the vision faded and I realized I had work to do.

With fishing line I tied his wrists together so I could see the cutting line clearly. The teeth of the hack saw broke into the flesh with ease. His skin flaked away and blood misted into my eyes. The hand snapped off and sinews of tendon hung like overcooked spaghetti. I put it in a Ziploc bag in my freezer. Rinse and repeat and the hands stayed beautiful even after death. They were to be the hands I'd hold the rest of my life.

"Would you like to come back to my place?" I asked a sweet-smelling guy across the dark bar.

He didn't answer at first, not that I cared. He had the bluest eyes I'd ever seen, and I wanted them for my pet project. Though we shared little conversation, he seemed like a genuine guy. I'd already spent half the night in the corner booth sipping Old Number 7 on the rocks through a little red straw, so what else did I have to lose.

"Well . . . sure," he said, dubious, "you seem like a nice guy, and you aren't that ugly."

I winced, hoping the music in the jukebox would turn louder, hoping that a glass would fall off the bar top and smash to a billion glittering chunks so to erase that awkward moment, to stop my face from turning instantly grim. I was starved, I admit, and my pallor had reached dangerous heights. I'd learned to stand upright and shake off the burst of stars before my eyes being that my blood sugar was so dangerously low. I often amazed myself at how we humans adapt to such terrible circumstances.

But the guy didn't, as the bar was ridden with shadows. Better for me, for I had exquisite plans to execute! So I promised him another drink and a good night in bed, no strings attached, as the men in this community love.

All I wanted were his eyes. They were forbidden gems, pride of northern Europe. They put Caribbean oceans to shame. I took a moment to tell the guy about myself, making up stories as I went along, as my brain was teased into pleasant drunkenness. I found myself being overtly charming, overtly calm, but on the inside I was screaming with loneliness.

"Horror movies are weird," he told me.

"My building's not far from here, but we can even take a cab if you don't want to walk."

"Sounds good. By the way, I'm Sean."

"Jason."

The lie slipped through my lips like dead weight. It seemed natural when the person who you're about to sleep with wouldn't be alive for much longer. Why not reinvent yourself for the fuck of it?

"Let's take a cab, it's quicker," Sean said.

We left in a jiffy, with my pants way too tight around my crotch.

I took careful steps to not damage the eyes.

Sean had put up a good fight. The first blow of the hammer sent him flying into my stereo, which turned off Daryl Palumbo's nascent screaming; the second only pissed him off. That should've knocked him out, but I was so drunk I'd not calculated the strength it took to kill a person with a hammer. Plus, my new diet of alcohol and cigarettes had left me with no strength to put on my pants correctly.

His blood sprayed my face as he darted for the door. I grabbed him hard, but to deflect me from coming any closer, Sean elbowed me right in my nose, jerking my head backward. I felt the cartilage crush like tomatoes under a boot and determined that my blood was not as delicious as others: it was sourer, watery.

As he clawed for the locks I wound my hand back and shot the hammer straight as an arrow, heard it connect with his head in a wet metal slap. The sound reminded me of a potato hitting concrete. His skull split like lips and his hair flooded rouge. He was out for the count. As I dragged him to the infamous bathroom, our little duel had left me wanting to taste his blood right away.

When I did I realized that it was faintly sweet. I thought maybe this was the flavor of fear, the grim finality within the second before you die. But I hadn't eaten in nearly four weeks by this time; my appetite was severely changing, my palate begging for any kind of nourishment.

Sean was so heavy in death. His arms and legs felt like they were filled with lead. I sat him upright and opened his eyes. They were still as spellbinding as when he'd been alive. I thought about popping them out with a butter knife, or even that little silver tool that you crack open fresh mussels with. But no, that would have flattened the eyes to pancakes. Instead, I chose a spoon.

Thin traceries of veins glowed through Sean's face, veins deprived of the body's electric. They looked quite sad, quite cold. I held one eye open with the phantom intelligence of a medical master, with the unflinching hand of a surgeon, and pushed the spoon in. It made a squelch like crushing a hundred worms in your hands, falling out whole in my lap.

I'd prepared a jar of cold water with a pinch of salt and dropped the eyes in. Thread-like optic nerve floated free. I was one step closer to my homemade lover, my forever. But something was missing: a body. I had the hands and the eyes, I had my cryptic imagination, but I wasn't a scientist by any means. I couldn't fashion a heart from scratch, I couldn't rewire the vessels in which blood traveled through. I couldn't take the brain, spongy and soft in my hands, and transplant it into another head.

That would take time and persistence, and I had neither. I was too sick. My diet was treacherous, equalized only by the seldom sip of water and Tylenol PM for the woozy feeling. What I needed was a whole body, one that could compliment the perfect eyes and hands. So I cleaned myself up and severed all of Sean's limbs. I bisected the legs at the knee, tore his arms straight from the shoulder and boiled his skull down to the bone before I stuffed him into an industrial garbage bag filled with bleach. From the depths of that bag I knew the eyeless skull was forever grinning, but at whom? Himself for being so stupid?

Then I felt something watching me, some entity from another universe. I turned and saw Sean's eyes swimming in the jar. The water magnified their size; I could see all the precious highways of vessels that supplied them with blood and oxygen, tears and sight, and they were carefully marking me. They made me think. Invoking life into a dead body would only take a little electricity and water, just like the movies. Drop a toaster into the tub and you have yourself a homemade defibrillator.

I set out on an adventure through St. Mark's. It's a seedy place at night, though I was so sick I couldn't focus on everything that I'd grown to love: the speeding cars, the smell of coffee, the loud music blasting on the corner of Astor and 3rd Avenue.

The wind bit through my clothes like a fucking little monster. I wrapped my arms around my torso, noticing that people staring at my bane form. I think by that point I was limping. Not too sure. I didn't know how bad the love-bug had infected me, how it had thinned me to such a skeleton that people feared me as the living dead.

I was in a bad mood anyway. I felt weak, ugly, un-wanted: everything that would bog my chances to bag a new cutie. Even the regular hobos of St. Mark's mistook me for one of their own, and that was the greatest insult of the night.

"Come," one of them said, a fetid woman dressed in moth-eaten rags lying in a nearby crevice. "We have room for you."

She offered me a bed of cardboard and a smoke, but I refused all her niceties. Away from that block, I stumbled into brilliant bodies shuffling along in groups. Boys with long corn-silk hair, white fishnets and black leather boots squiggled between yuppies and their perpetual sneers. Some boys held hands for the universal fuck you. The ground sparkled with spilled drinks; the sounds of bar laughter pummeled my ears. The air tasted black and drunk, ridden with perfume and lust.

It was how I preferred my nights.

I stopped at a bar called The Continental. Five shots for ten dollars was their special, according to the enticing sign, bold black letters painted on a bright white banner. I slipped past the stupid black velvet rope and took a seat at the edge of the bar where the wind blew in just enough to sober a person up through the heavy-duty curtains. The jukebox was obnoxiously blasting the universal bar song.

We're halfway there, ooooh! Living on a prayer!

I wanted to hear Glassjaw, my favorite band.

The bar itself was four people thick, all the faces tailing the two hard working barmaids to pour them shots, shots, shots! The girls' sports bras were soaked in alcohol and their nipples were like tiny pink diamonds. I supposed that big tips were in order. I downed four shots of Jäger, and it was like I'd drunk gasoline the way it singed my esophagus and rumbled my stomach. I just couldn't take it anymore. The alcohol left the sickly-sweet taste of cough medicine on my palate, but I found I wanted something more, something with texture: meat.

HUNGER!

The room took on an odd shape then, lilting and vibrating to the eighties music shrieking from the stupid neon jukebox. Darkness melded with the poor lighting scheme and made everyone look the same, but it all made perfect sense: I was simply drunk.

And then the miracle happened.

Just as I was ready to give up—and how ironic that some fucking piece of luck comes my way when I want to quit—he walked into the bar. A tall, shadowed boy with androgynous features sharp as a razor, high cheekbones and a great head of dyed black hair that reflected all the lights of the jukebox. A metal head. An emo queen. He sat two seats away from me, perhaps sensing one of his own. I took the opportunity to order Old Number 7. No one can refuse a free drink.

"Do you drink much?" I asked.

He pushed his hair away from his face and I caught the smell of meat sauce. "Not really."

His black eyes scanned me, as if liking what he saw. The bartender chick pushed the 5 shots his way.

"Old number 7, on me."

"Good. Fucks me up quick. This place is shit anyway."

"You're so right."

"I'm Perry, by the way."

"Arthur," I lied again; I'd almost grown a knack for it.

"I'm not really a club kid kind of guy," Perry added, "so I stick to bars. They're good enough for me, but my friends would argue the value of going to a club. I never listen though."

I watched his jaw move like an endless ocean as he talked, watched his throat constrict every time we cheered the next shot. I'd found the perfect one! His smile was evil as the Cheshire Cat's, though most people are brainwashed to believe that cat was a goody two-shoe. Then all the drunkenness in me came out and danced along with his hellacious grin, little teeth that would be good for chewing meat.

"Would you like to come home with me?" I blurted
stupidly.

"Got a bottle of Jack there?"

"Plenty."

"Then why the hell aren't we out of here?"

I spread him across the bed after feeding him the promised
bottle of Jack Daniels. It turned out that Perry didn't much
like the taste after the second bottle; he became so sick I
hadn't enough sheets and blankets to soak up the vomit
and heaping diarrhea that even faintly tasted of that dark
amber liquor.

Perry passed out with the intention of feeling the worst
hangover in the world when he woke up. Too bad he never
rose from my bed—well, not alive. I tied a wet pillowcase
over his throat, put a plastic bag over his head, pulling until
I saw his face go pale with death. I didn't want to damage
his face or his body, didn't want to use that stupid hammer
anymore. I was too weak; too starved. Perry looked good
enough to eat I was so fucking hungry, but instead I
dragged his lanky body to the shower and washed him up
good.

The loss of brain function made his limbs hug my torso
like dead tree branches and his bowels stick to my leg like
snot. A small driblet of blood ran from Perry's nose, and I
licked it off as I lay him down. The coolness of death
soothed me, the taste of Old Number 7 was still prevalent,
and the thought of Perry's last drink with me got me hard
instantly.

The hacksaw was waiting for me as if written in the
stars. I got to work straight away on Perry's wrists. His
bones were thin and feeble; his hands snapped away and
lay like dead spiders on the edge of the bathtub. The

amount of blood was phenomenal, and it had taken on an odd consistency: the creepy feel of new death.

My sewing skills were far from professional; I was a rookie in every sense of the word. I took the hands from the freezer, still so nice and smooth and savory, and matched them up on the correct bones, making sure the thumbs pointed inward. I punctured the needle through a thin layer of skin and it lifted from the meat of Perry's arm, pulling the limbs together. I used clear fishing line; it would leave a fleshy look. Black thread would've stood out too much.

Rinse and repeat and I laid the new hands on Perry's milky thighs, letting them get used to their new body. I scooped out Perry's eyes and rolled one in my grip, sad little fruit. The new eyes swam around the jar curiously, and I was surprised to see that they had grown in size, were too big for Perry's sockets.

They'd absorbed the saline solution, pickled, if you will. Yet I managed to squish them in, skillful enough to not damage even the slightest bit of iris, but was disappointed to see how slack they looked, how sad. One beautiful eye peered to the left as if not wanting to look at its maker, the other was pointing downward. But I figured that was nothing a little water and electricity couldn't fix.

Fill the tub and drop the blow dryer in.

It was time. The headaches were at their worst and I was thinned to a mere arrow; the muscles in my face had finally rendered me a living corpse and I could no longer escape the hunger pains.

I plugged in the blow dryer and stood above the shifting brown water like that of the Hudson River on a rainy day. I became hypnotized by this abominable act of bringing the dead to life, but the blow dryer howled all the way to the water, an old remedy used for murder, now being used to make life instead. It splashed into the tub, shooting a yellow-gold arc of sparks through air, burning my shirt.

The lights flickered like in an old abandoned building, and the body jolted. I saw its hand jerking, saw its head bobbling maniacally. Sputum shot from his lips, blurry eyes all of a sudden focused on something: me! Then everything went quiet, nothing but the crackle of languid electric and bubbling water. My breath became the only sound through the short-circuited darkness. No movement, no lover waking . . . yet.

I turned to open the bathroom door so to let out the burnt rubber smell, but that's when I heard the mouth crack open and deflated lungs take in a delicious breath of air. It was the sound of a person just saved from drowning. It spoke in a small, docile voice. Perhaps I was hearing things, perhaps I was simply too drunk, deliriously famished.

From somewhere distant I heard music and the laughter of boys long since dead in here, vengeful voices coming back to claim me. In death life can be born, I thought. But I needed to leave, and quick, or I was sure to be taken on a never-ending hayride to my doom. I kept dreaming about food, and thought that I might get some outside.

"Can you hear me?" I asked it.

No answer.

I was pissed off, hungry. I needed FOOD!

So I did leave, and found a friend that would feed me.

"You have to come over and see him!" I told Samantha, my punk-rock goddess of a friend. She loved leather jackets and ripped blue jeans, Mohawks and wore too many rings on her fingers. "Amazing and beautiful! We met at a club."

"You look like hell," she told me, but curious to see my new boyfriend. She'd gotten used to my boys lasting only from dusk 'til dawn, so she had to know what this one was about. "And when's the last time you've eaten?"

"Forget about that. I want you to see him."

It was perhaps my blind hope that if I brought Perry some fresh meat that he'd be alive when I returned.

But oh, was I wrong.

So wrong.

I opened the door to my apartment and was welcomed by a thick cloud of carrion. Sam held her nose and her eyes spoke of inquisitiveness, like she was wondering if I had truly lost it.

"I don't think he's here," Sam said.

A great shock of moonshine colored my living room gray as the grave. But through it I heard the sounds of frustration, all the pathetic pleas from victims past, my hammer smashing pretty face-flesh . . . hacksaw grinding into bone. I thought for a moment I heard chewing too, but Sam looked at me like I was playing a sick joke, snapping me back into reality. But those sounds were like heaven on a fishing line for me. They told me food was near, some-how, and that I needed it very badly or I was going to finally die. I didn't want any stupid human needs like hunger to stop me now that I had Perry to look after.

"What's really going on here?" Sam said.

But her voice was stolen by night, by my voracity. It all happened in a split second. The hammer came down on her head, hard, and I kept doing it until I felt her life gush like a warm river over my hands, my heart, my appetite. She lay on the floor, frozen in shock, her eyes turned up toward me as if I was some sort of an enemy. I wasn't. Perry was.

PERRY!

I ran to the bathtub to find him still there, calm and collected. His arms were limp and twisted as a doughy pretzel sinking into his own miasma. His torso was exposed and slicked with dead jelly; his cock shriveled into an ancient slug, hanging above the water for precious air. But I knew he'd be there once I returned with supper.

Zombie steps back to the living room, and little did I know that they were my own. Samantha's jacket came away easy with the switchblade; her t-shirt was doused in blood and tears; her chest smeared red. It wasn't a hard decision to make—because I was so hungry, such a ravenous beast for starving myself all these weeks because the love-bug had bit me.

I found that I'd become the monster! And I wanted that flesh in my mouth: sweet, honest, beckoning, safe as a womb. And taste it I did, at first with my tongue, then teeth, with no intent on stopping.

2011

Out of all the stories in this collection, this is the one that has received the most attention. It was selected by readers to be included in *DREAD (The Best Horror of Grey Matter Press)*. I think that's a high honor, better than being selected any other way. My first "best of," which is really funny, because this story was rejected well over 10 times. But I never gave up on it.

"Wormhole" was born out of looking at my own mortality in the face. I spent many years working in a hospital, which allowed me to see people die slowly and very quickly. It allowed me to speak to people I helped revive from death. It allowed me to ask them if they saw a light, saw anything. I won't go into the answers. I could go on for thousands of pages. "Wormhole" was written in 2011.

WORMHOLE

"The oldest and strongest emotion of mankind is fear, and the oldest and strongest kind of fear is fear of the unknown."
—H.P. Lovecraft

"I want to know what becomes of us when we die," Jason said to me. "The beautiful unknown; the fragile darkness."

His hectic whispers ignite the flame in my head: ecto-plasm, orbs, vortices and elementals. Together, Jason and I experienced lazy dreams, poetic nights and warehouse hunts in the refurbished ghettos of Brooklyn. Thrift shop rags painted on our bones; Geiger counters and cigarette smoke trailed ghostly in Bushwick; digital cameras clutched like pistols in Williamsburg.

Jason rambling about the best ways to die and the ephemeral existences we suffer here on earth. He couldn't help himself as the social scene he followed was that of the warehouse children who thrived in poverty, existentialism and gloom. Parties of shadow, candelabras in every win-dow and incense burning to kill the smell of the rats. I hated the sound of their snarky voices, but Jason's young face made up for it, the tight lips and frizzy black hair that tumbled over his eyes.

We'd just finished touring an underground gallery, one that made its name for capturing *life* in its utterly final stage: death. Photos slung up like ghoulish garlands in a forever-Halloween world, black and whites pinned to the walls showcasing long hallways of dust and vapor distilled in time, an empty doorway leading the viewer into the burnt husk of an insane asylum. Glittering things swarmed like stars, things that were said to be orbs, or the oily eyes of former patients.

"That's the place," silver fingernails in his mouth. "I know those eyes . . . the windows to a black soul."

Those photos lit a fire of jealousy in my gut: the strength and precision, the limitless angles. Photographers creating magic by the click of a button, but it was something I just couldn't do. I'd been shooting my own photos since the day I realized that photography was my only escape, the tissue protecting my bones and the air to my angry lungs.

Ghost hunting seemed as rational as any other form. What a thrill it is to prove the existence of things most people believe are locked inside books and movies. We spend so much time living in one reality while there are so many more that have yet to be discovered. I broadened my knowledge of ghosts, echoes and elementals with books like *Darklore* and *House on Haunted Hill*. I also bought the best equipment: temperature readers, Geiger counters, infrared motion exchangers and full-spectrum camcorders.

It was my big *fuck you* to the people who said I should be a good girl and leave boyish enchantments like death, the macabre and heavy metal music behind me. Enchantments, not influences, because all girls are supposed to be princesses, aren't they? But I am one of choice, the weird silhouette known as a girl.

I enjoyed the things that made others uneasy, matching my code of dress with that of my soul, the color of a raven's wing: skinny legs wrapped in fishnet; hair dyed every shade of a permanent gloom; my skin never in the sun long enough to get any vitamin D, pale to the point of being unhealthy.

Jason loved the way I dressed, said I was his black Madonna. What few friends we had always thought we were a couple, the kind that fucked in the subways or necked in the middle of Central Park—Elvira and her ragged prince of darkness. Yeah, right.

We tried to be lovers, memorizing the sharp curves of one another's faces, the pale jutting bones beneath our skin, the eloquent circuitry of veins in our throats and hands. But Jason's mouth left the taste of putrescence on my palate, and his skin was like touching a fish left in the freezer too long.

I realized soon enough that Jason was more like the brother I never wanted but always needed by my side. I adored his fascination for death. Naturally it became his only hobby, obsessed and oppressed by the memory of the bad-people-dressed-in-white who pumped his mother with a syringe full of liquid sleep and locked her in the loony bin. She'd rotted her mind with the bottle so much that eventually suicide became her only way out, being that they'd forgotten to take away her belt when they brought her in.

But it wasn't that Jason wanted to die. He just longed to discover death, which he said was simply the soul breaking free from the living chrysalis of bone and flesh. The final freedom. After all, his mother had done it, and his plan was to at least meet her halfway.

Jason often filled my head with stories of her, his hate and regret, the anguish that a child feels over a mother who never wanted to *be* a mother. But even though she had fucked up his life beyond measure, Jason's mother was the only person in the world he ever talked about.

She was his personal poltergeist.

Oh, how he would recall the memory of her, those piercing blue eyes as if the tips of needles, and the twisting dark red curls atop her head. When you love someone enough to hate them, you find that you become their slave, and everything you say and do revolves around them; you aim to please the insatiable. It's a sick but true part of the human condition.

And then there was me, the weird best friend trying to understand how she fit into the fucked-up portrait of Jason's jaded life, the paltry ghost hunter willing to sell her soul to capture the dead, in any form, on film. Whenever I talked about ghosts, elementals or orbs, Jason would listen closely. His love of aberrance flowered into a deep under-standing that there truly *is* life after death. We connected greatly on that level.

But I didn't yearn for the ending of life like he did. Rather, I simply wanted to prove that it existed with the click of my camera, bringing to life the final moment when a person closes their eyes and accepts that there is no light at the end. That's the moment when there's only the one great expectation: the dirt nap.

Looking Jason in the eyes was like a puzzle. I wanted to know what was going on in his head. In the spiraled valleys of that special brain, perhaps there would be a symphony of death written by careful hands. Many people assumed we were nuts or watched one too many scary movies. I feel terrible for them and their small minds, so complacent in judging others, wholly ignorant to the many realities beyond our own.

"*When I am here death is not,*" Jason would say. "*When death is here I am not.* I want to find the middle ground!"

That's only a taste of the poetry he wrote in scrappy notebooks until that horrible purple hour called sunrise. The promise of poetry is so much greater than that of ghosts. It will always be there if you want it to be; ghosts have a mind of their own. I learned this as no matter the equipment and no matter how many hunts we went on, I never came up with any hard evidence.

This drove me to become sick of my art, sick of never being gifted with the promise of orbs or vapors, not even a sparkle of dust. And so it was then that Jason dropped the bomb on me. He wanted to visit the insane asylum where his mother took her last breath, where she had convinced herself that suicide was the only way out. That was to be my big payoff. But the place had burnt down, destroyed by arson.

"Why seek something that we'll all encounter? I mean . . . we're all going to die." I said this to him nonchalantly, but curiously looking forward to his answer.

"We're all born into a temporary world." Jason pulled on his crazy hair, lit a clove cigarette, and clicked his nails against a bottle of beer. "After our body and mind die, our soul joins our ancestors in the permanent world. I'm not seeking this end of *process* we call death. I'm merely its biggest fan."

Ever feel like you're being watched? Ever feel that tickle at the back of your neck? Everyone has. In the ghost-hunting world it's called a vortex and is defined as a tiny explosion of energy. We wanted to feel the ultimate vortex—Jason's mother. So we stretched our faith to the point of no return, living by the firm belief that life after death was a reality and that it could all be caught on film. And why shouldn't we?

People never ask why they feel like they're being watched, because maybe they're too afraid of what might answer them through the depthless dark. People just don't want to know that this reality we blow holes in and deplete like it's some renewable resource isn't the *only* one. They don't want to interrupt their careful equation of perfect hair, perfect wife, perfect kids and perfect life. The Born Again Americans.

I decided I was finally going to be somebody.

But I knew deep down that this was something that could lead us to the *big come down*. Having too much faith in something can hurt you, can mock all that you stood for in first place. In this sense, faith is very much like a wormhole. It transports your mind to another place so you can stare at yourself as if through a glass wall, trying to break out, remembering when you once had your sanity.

It was mid-October and the mist was still a swirling-gray phantom atop the Hudson. We watched the water scintillate against the moon while drinking whiskey from the bottle. Oh, that amber burn in our throats and how it helped us sleep!

Halloween was in full spring. Gossamer webs spread across tenement doors, black and orange lights pricked twilight like children's daggers. That night we left a calamitous heavy metal show of rattling guitars and psychedelic lights. Mosh pits swirled with torn clothing and costume jewelry. It was our wasted scene.

Dusk washed over the towering buildings like a great spill of quill ink. Our tussled hair whipped the star-wind as we sped down Tenth Avenue on our Mongoose bikes, cursing the busy city streets. Sharp limbs swathed in black, Souls on the Road, like Kerouac wrote. We tipped a scraggy street musician who was shattering notes in the air with his violin, then halted to glimpse at what we thought was a specter in a lone alleyway, finding it was only thick grease vapors pouring out of a food truck.

Down a half mile, zipping under the brand new High Line Park, and we smelled spicy smoke and heard the paranormal echoes of scuttling, crazed forms running into the nearest bar they could find.

"These kids get annoying," I told Jason.

"They run from the night as we run into it."

Jason leaned over to kiss me but I backed away. His breath was rancid even with the lace of whiskey and cloves. Bad teeth jutted out of his frown. In that moment I pitied him because I knew that when one is poor they don't have time for the dentist; the will to care is a phantom memory.

All that shines turns to rust.

It was then that our eyes became tortured by the dilapidated sights of the industrial section. The air was weighted with coal ash, diesel fumes and charred timber, the clear smell of a recent fire. Hidden between buildings scarred by flame, buildings so old the next wind would send them crumbling to the cobblestone street, our insidious destination had been met.

We parked our bikes illegally and took a moment to gaze at the asylum tipping forward like a sentinel rising from a gravelly grave and judging the city before it. Bashed windows and a hundred-thousand glass shards glimmered against the cobble; the moon lit its bare-bone insides and I thought that this was as close to a 9/11 ghost as I had ever come. Chain links crisscrossed the huge front door, but Jason picked the lock and we were soon ducking beneath a black nylon cover.

"Take a picture!" Jason said. "Mother may be right here in all this cold fluorescence."

Gods, he was really always talking about her!

Finger on the shutter button of my digital camera and I soaked the huge foyer with a bright ball of light. A sibilant group of rats scurried; black dust became unsettled and peppered our clothes. Unhappy with the results, pixels showing no promise of orbs, vortices or ectoplasms, we continued our journey into the asylum.

I imagined full skeletons alive on their feet, bones not like you'd think, not birdcage torsos white as the moon, or skeletal hands reaching out for a place in purgatory, or skulls with permanent grins. No, I imagined the dirtiest, grittiest whole skeletons seared like skewered meat, tiny bones curled in fetal positions avoiding the fire; osseous matter splattered like bird shit.

Jason lit a poorly rolled joint of salvia, throwing fruity smoke loops in the air. I took a hit and it made me feel quite fruity right away, imbuing in my brain, playing tricks on my eyes. The first sign of a good salvia high is hallucination.

"There are things in this world that can't be explained by the rational mind," Jason said. "They have the power to appear or disappear when they want."

"No matter what, it's time to prove these suckers wrong, the zealots and the atheists."

Eyes like chips of moon and him holding me close, he agreed.

I've always believed in the *We are One* idea. There's no real logic behind it. When we die, we go back to that one universal soul. Our bodies and brains are simply the vessels in which we travel. All life is energy, time and space, thus we are all one in this tired game of death. But this went against everything I stood for as a ghost hunter. I *had* to believe that there was something to capture, something that would make me a hero in the art world.

Jason pressed forward, humming "10,000 Days" by Tool, a song written for mothers. *Daylight dims leaving cold fluorescence, difficult to see you in this light.* An ode to heartache, remembering each time she picked up that poisonous bottle. I couldn't understand why he loved someone who treated him so terribly, who loved the drink more then her own family. That's the real unknown, if you ask me.

"I feel like I've been here, as a little boy," wilting bones touching the ashy floor.

Our Docs skidded across the complaining floorboards as we entered a room so dark, so utterly vacuous of light that I needed to switch to my full-spectrum recorder. I took it out of my backpack—a craggy, bulging, oval thing decorated with **XXX** stickers—and turned it on to see the room under a different angle and different light.

The room itself was destroyed. The bed was turned upside down; doll heads with burnt hair and gouged eyes piled in every corner. There were so many, and all were missing their eyes. I read once that insane patients play with dolls to recreate the life they think should be living. But you can't behead every doll you have and live in peace outside these crumbling walls; such is why they're locked up.

It was then that I smelled beer and the sweet and sour aroma of white wine. And when I looked into the small LED screen, I saw something I shouldn't have seen—a pair of blinking, blue eyes. But when I moved my view away from the screen I only saw that complete blackness again.

"Mom?" Jason called as if he knew. "This was your room, wasn't it?"

The eyes rolled in their spectral sockets and took one long, wet blink before vanishing. A pale vapor rose around us, thick as ectoplasm. I suddenly recalled the pictures with all the eyes from the gallery and wondered if they had been taken here. When I came back to my senses we were doused in silence, and oh, if I could describe it. Not devoid of sound but the absence of it, pure nothingness, the way you would say black is the inexistence of color. But I knew we weren't alone; I knew her eyes were carefully marking us.

"I have the chills," Jason said. "I think I need to sit down."

"No."

I didn't want to sit. I had to get into the heart of the building. I felt so close to that pivotal point where a person meets their own tragic dreams that I couldn't stop myself. Davy Jones' locker full of the blackest treasures. I pushed Jason forward, planting my hand against that impossibly sharp shoulder, nails digging into his scrubby shirt. But all he did was stare at the doll heads.

"I remember how she looked at me . . . before she turned to the bottle. She had a way of making me do anything she wanted."

Then we jetted out of the room, taking the longest walking tour of our lives. Each corridor after that was weighted with the sense of loneliness, loss, the hope for a friend or family member to come to the rescue. But no one had ever came. I could feel it. Everywhere I turned was only a pitchy silence, the sound of dripping water, of a million collected tears. It was then Jason proclaimed that we had come to the asylum in vain, that we weren't destined to see anything.

"I've let you down. I'm sorry," he said.

"I already saw something. Big, blue eyes . . . curly hair. I smelled alcohol—"

"Don't tease me."

"I'm not!"

My voice took on an echo that seemed to never end, curving into another part of the building until it was above us, rushing out into the still-dark night. I thought about something that I'd read in a book about ghost hunting, that we are all born into a temporary world known as the *spirit incubator*. I recalled Jason's words. *After the body and mind dies, our soul becomes the spirit and joins our ancestors in the permanent world*, the world Jason wanted to get into, the world I wanted to record on film and show off in all the galleries across lower Manhattan.

It was that very notion that drove me to my very unforgivable act. I begged Jason to call her out, tease the spirit, take away the incubator before hatch time. It's well known that if you fuck with the dead, they will fuck with you right back. Jason was a good boy and did as he was told, with the help of a jet-flame lighter and a quick pull off the salvia joint. He began to spit and cry, his face a white sphere of light against the pitch black.

"She was my everything," he said, snot like worms running down his face.

I wiped the slime away with my hand, sparkling slush on my pale palm, and I kissed Jason on the mouth—first time in a long time—and his lips burned, much like his voice. He kissed me back; a big, sloppy kiss that tasted of tears and boogers, and that was fine by me. I realized that I truly loved him and didn't want him to hurt. But it was time to get the show on the road.

Fuck faith and how it tricks the mind into believing there's something greater in the world than us, some great cosmic force in the shape of a puppeteer god. Nothing is greater than the *big come down*. Nothing is greater than the end of days, the loss of friends. The afterlife is yet another construct of mankind's fear of the unknown. Death is merely the end of life, and it's nothing to fear! Like pages in a book with a beginning, middle and an end, so predictable.

Get it?

Jason didn't understand this. He never feared death because he was so set on finding his mother.

"Come out," I heard him say over and over. *"Difficult to see you in this light."*

But then . . .

A pale void, angel's brilliance. Deep glow of a space and time that smashed all the rules of physics to jagged pieces of universe. Eyes moving rapid as bad thought, ones that I could only see through the view of my full-spectrum recorder. When I looked without the camera I saw only the inky black of the asylum.

"I see her," Jason said.

He ran, didn't stop even as I begged him to turn around, to come back with me, that we'd seen it all and we needed to go. I didn't want to be alone, not in here, and I didn't want to follow him to that bane light. I couldn't. Was I truly a believer?

"This little light of mine, a gift you passed unto me. I'm gonna let it shine . . ."

At the end of the narrow hallway I saw her showing Jason the way to the noose. Jason was standing on a stool, hair falling over his face, bony hands itching with relief. Freedom in the arms of his savior?

It was that moment Jason kicked the stool and I saw his trembling feet in midair. When they stopped moving I realized that this was no noose, but a *belt*. He'd found the beautiful unknown as I was made into a true believer.

Death is a shortcut through space and time, ending at the blunt finality of nothing. It's a road I cannot bear to take just yet.

The last I saw of them was the clasping of wispy hands as they disappeared into the fiery wormhole, leaving me alone in that dusky asylum, to question my sanity forever, the proof in my hands, but the loss of my friend like dead weight in my heart.

Never took a life, but surely saved one.
Hallelujah, it's time for you to bring me home.

2011

"Unveiled" was written in 2014 and was my first "pro" sale, whatever that means. I was asked by Steve Berman to write a story involving a "Handsome Devil" for an anthology he was editing for the popular publisher Prime Books. Lucky for me, I was able to do whatever I wanted with the theme (which is how it should be for all writers). At that the time of brainstorming, I was still obsessing over Delilah Dellinger, the girl who is me in so many ways. Clive never really got to say goodbye to Delilah at the end of *The Absence of Light*, and I guess I maybe owed it to him to see if Delilah would allow it. This is the result.

UNVEILED

A painfully skinny androgyne sits at the drab third floor window of her drab third floor apartment, tobacco stained tongue running across lips striped black. Copper skull with smoke running out of its forever grin, scrungy couch taking over her body, and the Manic Panic hair dye reeks like poison. The record is on repeat.

Dreaming . . . thinking . . . demon . . . monster. *I'm a monster.* But then the curtain flapped, Salvation Army special, unveiling cryptic lyrics that she'd scrawled in scarlet across the pane: *BELIEVABILITY—MENOCIDE— UNVEILED.* Decrees to summon the goddesses of glum: Lilith, Eve, Isis, Kali.

But she would evoke none of them. What came had no name, no marks of cultural shame or inferiority, and no decay to speak of. A preternatural force that lived within her music, one that spoke the language of the dead.

Incubus, Fiend, Goblin.

It had many names and many faces juxtaposed and needy; it had a thousand hands to touch her, a thousand fiery mouths to talk to her, but she did not react to him as expected: a scared girl in need of company. It was the maddening melodies of her music that had ripped him out of his personal hell to meet her.

"You grieve long and hard," he said.

"No I don't," and she brought the bottle of wine to her lips, leaving a black smear across the tip.

"I know when one hides their feelings. You hide yours quite overtly."

"No kidding," sharp little face hidden beneath still-wet dreads.

This girl was a master of the rictus grin, and there was no possible way that he could read her thoughts because she'd already blocked him out of her head: the little wisp was a gifted child. But the look on her face was that of pleasure when he said her name, even though it was already stapled to the walls on cheap neon poster prints and inscribed in gold on all of the records that she'd recorded with her band: Delilah Dellinger. Devilish name to compliment the silhouette clad in black on black on black.

"Are you in mourning, Delilah?"

"Nope."

"I think you are. You've lost your one true love. I can feel it."

"Ghost drawl."

"Would you ever consider loving someone other than yourself?"

"I don't do love."

"Independent movement?"

"Rational thinking."

There is a bible-like book of rules that states a proper incubus must covet his succubus while she is possessed by the swirling paralysis of REM sleep, or drunk on a week's worth of rotgut, but Delilah never slept well, and she only drank Jäger. This could be seen in the bruise-dark bags suffusing beneath eyes the color of blue fire, the frizzed hair and the constant bitterness that would rightfully flower within any insomniac.

She was running from her own dreams. Consequently, without the proper amount of sleep, a mammal can and will die; as complex as the human body has evolved to survive, it also needs to repair the damage brought upon by stress, rage, depression and intoxicating substances. Sleep is the only way to fix all that is deemed terrible while awake.

"When you sleep it's like your body is suspended between pain and regret," the ghost said. "And when you wake up screaming, the only way to stop is to drink again."

"Congratulations. Want a lollipop?"

Even though Delilah had a penchant for insomnia, she was able to half-function thanks to self-medication and music therapy. And even though women are considered the weakest link in the game of gender equality, the incubus knew that women were twice as strong—he just would never say it out loud. They bear children, are the pillar of every family and their emotions can render them extremely feral beneath the veil of complete control. A man could never handle such responsibility.

"You still dream of Clive."

"That's if he can catch me in a deep sleep, that asshat," and Delilah slipped a crazy-colored CD into the stereo.

"He's what I would call your personal poltergeist. Dead . . . but not dead enough."

"What are you, his liaison? And I already told you to stay out of my fucking dreams."

Her tattoos bulged furiously—bats, a squiggling road map, musical scales—and her demeanor did not match her mystical outer grace. She almost had a Stevie Nicks flair about her, that is until one realizes that Delilah is generally cold and oppressive, the natural characteristics that hide vulnerability.

Too smart for her own good and far too mentally bruised for her twenty-two years, Delilah was very open about her frustration with death and her rejection of it. She flat out refused to die, refused to sleep. She refused to stand fucking still. Her sentences were flawed by words like *ghost hunting* and *Shadow Man* and *astral projection*. The haunted parts of her life she wanted to erase. Plus, ghost hunting was Clive's thing. Delilah might have ruined their relationship, but what she never said out loud was how bad she felt about it. But Clive was talking to the worms by now, and so there was nothing left to do but privately grieve.

"I'll never speak of that moment so long as I live," she whispered.

"Your anger fascinates me. If I could only touch you . . . I imagine you'd incinerate me," breathy voice as much as it was dead.

"Such a passive-aggressive poet you are. Though I must ask . . . why do you care? I've spent my whole life running from things like you."

"Because I admire you, Delilah."

"We've had our fill, Rez and I. Why do you think he spends all of his time with Alex? I'm a fucking plague. The Rage Plague."

"Rez, your twin brother, he loves you so. You know this. And your best friend Alex . . . is that his name? Wasn't it his piano skills that first woke the thing in his basement?"

This was Delilah's second year in New York City and the memories of the Pennsylvania boondocks—of music and mayhem—were about as fresh as the day-old fish sold in Chinatown. The diseased soul of that once small-town girl was replaced by that of a city girl's fervor, of nights sulking in damnation and days ruined by the insouciant nightmares that live within a bottle of cheap red wine.

Upon arrival she wasted no time in getting to know the city's local denizens. Her apartment was often berated by drug deals and squatters, scrawny metal heads snorting whatever they could crush for a good time and Brooklyn hipsters using their parent's cash to score a taste of the real New York narcotic scene.

Delilah never liked the hipsters; she had her fair share of fistfights with them because they claimed to know what hard work was, what living on the edge really felt like, so long as they had the cushion of their parent's trust fund account. But once Delilah's fist met their teeth, they never spoke like that again.

She also shared the apartment with the only men in the world she loved because those two men were not interested in her sexual companionship, prerequisite fulfilled. Delilah called the frayed-looking one Rez and the girlish-looking one Alex. Rez was her twin brother and Alex was her best friend. All three of them shared the same disposition of angst, dread and depression that tends to plague the few fringe scenes left in this city.

Also, Alex and Rez were partners, which often meant Delilah was left alone while they prowled the dreary sections of Brooklyn and the Lower East Side. It wasn't that she didn't want to tag along; she just hated to be the whining third wheel, the wraith-like presence between a pair of boys who were so sickeningly in love it literally made her insides boil. Delilah knew not one thing about lust. It seemed she was asexual.

"Shut the fuck up about that," butterfly knife pointed, kohl-smeared eyes glossed with tears.

"I don't want confrontation, Delilah. I just want you to be whole again. Don't you know that I love you?"

She'd heard those words in a past life.

"Horse shit. Sounds like something I've heard before."

"Maybe it's something I've said to you before."

"I don't recall having a conversation with a ghost."

The incubus chuckled. "I mean what I say. I can fix you. I can take away the pain."

"You'll never get in my head. You'll never know the truth. I know all about you bastards and I refuse to wilt to your advances."

Delilah chugged from the wine bottle, then looked up at the ceiling, at all of the posters hanging like butcher meat. The Heavy Metal superheroes she'd come to adore over the years stared frozen with gawked mouths and fuck-me eyes; it spread a universal comfort inside.

Admiration was the most lenient term for her love of music. She could have been any of those oily forms in black leather and spiked jewelry, but there was also an ocean of indifference between them. Delilah was possessed by passion, terror and rage. She was an amalgamation of the finest ingredients that all song writers wish they had.

"Sometimes you just gotta smile, pretend and forget," Delilah said, the butterfly blade in her hand fluttering as if alive.

"Doesn't it hurt . . . to cut that way?"

"You mean you can't feel pain?"

"I don't remember life, yet I'm so alive when I'm with you."

She closed her eyes and began to bite her dark fingernails. "Physical pain belittles the emotional."

There came that shit-eating grin again as the knife created a tiny squiggling worm of blood across her wrist. It reminded the incubus of how they first met. In the dark, naturally; candlelight bathed the hollows of her face and the moonlight was soft as fur reflecting off the surrounding tenements. Delilah had just cut herself behind the knee, right through her black jeans as her body gyrated to a sinister song and her mind swayed between the temptation of insomnia or completely passing out.

The warm autumn wind brought in the smell of piling garbage, spray paint and spicy marijuana smoke. The tune playing in the background was her own, "Flesh of Eve," a song off of the debut EP from her band Electric Orchid. Delilah's voice crawled out of the speakers like a séance, an original masterpiece poisoned with sorcery and malice. Her lyrics pounded deep as a subwoofer, words to clatter bones and teeth, words to make an eternal being question his purpose. But it wasn't until he read her lyrics on the windowpane did his interest truly peak.

I'll never speak of that moment so long as I live.

"You will speak of it!" he said, lowering the music.

"I just couldn't be with him."

"So then why are you such a wreck?"

She rocked back and forth, staring at the window. There he caught his own reflection clouded by hers: faint ecto-plasmic smear, soft as spider web, much like Delilah's soul. He turned away because the best seat in the house was in front of Delilah, not looking at his reflection. Her outburst did not change the fact of what she'd done. He'd read her diaries, her forbidden book of lyrics. She'd written about it a thousand heartbreaking times how she'd done it, how she'd showed Clive her murky dream world, but then how she took it all away from him.

And at the bottom of every page lay an asterisk sur-rounded by a frown-face emoticon: *ShOuLd It FeEl tHiS gOoD To BrEaK SoMeOnE's HeArT?* But one must realize that to understand Delilah is to understand pain and suffer-ing, to have the weight of the cosmos force your bones on a downward spiral until you're six feet below the surface of the earth.

"Shall I repeat myself again?" she scowled.

"As drunk as you are, you're still the most eloquent girl I know," and the incubus sipped Delilah's boilermaker.

"Do you still taste . . . in death?"

"Absolutely. Taste you so well," body elongating around Delilah like shadows long cast.

Then Delilah started talking to herself. The ghost listened carefully as she argued back and forth, an uncontrollable tide: the temptation of suicide but her pure fright of the act, the wounds from the butterfly blade on her wrists and calves forming a new set of scar tissue. *Life does not have to be lived like some broken record, like some bad film on replay. I can escape it. I can be my own person.* It was as if the song she had written seven years ago had come back to haunt her . . . her own Personal Hell, and in its new wake she was swinging haphazardly between dream and nightmare, between choice and circumstance.

"Lying is a sin, is it not?"

"There're no sins where I come from."

"And where's that, Hell?" Delilah chuckled hollowly.

"You wrote an entire song about it."

"Fuck off . . . just fuck off!"

"If you just let me in we could—"

"We?" She began to cackle mockingly. "There will never be a *we* in Delilah Dellinger's life."

"There can be a *you and I*," his voice growing deeper, impatient.

"I'm not your concubine or your succubus," she spit. "We're in the real world, and your reality means shit to me."

"Cold as always, Delilah. Scared little girl refusing to explore her wants to save face."

Delilah bolted to her feet and grabbed her pack of smokes. "I'm out of here. I forgot I have a show tonight."

Too hot for October, humidity like August and sudden smell of rain; the reality of it iridescent on the black top.

Delilah ran as fast as she could, Vector microphone clutched to her chest, huge clump of girl-flesh as he tailed her through the streets of Alphabet City. Easy to track: just follow the smell of clove cigarettes and the forever turmoil of a pissed-off girl lingering in the heavy air.

Most of the blocks were alive with the usual street hustle and bustle; the rest were dead as doornails. Not such a scary place anymore as it was scarily safe. The graffiti was sparse and the windows had lost their runny coat of grease vapors. One did not catch the sight a bum pissing in a random alleyway, or a strung-out junkie.

But the tenements that weren't filled with transplant posers paying holier-than-thou rent prices still spoke of bad times, of poor families three generations in, of the city's bureaucratic capability of keeping certain people of certain color and status on this side of the jaded street and everyone else safe on the other side.

The window to the bar was clouded with a massive amount of posters that read *ELECTRIC ORCHID TONIGHT!* Delilah noticed that someone had burned her band's name into the door; that's how serious her fans were. Past the entrance and the doorman who was pleased to let her in without fault. Like many girls, Delilah denied her outer beauty; the grace of her naturally high cheekbones, tiny chin and straight teeth without the help of braces. Feral features were sought after by most. But all that beauty didn't change the fact that she was the lead singer of tonight's headlining band.

Dark inside, unpredictable as some fucked-up x-ray; a world without color, the absence of light. Pipes lined the ceiling like varicose veins and the punky floorboards rattled beneath her Grinders. The deafening PA system vomited nu-metal and British punk, a way too up-to-date a system, given the ramshackle culture. Delilah eyed the poor excuse for a stage as random metal heads clad in dirty clothes called out to her; hipsters gave her many thumbs up, and the usual goth-grunge-punk poser sat alone on a stool while sipping a bright green cocktail that made her lips shimmer.

Same fringe kids, but a good turnout.

With twenty dollars in her pocket and happy hour slipping into its last moments of smiling faces, she planned to order her cold black heart out. Drinking before a show soothed her because alcoholism did not exist in her vocabulary. But the bartender would not take her money. *For you, everything is on the house!* Bad juju to charge the headlining band's lead singer. Delilah accepted her offer and the Dogfish Head "90 Minute IPA" was like carbonated floral heaven as it invaded her tongue, full of hops and the golden thickness of barley. She licked the wet remnants of the filmy head from the glass in such an erotic fashion that three hipsters turned their heads, but then looked away when the girl snarled.

"I think they liked you."

Delilah swung her Vector microphone toward the sound and clocked a depressed looking girl in the face by mistake. The girl dropped her beer and covered her mouth that had instantly slimed the color of blood. No one made any sudden movements, as Delilah's temper was somewhat famous, and the fact that she just stood there vexed rather than offering a fucking napkin surprised nobody.

Damn voice, Delilah thought. It pissed her off that he could follow her wherever she went. Weren't ghosts supposed to be bound to the place where they died? Why didn't the incubus follow the ancient laws of the underworld?

Delilah finished her drink, then indulged in some good old fashion sweet leaf. Beneath the guise of a gaudy hookah, one could order any strain they desired and smoke it scot-free in here. It was a smart way to bring some of the culture of Amsterdam to a small dive in Manhattan. Delilah's hookah was gold-plated and ornate as an Arabian king's throne. After the third pull flowers bloomed in her skull, making her unusually conversant.

"Aren't you supposed to haunt the last place you were alive? Aren't you supposed to be stuck there?" she asked, annoyed.

"Not when such gifted beings like you can talk to us."

"Fucking hell," and Delilah chugged her beer.

"You're killing yourself to live, Delilah. What a waste."

She pulled on her hair and her eyes widened. A few kids embraced one another as if she was going to explode.

"I still see him in my dreams. I can't get him out of my goddamn head. I wish I knew how."

"I can get him out, Delilah."

"You're a fucking haunt, not God . . ."

"Let me *inside* you."

Inside you.

Those were words she'd heard before.

"NO!"

"Well then do as you always do: drink yourself into a stupor and dream like there's no end."

"I have a show to play. I can't talk about—"

"I can bend the rules. I can go in your head and turn off your thoughts."

"Stay out of my damn head! My thoughts are my own. I'll keep blocking you. Rez warned me about things like you."

"The sensitive, your brother, I know. But he has it frightfully wrong."

"What do you mean?" Hair whipping out of control, scarred hand rubbing her temple.

"If you see Clive in your dreams, perhaps *he* is your incubus. Your living nightmare."

Delilah held back tears. "Not just in my dreams. I see him on the astral plane. Do you know about astral projection?"

"You must confront him."

"Don't you know the first rule about life after death? 'If you make contact . . . THEY will contact you.' I've already been through that and don't want it again . . ."

A few kids stared at Delilah with blank faces, lips glittering with alcohol. From their view she was talking to herself, but from her view there was an intelligent essence that she could talk to. Then everyone turned when the door slammed and Delilah's band came straggling through in a cloud of cigarette ash—three dark bony blots with instruments on their backs, three dirty bodies leading a new trend—bringing with them the stench of Jägermeister and warm summer nights. Billy, Jimmy and Sheigh barely exchanged Delilah a glance before they set up in the equipment in back of the bar.

"You think she would've helped us bring the equipment in," Delilah heard Jimmy say.

"She's in one of her quiet moods again," Sheigh said.

"Or maybe she's become a diva now."

"We pack dives throughout Brooklyn and the island of Manhattan. We've hardly had success."

Blah. Blah. Blah. All talk. Delilah just wanted to play, wanted to tear into the world so deep that she'd be able to smell the dark force that keeps the universe in balance. And then finally she saw Alex stroll in, beautiful as always in his genderless fashion, long hair tied into a pony tail and that same huge trench coat hanging heavy on fragile bones. Rez was not far behind him, chatting with a couple of friends about the advanced reading copy of some beat poet's novel he was obsessed with.

"Alex!" Delilah screamed for his attention.

"Hey, D. You ready?"

"I don't know if I can do this tonight."

"Still having those dreams?" Alex wrapped his skinny arm around her shoulders.

"Clive's usual begging," and Delilah's head craned to lean on Alex's collarbone.

"He hasn't changed, even in death."

"You're the only one who knows that he's haunting me."

"Remember what I told you: as long as you ignore him, he can't get to you. He can always look, but can never touch," Alex said.

Then it got quiet, doomsday lingering, and the shadows in the bar began to flower, ravaging Alex's pinched features. On the way to the stage Delilah watched the bobbling drunken heads of the crowd lose themselves in talk, cheap beer and a universal love for music. They smelled of dirty clothes, stale cigarettes and teenage dreams.

Now Delilah felt that same calling like when she'd first played in New York two years ago, that night still so fresh in her mind: downtown club full of wasted youth much like this one. Would she still wow them? Would she still be the reigning queen of the underground music scene as all of those downtown and Brooklyn publications labeled her?

Only one way to find out.

Time to fly.

Smoke machine out of control, thick as butter cream, and the lights a stroboscopic rage. Sheigh's distorted bass shook the stage madly; Billy's drumstick kissed a cymbal three times before Alex's synthesizer rang out like something derived from Black Sabbath's *Sabotage* album.

Delilah closed her eyes and allowed the music to overtake her, lips brushing the edge of the Vector microphone. Before she knew it Jimmy's fingers were charging steadfast, his feet fiercely manipulating guitar pedals, un-leashing pinch harmonics like screaming birds. And so Delilah let her voice flood the room.

> *Green slate sky dark as pain*
> *Manifest the decadence*
> *I call the Goddess to reign*

It was a big risk to open their set with a new song, and it took hours of Delilah's begging to convince the band to do such. They argued with many good points: *too risky* and *our fans like our shows a certain way.* You have to start a set with a hit in order to reel the crowd in, to make them feel like they should stay.

But Delilah liked to take chances.

The song was called "Ambigrams & Palindromes," inspired straight from the pages of Rez's speculative short fiction. Jimmy had written the chorus and bridge within an hour after he'd read Delilah's lyrics, the bottle of Jäger already blazing in their stomachs, which to them was a writing milestone. Sheigh threw her bass line over it as did Alex and Billy with their respective instruments. But Delilah's melodies were the most controversial.

> *The night is in control*
> *Under the guise of demons*
> *Her mind will open into a black hole*

Voice of purgatory, of the stairway to hell, and in a matter of moments the crowd disappeared, even though the song was still raging. Did they not like the new music? Did they not understand that an artist must evolve, must keep moving forward in order to not make a joke of herself?

Delilah continued the vocal line, but when she opened them again she saw dozens of tall, lanky kids with disheveled hair and ghost-hunting cameras swaying like necklaces across their torsos. Had she fallen asleep? Had her body finally given out?

Only one way to find out.

Delilah began her molt, ripped herself free from the skin of reality and stepped off the stage. Behind her, the other Delilah was still singing as her dream body sailed through the sea of faceless bodies and entered the astral plane. Labyrinthine, and this place might as well have been the underworld of Kur, the loathsome lair of Lilitu and Alu.

Maybe the goddesses of redemption and plague would finally come, her muses, her salvation. Honeycombed descent, and the sky was the color of pumpkin teeth; the moon rolled cold above her.

Walking in no certain direction, slate-colored road pale against her black boots, Delilah knew that no direction was safe; in this world, every road was the one of needles. Suddenly aware of what she was about to do, Delilah lifted her arms to show her tattoos gleaming and insidious, the razor scars a beacon to all the suicide ghosts that lingered here.

She kept singing as her music attracted the dead, because in this world each word was a weapon, each sound another building block to the answer. There was no way around it: if she was going to stop the dreams, if she was going to become whole again, she'd have to make contact. She'd have to let them in. Fuck what Alex said. Enough was enough.

"I know that voice."

He had startled Delilah, and she actually *flinched*, as much as she hated the fact that she did. There was no denying it. Clive stood as tall as she remembered him, a long time since she'd seen his face. The fancy ghost-hunting device was held in hands covered in thieves gloves and the MISFITS t-shirt hung loose on his torso. The usual beanie covered ratty English hair. His lips were pursed in thought and his eyes still tired, mysterious. Was he still hunting ghosts in death? Could a ghost hunt another?

"You got your wish. Now what the hell do you want?"

The scar he'd left in her side with the knife began to throb like Voldemort to Harry.

"To finish what we started, love. After all, we've been talking for weeks on end. You know you feel guilty for what you did to us."

Delilah saw a shape-shifting presence behind Clive, his own wasted shadow. Thin, wretched.

The incubus!

"I should've known. All that whining, all that pathetic poetry. Just like when you were alive."

"You've given me a new life in dream, Delilah. But I'm alone," big blue eyes bright as earth viewed from space. "All I want is you. Always you . . . *mon fleur vénéneux.*"

"I'm only here to tell you to leave me the hell alone."

Clive let out a terrible laugh.

"In this place the rules are not your own. My dreams are yours, and yours are mine. I can feel your anger in here, your guilt. You liked what we once had. But as with everything else . . . you ruined it. Why, Delilah? Why?"

"Because . . . I just don't want it."

Clive shook his head waywardly. "An empty, indecisive answer as always."

"Please just go away. You're no Freddy Krueger; you're not a living nightmare. You're just my fading memory."

"Don't talk about us that way. Don't you miss me, Delilah? I miss you. I miss your music and the sound of your voice; I miss its power, how it brought us together. Don't you remember bringing us here?"

She couldn't answer him. The memory of their innocent night hanging out in the alleyway across from The Cabal art gallery came back strong. Oh, the way Clive manipulated her flesh, the way his strong hands stroked her hair, her breasts, and oh, how his words coerced her legs to open and her panties to slip off! It was so easy to give in, to let hormones pave over critical thinking: she wanted him then, wanted him so bad. She wanted to feel love, wanted to feel protected, desired.

"I remember how you looked at me," Clive said. "I remember how you let me touch you."

The Jäger was still fresh on their tongues and the cloves had been smoked past the filter; all of a sudden they were kissing, long and deep, tongues and teeth, mouth-flesh, and the walls of her vagina began to throb in time with her confused heart. The rain was warm as the sweat between them, but tasteless as their lust. The light that night just wasn't right, and the way Clive grew obsessive was too much to handle. He was going to love her forever, be by her side forever—until she put a stop to it.

I don't need a man to make me happy. The complacency of marriage will not swallow me whole. The hollow matrimony of man and wife will not infect me. She never said those words out loud, but it was all it took to change Delilah. She wouldn't fall for Clive, and the only way she knew to escape was through song. So she began a vociferous melody, let her very cells stop dividing as her soul slid free from her body like umbilical residue. She grabbed hold of Clive tight and they entered the dream world she had been visiting since she was a little girl.

"If you would've let me have you this all could've been avoided. I'd not have to sneak into your life, into your dreams in disguise," English accent beginning to unveil, hard-boiled Birmingham drawl.

"We don't belong together. You were bad for me then and you're bad for me now."

Hangover pain like someone had dropped a brick on her head, and Delilah was brought back into the night Clive almost raped her. They were trapped in a burning building in Long Island City that was kept alive by the magic of aerosol art and old ghosts. Clive had already beaten Rez to a bloody pulp, and he'd manhandled Delilah to the point of her nearly passing out. The anger of Delilah's refusal to love him infected Clive with rage, telling himself that if he could not have Delilah in life, then he'd have her in death.

The knife gauge in her side was pulsing darkly and the blood felt molten. Her legs were open and her skirt was ripped; her body was so weak she could barely fight him off. It wasn't until his hands had slid up her thigh, teasing the warm heat of her, that Delilah knew Clive could do whatever he wanted, that no one would care, no one would help. He would pluck his sweet flower and then crush her in the end.

"I thought it was a rather good disguise. All that moaning, creature of discomfort, creature of seduction," Delilah said with her hands molding into fists.

"That's not what you mean. You see me as pathetic and stupid. And yet for you I still wait, because I want nobody else!"

"You wait for me? After all you did? After the scars you left me, after the dignity you stole?"

"Fuck you, Delilah. Just fuck you!" Clive screamed.

"You can't hurt me; you're a powerless, bitter ghost unable to move away from the hell you cursed yourself into."

Clive stepped closer, his limbs elongating, his hair lengthening and his shadow shrinking.

"If I can't have you, no one can!"

Clive rushed toward Delilah, increasing in size. His face was mangled by rage and jealousy, and it was the last thing Delilah saw as their bodies clashed, skin to ectoplasm, bones snapping and blood spilling thickly as the ghosts of her past invaded without permission. One of her legs fell limp in pain, but she was on the offensive fast, and Delilah's nails ripped furrows into Clive's face. Their mingled blood had the consistency of jelly and smelled of a sewer.

Old death.

"You killed me, Delilah," hectic whisper. "You actually broke my heart . . ."

Delilah felt her own heart wrench.

As much as she'd have loved to take Clive on in a street brawl, Delilah knew that there was no point. That story had already been told. That story would involve keeping his memory alive when all she wanted was for him to be truly dead. And so she called upon the only thing that had ever saved her when she needed it the most: music.

Her voice belted like an anti-melody in this dream-world. Everything writhed uncomfortably as the image of Electric Orchid on stage came closer and closer, as Delilah rode her musical ascension towards reality. She watched in pity as Clive was unable to follow; it seemed he was locked within his own shadow, never truly able to see past the dark times, much like a shadow is always dark.

And so he disappeared as if she'd never even known him.

Because her words were about rejection, of not needing old ghosts and never letting her feelings get the best of her, Electric Orchid played an extended set. There can be no explanation as to how music can cure a bad feeling, a virus of guilt or a plaguing past. It just needs to be accepted.

Delilah finished the last song with a throat-tearing scream and the sea of faces was left astonished, mind-fucked, their mouths hanging open like atrophy.

2014

"Dark, Fire, Kiss," written in 2012, was born after I went to an art gallery in the Lower East Side that featured a unique photographer (no need to share her name). The things in there that I saw stayed with me . . . haunted me. Cold, frozen images. Dreamy landscapes, distant shorelines. For me, there was something more to those photos, something inside. Then the mania began for me.

This story sold to two professional anthologies that folded before publication. Such is writing life. I should also note Lana Del Rey's "Dark Paradise" influenced this story way too much.

DARK, FIRE, KISS

Red drool stain on the pillow, mouth aching—been grinding my teeth again. The dream comes: Blake and I playing like children, the world too bright and he a gaping black hole.

How was I supposed to know what love was? Dark little pill we all eventually ingest, only to find out that it is bound to kill you. But by then it's too late; you become its prisoner.

Love can make you do crazy things.

Craft beer, and that night we drank it down flat and warm like satisfied Brits at Tarots, a local dive that attracted the admirers of delirium and death—gay, straight and questioning—kids lost within their shabby choice of clothing and who believed that their apathetic attitudes wasn't cliché.

Multicolored lights of green, purple and orange cast neon shadows behind headbanging bodies. The dusty records blasted on repeat, thrash, nu-metal and alternative, and with the price of the beer you will find yourself quickly in the state of black-out-drunk.

"Can't believe that asshole is here," Becka said with resent.

The dark angel was sitting at the bar toying with an expensive looking camera, pale hands cradling it like an embryo. The camera's flash rode along his heinous smile, casting no shadow behind him. I thought it a queer observation, to be subject to phosphorescence and for it to not pinpoint your humanity. But I was too focused on wanting to talk to Blake to allow any kind of forewarning to get in the way.

"He's breaking new ground," I said bravely with drink in hand.

"You don't know anything about Blake."

"Whatever," I said.

Becka grabbed me by the chin and made me look at her. "Blake isn't a good person. He'll destroy you and anyone who enters his sick fucking scene. Everything to him is ephemeral: his art, himself . . . someone's innocent heart."

"Don't be a stupid boy, Edo," Lindsay chimed in.

Becka gritted her nasty teeth. "Stupid like my brother."

I pushed Becka away, picked up my "90 Minute IPA" and walked in Blake's direction. A smile took over my face and a strange drunk courage moistened my words. I could hear my footsteps even above the loud music, my own melodic jangle. I saw Blake's shoulders shrug in drunken relief; his fauxhawk sagged, the piercings in his brow looked like metal acne.

Rumor had it he was a bleeding queer with a napoleon complex.

And so I put my hand out to touch him, like Gatsby reaching for the green light, longing for something that would surely hurt me. Johnny warned me a long time ago, and I was in no place to betray him so, but one cannot stop the heart or hormones even in their most rational mindset. *He'll suck you dry, right down to the marrow of your bones.*

"I said no," Becka's hand pulled me back by my shirt.

I made a noise equating to a sad grunt.

"Don't give me those puppy dog eyes."

Unfortunately I had to listen to her, so long as I wanted to keep my friends. Becka was our fearless leader, dark and hard as granite, but more importantly she took care of us when we needed it. And we needed many things in life. Lindsay, her reprobate twin, was second in command and sometimes it showed upon her sneaky smile that she was simply waiting for the day she could claim the throne for herself. My place in the clique? The pathetic jester, forever Becka's pupil in her unwelcoming kingdom.

"I know what's good for you," Becka said. "How could you do that to my brother?"

"We don't really know if Blake did anything to him."

I pounded through more two craft beers called Arrogant Bastard. The ale was aggressive and slammed into my head like a fist. I was drunk before I knew it, my brain a sad lump of meat between my ears. Then Becka made me sit next to her, putting her sharp finger against my spine to straighten my back.

"Story goes like this."

Her words flooded my cranium. Sweaty summer nights, photographic insanity and two hearts destined for different paths. She told me in angst about Blake's mystical reputation, how his forlorn art only attracted the cynical crowds. She loathed their pious dispositions, their outré sense of style, which naturally fed their narcissism. The only thing they cared about was their pathetic creative missions, no matter the cost. Tears assaulted her eyes when she spoke of Johnny, but anger conquered her lips when she confirmed that Blake never loved him.

No matter the cost. That rang in my head

She missed her brother, and so did I. He was my best friend. But that was a long time ago. Time heals all wounds? When Becka stopped to catch her breath Lindsay laughed sheepishly, but Lindsay was stone cold stupid and had zero social skills. When people like Becka have someone like Lindsay to feed their anger and resentment, to worship them like the snake she is, there is no stopping the tirade.

When I lost all hope of blacking out I walked home alone. At sunrise my head finally hit the pillow. My nightmares were only of Blake.

For the next four weeks I led my life by lies. In Becka's head I was a full-time slave to coffee addicts, brown stained teeth, caffeine crashes and flickering laptop screens. Therefore, shortening our hangout time made sense.

It wasn't hard to find out where Blake spent his time. Somebody knew someone who knew Blake, but most of all they had all seen his lugubrious work and were more than willing to sacrifice an ignoramus.

"Art is more than expression," Blake said to me. "It's a way to explore . . . then cut."

Blake took me down to his ramshackle for a photo shoot. We bought a six-pack of Natty Ice and some mind-altering substance to loosen the mosh-pit of our thoughts. He put a tab on my tongue and I drank back my beer. The effect made me feel very distant, slow, as if the earth's gravitational pull had suddenly weakened.

"What do you see?"

It was in this moment that I took the deepest look into Blake, let his essence completely take over my own. Eyes the color of blood, razor teeth. Skin like a tortoise shell. His face was a melody that would never leave my head.

"You," I said.

Blake smiled. "Lay down."

Hands seized my skin with rough command; words tongued the sticky rings of my brain. The camera flashed like porn lights. But sex was not his mission; he hadn't even leaned in close enough for a kiss.

But imagination deceived me. I wondered just how rotten his lips, his teeth, his tongue, would taste. Rotgut and black squid ink. His touch? Nothing less than electric crackling all over my skin, rhythmic as a pulse.

"What attracts you to my art?" Blake said.

"The chaos."

When I first saw that cursed work I was too young to understand it. The air that night was permeated with the odor of red wine and cheap cigarettes. Johnny and I had already drunk half the bottle of Syrah, thus opening the door to his secret world. It began with pictures that I saw on his cell phone, of an insidious nature. Strange things that I cannot describe in words, but if darkness was light and light the pathway to darkness . . . that's the only way to imagine it.

"These will drive you insane," Johnny said assuredly.

All of them were originals: Johnny pale and vulnerable, his skin marked up with bruises like dark freckles. The backdrop was a slick surface of scales and petals. But I noticed something off about all of them. The pain in Johnny's face did not match the pleasure in his petite body. And then the picture moved. Not enough for me to question my fleeting sanity, but when the cold mist hit my face I screamed. Johnny smiled like the joke was on me. But it wasn't.

"These are going to make me famous," he said.

I nodded. "Is Blake the one?"

"Yes."

Johnny's eyes were lucent fire; his lips glittered with desire. A life without Blake would be futile, and I haphazardly agreed. I could not imagine what it would be like to be loved by such a man—that heart beating against my own—but I knew that I wanted it. The more Johnny told me, the more I fell in love.

Then one night I came home to find Johnny in funeral attire, his eyes caked in shoe polish and tears slugging down his face. Blake had broken off all relations and Becka had already written Blake's name in blood on the kitchen wall. Months went by, and Johnny could not release himself from mourning; he abstained and wet the bed, paling to the color of death. Soon enough his young face became emaciated and his bones took on a rattle as if his insides had dried to hollows. But I'd subconsciously chosen to ignore him because I had successfully let Blake in.

Then Johnny disappeared.

Becka was the one who found the note. She cried for three weeks straight, forcing Lindsay and myself on the streets in a giant search effort. We rang every doorbell, threw bricks through windows and called every number in the phone book. But Johnny was gone. Forever.

My only chance to become friendly with Blake had come.

The advertisement was emailed to me from a dummy account. A chasm filled with teeth, claws and eyes. When I arrived at the warehouse I began to feel somewhat vengeful. But upon first sight my dick got instantly hard.

The gallery was like *The Twilight Zone*. Blake's mind surges the planes of the inhuman psyche that people do not understand . . . most will not even come to fathom an inch of it. His work is a black paradise; darkness and light swirl like evil candy canes.

"I know you," Blake said from behind. "Johnny's friend."

I froze; my cigarette burned down to the filter.

"Do you talk?" His big eyes would not release me.

Where is Johnny? I wanted to say, but instead I cocked my ear and let him convince me of doing something drastic. Later in the day, I found myself naked, engulfed in the chiaroscuro web of his camera. The lights dazed and confused me. The fancy strand of weed we smoked tasted like burning leaves.

"Now hold still . . . hold so very still . . ."

Did I see his forked tongue snap free from that reptile mouth? Did I feel it reach every inch of my body, covering me like ectoplasm?

Why is it that everything that is bad feels so good?

It made me happy. It made Johnny happy too.

At least I thought so.

"Did you see he made *The Underground*?"

Becka's growl shivered across the local avant-garde newspaper. I played hookie on Blake that day to satisfy the requirements of friendship. Though my body might have been at the espresso bar, it was a mere flesh doll being that I could only think of Blake.

"He'll suck a person dry for all they have, then demand more," Becka said.

"And he gets praise for it!" Lindsay added.

Full page in the art section. Digitalized labyrinth schemes, inkblots and studies in vitriol. In the backdrop a dark sky was pinned with stars, red and soft as meat. The reviewer spoke about how the pictures themselves took over any wall they hung upon, and that no one could figure out if Blake painted them himself or manipulated still photos.

"There's no one like him," I said.

Becka rolled her pale eyes. I paid her no mind, drank my espresso without the lemon wedge and continued reading the article. *Blake's work beats like a living heart. This can be noted as the opinion of each observer comes to a unique conclusion. You hear things that you shouldn't be hearing; you understand that you must turn your face, shut off your ears and walk completely out of the room for fear of falling deep into the hell that is Blake's brain.*

"He's allowing me into it," I whispered.

Then I felt a warm tingle, saw the fresh hematoma on my arm, swollen so that I couldn't even see my own tattoos. I had no clue how it got there, and all that came to my mind were weird reptilian visions.

"Allowing what?" Becka said.

She ripped the paper out of my hand. A few heads turned our way; Becka's temper always made her look childish. She might have wanted an article like that written about her, but everything she attempted to create always ended up in failure. Jealousy is an ugly attribute, especially on someone who wasn't afraid to show it.

"His genius," I said reluctantly, "lies in his passion. Blake knows what it means to create from the soul."

"And how would you know?" Becka smacked a fly with her hand and smeared it across the window. "That's exactly what I want to do to him."

I came to the conclusion that her favorite hobby was to lambaste Blake.

"You're right. I wouldn't know," I lied.

"Edo, you're a great guy, but you're foolishly in love."

"No, I'm not," I said.

"And you're betraying Johnny. But I know it's not your fault."

I got up from the table and flew out the door. It was so hot out that the city itself was dripping with sweat. I found a seat and daydreamed about how I would pose for Blake again . . . how he would drastically manipulate the final product. He could tear my soul apart, string it back together in bleeding beads, and I was fine with that. It was the only way I would allow him to have me.

One day I'd make the papers; one day I'd be famous.

"Every landscape is a dark magic dream."

The same ruinous nightmare replaying in my head: Blake's empty gallery a sloping pale land, rich wintered foliage of wildflowers, lilies and inverted weeping willows as if the world had been tilted upside down. Rising columns of ice were crowned with gas lamps that threw no shadows. The heavy moonlight came down in spangles.

I am in a very bright room. The floor is crinkled like aluminum foil; above my head is a carnival mirror that changes Blake's face into something haggard. He takes my hand in his, so cold, and so it must have meant that his heart was where all the warmth lay. But it was not so because I saw no love in his fiery smile.

No pulse in his grip.

"What is this place?" I asked.

"The chambers of my mind."

Blake's art hung upon a wall that ascended to heights my eyes could not fathom, and descended to depths that matched the pain of Hell. I focused not on the enormity of what was above and below me, but on the living abyss in which laid the boon of his artistic mission: darkness.

Each frame was bejeweled in icicles like a sharp grin. As I passed each one I felt the ghostly force of something resisting his art. Then I heard a voice so familiar it chilled me. A pale shadow climbed out of one of the pictures, a young boy with snagged hair and ripped clothes; he screamed with a voice scraped raw by hurt.

For some reason I could feel what he felt, hear what he heard, see what he saw. I knew this boy, as did Blake, but there was no mercy to spare. I reached out for him, understanding that there was no way out.

Then Blake pulled me into his hot embrace, skin unzipping to reveal the rank inner decay. He opened his carrion arms like a budding flower, holding me tight to poison me with his dark fire kiss.

And then everything clicked out with the eerie sound of silence.

I woke up coughing ash, blood and smoke. My tongue was charred and my feet numb. Becka had called me six times. *Where are you?* Typical scowl. *HE WILL DESTROY YOU.* I threw my cell phone into the toilet and vomited right into it. A cold milky liquid and tiny crystals of ice.

In my living room the posters on the walls judged me. Their eyes were daggers of light; their hands reaching for my brain to render me insane. Two o'clock said the microwave but I cared not to figure out a.m. or p.m., let alone shower or brush my teeth. Instead, I ripped the socks off my feet and smelled the proof of poverty, telling myself that there was no better time than now drain myself of dream and come to the terms with this love-germ building inside of me.

Malediction.

Constriction.

Addiction.

Blake and I met up at his apartment. Below us the sounds of a dying music shop played vinyl records: Avenged Sevenfold and Tool. It was so hot inside I thought I was going to puke again. No fans, no air conditioner; the humidity was a tumescent tongue that would not stop licking. Once inside I saw that he hadn't cleaned up for what seemed like months. There was garbage everywhere; the smell of ink was like grease in my nose.

I found Blake in the fetal position beaming with sweat and darkness. He was backtracking through a catalogue of photos, simultaneously running his fingers through a black pool of developing liquid. When he took his finger out I saw that it was bleeding.

"Can't breathe in here," I said. "Is there a window?"

He pointed to a place that could have made Lovecraft's *Dreams in the Witch House* question itself. Either my eyes deceived me or the world I knew no longer existed. Like some trick of the Wonka factory, the ceiling and floor seemed to slowly close in on me. By the time I got to the window I was out of breath and dripping.

"*Absurd Clarity*," Blake said. "That's what I'm going to call your photos."

I came back to the thrift shop couch. He stroked my longish hair, my ears, my lips. He was temptation incarnate. Danger was set to follow. One stroke, two . . . the oils of his fingers like a mating call. I couldn't hold myself any longer. A monster welled up in my throat and a tortured angel swelled inside my pants.

I attacked him with my mouth and scissored my legs. Becka's voice of warning pounded in my ears. *DESTROYER. USER. LOSER. ABUSER.* Nothing mattered. It had been too long since I'd been with a man, and oh, how I missed the feeling of their skin, the bittersweet taste of their sweat. But what I discovered was that Blake could not be tasted nor savored; he could not be categorized or fit into a little box tied with a bow of blood.

And for that Blake drove me insane.

His pajama bottoms shredded in my angsty grip and his penis rose with the beautiful stink of dead flowers. I swallowed him whole. I wanted his juices to freeze my heart in static rhythm. His fingers seized my hair, some-thing monstrous taking control, to which he squeezed as if trying to turn my brain into goo.

A pleasurable growl started in his throat. Long nails cut into my scalp as he pushed my head down until I felt a sinewy snap and the warm trickle of blood in the back of my throat.

But I cared not for dignity. Living in the moment felt natural. I saw the lightning strike of the camera flash and then heard that horrid roar again as Blake's orgasm singed my throat with the flavor of brimstone. I pulled away, lips wet with spit, blood and come. It all tasted the same. That's when I saw his forked tongue.

"There's no release from me," Blake said. "You'll find me in your dreams."

And then Blake hit me so hard everything winked out.

"Freak!" Becka's voice skyrocketed. "Black eye, a few missing teeth . . . maybe a broken jaw. Look at the way his tongue is hanging out the side of his mouth . . . bleeding."

Déjà vu.

I am the emotional nightmare.

"Did he get beat up?" I heard Lindsay say.

Becka pulled my band shirt so hard it ripped at the neck. She made me sip a horrible energy drink that seared my sore throat and crashed into the pit of my stomach. I could barely hold my mouth open to drink. Blake had hurt me. HURT ME . . . but it was so worth it.

"He left you on the fucking street," Becka said. "Is this how you like to be treated?"

"It's not his fault," I said.

Becka tsked. "And you crawl back for more!"

"I'm fine."

"I can't let this happen again. I won't let this happen again."

I let my hair cover my red face as she scolded me.

"You've been lying to me. Don't you know what this will lead you to? *Nothing*."

She had made me reach my boiling point. At first I wasn't even going to say it, but being that she had no remorse for my tainted love, I let it slip.

"I saw Johnny!"

Becka gripped my shirt and pulled me towards her. "You didn't see a thing."

"He's alive."

"Liar!"

"I know what I saw."

"Is that so? Tell that mother fucker to come outside and explain it to me."

She pulled a bottle of 151 out of her messenger bag, doused a washrag in the liquor and then shoved it into the neck of the bottle. The smell seared my nostrils, made my eyes tear. Becka looked right at me when she set the rag aflame with her cigarette. It was an exquisite sight . . . until I discovered what she was about to do.

"It's for your own good."

The Molotov cocktail shot out of her hand like a roaring cannon ball, bursting through the window of the music store below Blake's apartment. I could not stop the horror I felt for fear of losing Blake. My countenance betrayed me; Becka began to laugh and cry, somehow vindicated.

"You're on his side!" tears falling like rain.

There came the smell of melted glass and vinyl, the crackling of old wood. Above, Blake's window flickered with ghost-shadows. I heard his monster growl fill the room. I caught the memory of his transformation as it exploded.

"Run!"

A black mist hurtled toward us. I heard Lindsay's terrible scream just before it swallowed her whole. Becka and I darted for the wide street, but the swarm was too fast, too fluid. It came between us, dangled over my body like hair and knocked Becka to the pavement as if a rug had been ripped out from under her feet.

I lay back in shock as the blackness covered her, caught the reflection of red eyes and fangs . . . heard the werewolf howl. Becka's feet disappeared first, then her legs; her sharp face fell into a contortion of remorse and pain as she pleaded for my help.

But I ran for my life.

It's been three years and I still haven't forgiven myself. But this is how Blake makes his move: he opens his cold black heart to you, makes you love him, and then when you are his, he spits you back onto the lonely streets from which you came. I want to say that I learned from my mistake, but I couldn't be sure until I went back to see Blake.

I ate a shit-ton of sleeping pills. At first nothing came. The walls of my room seemed to gently flow; my bones became brittle and the tattoos on my arms stretched to impossible angles. The next moment I opened my eyes I saw an abysmal mist flooding the room.

In its depths I could see a pair of crimson eyes, a forked tongue and a frayed pale youth running away from the camera. In the distance were rising columns of ice, but at my level something clamped upon my inner thigh, leaving an ectoplasmic glow along the length of my penis.

Then Blake's hand became entangled in my hair, cupped the beads of my spine as if they were Fabergé eggs. I could not extricate myself from his touch. We moved in fathomless directions as the smell of ice and fire ensconced us.

We stopped in front of an art gallery. Shadows careened, each one I knew was a boy that had loved Blake. Each one a victim of self-loathing. And then I saw my own fate, the face that I had fallen in love with, scales and orchid petals. The photo's backdrop was an endless black sky with no stars or moon. But if I stared close enough I could see the beginning stages of a sketch: the sketch of me.

Blake planted his lips upon mine, filling me with his dark fire kiss. I closed my eyes and cried because I knew that I was too afraid to know what was on the other side. I didn't want to be like everyone else. And so I let go of Blake, pulling myself free of the nightmare as if through a funnel—

—to never sleep again.

Love is like a walk on the wild side.

Love is also the sweetest lie.

. . . There is no dream but you . . . and I don't want to wake up from this tonight . . .

2012

Another appendage to *Blood Kiss*, this was very hard for me to write. I knew that there was another story concerning the world of *Blood Kiss* in me ready to come out, but just couldn't really find where it needed to go. Maybe it was the fact that I wrote this story *after Blood Kiss* was completed in 2013, and due to events within the novel, maybe this story felt a little fake. But then I realized that there are no limits in fiction. I am the Gods when writing these stories. So I just started writing and got it done. If I wanted to put this story in some kind of chronological order, it would probably take place between chapters 7 and 10.

Now that I look back on this story I really like it. One that is morally important.

THE LONG LOST AND FORGOTTEN

South Williamsburg, far as one can go before they swim. September, says the calendar, but summer won't shut its greasy legs to let the cool breath of autumn roam free. Here it is far too quiet to be considered part of metropolitan New York, even with Manhattan's lights slathered like grease upon the shoreline, or the endless adventures that live within the abandoned factories.

Two hooligans prowl the streets looking for fun or trouble, most likely a little of both. Their friendship was founded upon a mutual love of creation, perpetual laziness and ridicule of the current art scene. They had been introduced by their lovers and quickly found that their obsessions complimented on another quite well: the girl's painful poetry to the boy's surreal art.

Tyria was fair and driven by anger; Dorian was dark and wretched in nature. But when the two of them put their heads together they could spin straw into gold, turn creative energy into defiance and unravel the entanglement that we call reality.

"I really hate Brooklyn," Tyria said.

Dorian looked at her with eyes made of dark stone. "Then why do you live here?"

"I'm in a much better neighborhood than this."

"Horse shit," Dorian tugged at the piercings in his lip.

Tyria looked at him square in the eyes. "Is your boredom killing you finally?"

They stopped walking. Dorian lit a joint, inhaled a spicy cloud of THC that put his mind into a more patient state. The smoke swirled about everything, claimed the air. Tyria watched him with disdain, lit a hand-rolled cigarette. They both enjoyed the full minute of silence, losing one another in the dreams that lived behind their eyes.

"I've something on my mind," Dorian broke the silence.

Tyria rolled her eyes, put on her black Ray Bans. "Entertain me then, *Dangerous Dorian*."

"Hate that name."

The way Dorian looked upon Tyria was a most maddening sight. It was not admiration, protective instinct or even lust. It was fascination. His almond eyes bowed to her every move and word. He was Tyria's greatest admirer and, admittedly, wanted to cut open her head and live inside her.

But Tyria would never say how much Dorian marveled her. He was a unique painter with a macabre slant that put all of his competition to shame. When you entered a gallery you knew immediately that the one painting that rubbed you the wrong way was a Dorian Wilde original. It was his unique technique, the relationship he developed with the paint brush: one moment you could be looking at Dorian's work—the sure admirer—but then all of a sudden find that your God-given free will is no longer yours and that Dorian's work is staring *into* you.

"Out with it," Tyria said.

Their walk had taken them to edge of the borough so that the sulfuric smell of the East River tongued them passionately. Unstable territory, Tyria knew, as peace on this side of the street was intermittent and drug deals were exchanged as if currency. Popular real estate had yet to enslave this part of town like it has done the north side, probably because the pavement was so uneven and that the creepy warehouses were hunched together in attempt to hide from the neighborhood's volatile populace. And then something caught her eye: *Salvage Warehouse*, in bright pink aerosol paint.

"Isn't that—"

"Oh yes," Dorian said. "And look."

He pointed at a flickering window. There, Tyria saw something dark. Not shadow, nor a shred of universe, but something *wrong*. It looked back at them, into them, the face of something forgotten, lost. Dorian didn't waste a moment, taking out his sketchpad and pencil, immediately drawing parabolas on the page. There was no true way to make sense of the horrible thing, but his hand always moved before his brain, circles and dull ends and spirals before he realized that something had taken shape: a mouth, a cyclopean eye and a tail. Tyria grabbed the sketchbook from his hand and threw it on the ground.

"What was that for?"

"Not everything wants to model for you," Tyria hissed.

"Don't you want to see it?"

"Not for the life of me."

But that was not where her rage was stemming from. Somewhere inside she was scared as hell, and the only way she knew how to protect herself was to get mad, since there was no getting out of this, not by a long shot. Dorian's mind was set, and he was ready to do something terrible.

"You coming?" Dorian said.

The front door was bolted and the side entrance was gated off with rusted barbed wire. No matter, as Dorian was already scaling the fire escape, dropping his hand for

Tyria, and though she huffed and puffed, she took his hand and he pulled her up without effort. They faced a window that was cracked by sun and snow and moonshine.

"Thought you had the key to this place?" Tyria said.

"Where's the fun in that?"

Dorian's fist easily punched through. They climbed in carefully, throwing pieces of glass onto the metal staircase. The floor below them was a dark maze of spired gates, x-ray films, antique keys, desks, ornate light fixtures, art supplies and stone animals. No light inside but what reflected off the river, and as Dorian illuminated his cell phone, Tyria saw one of the stone animals turn its head away.

"I'm not going any further," Tyria said.

"Don't be shy."

Dorian took her hand and pulled her in.

From 1980 to 2000, the Architectural Salvage Warehouse was the only place in Brooklyn that accepted the remains of demolished structures from around the city. Precious detritus revered by historians, nostalgists, and even bloggers; priceless ghosts of a past that was unable to be preserved since institutional Alzheimer's became some-what of the norm in New York City.

For restorers, this warehouse was a place they could call home, a luxury their craft hardly ever had. Griddles, fire pokers and street signs could be melted down to create something more modern, or simply restored and put up for sale to anyone who appreciated the painstaking work. But to developers, the once city-operated business was just taking up space on their future goldmine.

It didn't matter what relics were stored inside, or how much cultural legacy could be wiped clean if and when it was demolished or sold to the highest bidder. It didn't matter that the origins of each item could no longer be traced as fiscal constraints had cut staff down each passing year, which meant that bookkeeping had been grossly overlooked.

Thus, the landscape of the Architectural Salvage Warehouse changed from historical heaven to sudden purgatory. The lights cut out and the doors were sealed. Everything began to collect dust. Pieces of history piled upon more pieces of history, and once put inside, no item would ever find its place in the world again.

It was a summer to remember, insofar as summers are to be remembered. Dorian's art had sold well through July, and his first four shows in August put so much extra cash in his wallet that he was able to pay the rent two months in advance. The leftover cash was invested in craft beer, completing his Black Sabbath vinyl collection, painting the brick walls of his loft silver and black, and more art supplies, natch.

Riding on the success, a local Brooklyn paper called *Eyesore* ran an article about Dorian. Within it the writer theorized that if photographs were an inexhaustible source of material for Francis Bacon, than reality—even nightmare—was for Dorian Wilde a depthless well of inspiration. How else could the oils have bled together with such vigor, or the jaws of a fossilized abomination snap open? Dorian made his audience question the external world in effort to justify their own perversions.

But popularity soon dwindled as it always seems to do, that white-hot moment of stardom cooling so fast there was no point in trying to redeem himself. If you don't keep up with the in-crowd—if you don't make small talk and smile—they stop buying. Self-promotion was an act that Dorian knew he could never ace, and so now he was suffering the repercussions. Lucky for him Tyria only lived ten minutes away by foot, which eased the transition from skyrocket to skyfall.

"When will the artist ever be challenged?" Tyria said, sliding her finger across the centerfold of the magazine.

"Do you not live in the same world as I?"

Tyria smiled. "The rational world or—"

"The one that forces us to pay rent to slumlords and buy food because we can't grow it ourselves in this city."

"You sound bitter."

Dorian snapped his face toward the sun and the reflection caught Tyria right in the eyes.

"I have to get a fucking job. Do you know how that feels?"

"No," Tyria said, wincing in preparation for Dorian's reaction. "And don't call me a brat because Adelaide takes care of everything."

"You're very lucky. Leland, as you know, is upstate on that fucking Zen retreat. I have to find a quick way to get paid, quicker than schmoozing."

"Leland didn't leave you any cash because you were doing so well when he left."

Dorian took a sip of his early morning IPA. "Yeah, well, he also didn't give me a fallback plan, and I guess that's partly my own fault."

"Hey, you wanted the rock star life, but artists rarely enjoy all the sex and drugs. The rock n' roll is there for sure, but without the glam."

A spoken word poet by nature, Tyria almost always had the upper hand in any conversation they had. Though her talents stemmed from a tragic childhood, having lost her innocence too early in life by a father that showed his love by touching his only daughter in places no girl should be touched, she had those memories to thank for her passions even if they weren't the greatest. But this is why Dorian and Tyria were friends, and this is why they would continue to work together so long as they dreamed.

"The fuck am I even good at?" Dorian looked at his studio door that had just creaked open slightly. "Everything in that room contains the life I need. No more, no less."

Tyria lit a Camel. "You say that like it's my fault."

The small talk went on for another two hours. Brainstorming and surfing the internet for job postings, Craigslist and LinkedIn, two web platforms Dorian never thought he'd find himself needing. By moonrise Tyria was a six-pack in and Dorian switched to a wine that stained his tongue red. Another hour flew by, and maybe it was the rush of beer drunk, or the fact that she hadn't laughed so hard in a long time, but Tyria made Dorian a promise to hook him up with a guy that Adelaide used to buy her dope from.

"I don't want her hanging that over my head," Dorian said.

"I'll make sure she doesn't."

"Yeah, good luck with that."

The hook up was an Italian relic from the north side, Johnny-No-Thumbs, aptly named because he had lost both his thumbs to garden shears after not making good on a gambling debt he owed a certain family. After that incident, Tyria said that Johnny had left the wise-guy stuff behind and went all out American hustler, buying buildings on the south side while they were cheap, housing a junkyard, a factory that made propellers, and using one of the buildings as a storage facility of the strangest nature.

"If ya want work you gotta work for it, ya lazy bum," Johnny said to Dorian. "I hear yous a good guy, but I also know you make weird shit up."

"I'm a painter," Dorian said.

"I don't know nothin' about painting; but what I do know is that I got shit lying around and nobody to clean it up."

Johnny was a small man with an abysmal demeanor. Whatever guilt or empathy Dorian had felt about his radial nubs had faded to the reality that for an indeterminable amount of time he'd be slaving eight hours a day hauling shit he couldn't care less about, ultimately taking time away from him being an artist. But cash was king; emotional livelihoods had to wait.

Work started on the hottest Sunday of the year. The sun blazed against Dorian's back, and he hated himself for wearing his *Ozzfest 2001* tour t-shirt and black jeans from *Yellow Rat Bastard*. By the end of the day he had never felt so abused, never seen his skin so red or his dark hair stick up in so many directions. He wanted to choke Tyria for all this stress, but the crisp $100 bill in his back pocket was something he could get used to.

Though he felt completely out of his element due to the humiliation of the job, not to mention the language barrier of the immigrants—the fact that they laughed at Dorian and made fun of him under their breath—could not touch the electrifying inspiration he felt when he first entered the building at the loading entrance.

The warehouse on Berry Street lay in the shadow of the Williamsburg Bridge, nestled grotesquely between a bar, a junkyard and two small apartment buildings. A brick-and-mortar time capsule unlike anything he'd ever seen. No museum could compare. Literal pieces of the city were inside of it, torn down facades, shredded subway tracks, antique doorknobs and stained glass that would never see the light of day again if the current administration had their way. They had no respect for the past and no hope to restore it. Whatever made its way inside the warehouse was to remain, to decay, to gather dust.

Johnny was paid a handsome salary to keep these strange keepsakes away from the general public. While some of the stock like the original street signs or skeleton keys for padlocks that secured the first storefronts of the city remained priceless, there were some items that Johnny had mentioned that rubbed him the wrong way. He was not a believer in echoes and specters or ghosts and goblins, but he figured since Dorian always walked around with a rain cloud over his head that he'd be into some of the spookier things that the warehouse stored.

"I'm a man of Catholic faith. I grew up reading the Bible, which I will say has some scary shit in it. But I never seen anything like this," Johnny said.

"I don't believe in spooks either," Dorian finished his Marlboro and crushed it against the warehouse's metal door.

"Yeah, right," Johnny said. "Here's the key if you ever want to check it out when no one's around. Tell Ty I said hello."

That night he tried to call Leland but couldn't get through. When he called Tyria Dorian could feel the immense annoyance in her voice. Adelaide was in the middle of painting her nails, but he let it all out anyway, going over and over about the warehouse as he supposed Tyria would like the idea. But five minutes into the conversation she slipped an invisible DO NOT DISTURB sign between them by hanging up.

He would have to do it alone.

It was the ass-end of a typical Brooklyn night, the East River scintillating and Manhattan's glass and steel facades seemingly unreal. He checked all of his things before leaving his apartment, didn't need much other than his backpack, a fresh sketchpad and two No. 2 pencils. He weaseled his way west on South 4th Street, making a slight left on Berry, stopping directly in front of the warehouse.

The building had been freshly tagged, something Dorian hadn't seen earlier in the day. Swooping white paint and black bubble letters, the beginning of some kind of mural against the establishment, from what he could make out. He fished his pocket for the key and had to give the lock a few good twists before he heard the rusted cogs unhinge to let him in.

The warehouse had changed, stretching further than he remembered, which was damn near impossible, but somehow plausible. Maybe it was just too dark inside. For a good five minutes he couldn't bring himself to walk fully inside; weary of something that hadn't even shown its face yet.

He used his Zippo lighter to guide him into the labyrinth, barely enough light to get him to one side of the main room. Immediately he tripped over pieces of sheet-rock, smelled insulation and the cinders of buildings that had been brought down by fire. Sounds infiltrated his ears from all parts of the room, not wind, not rodents, or even the wings of insects. Just sounds. He placed the lighter on the floor and opened his sketchbook, blindly drawing all the things he was hearing.

When his pencil broke through the pad he knew that there would be no hole to prove it. Now his hand was going in, deep into the mouth of something he could not see. He heard a footstep, cloven hoof made of stone, and the sound of mortar being chewed by steel teeth. The Zippo light blew out, forcing Dorian to take cover in an old glass phone booth. When he sat down to catch his breath he had accidentally pulled the chord out of the phone—

—as something on the line began to speak.

Third Wednesday into August and the swelter had hooked itself so deep that nobody could escape their own stink. On the street odors mingled madly, everyone holding their noses, bags above their heads to block the sun but their hands burning against UVB rays.

Down below the surface there was still some candle-light left in the old book shoppe. Tyria had been perusing its aisles since dawn, transporting herself into multiple galaxies far, far away, ones that would never change inside their paper bindings and flimsy parchment. Opening a book is sort of like opening a wound, splitting memory; always there to haunt you, it just needs the right touch.

Now her stomach began to growl and her head started to ache; her tattoos itched, especially the bright green ouroboros around her left wrist. She wanted a cigarette. But she was safe in these long halls, a strategic move to partition off Adelaide's clinginess and Dorian's madness as there was no cell phone service down here. No way for them to poison her mind with their rhetoric, their aches and pains, their artistic debts to various entities and organizations. As much as Tyria loved Adelaide, and as much as she respected Dorian, she did not have to be at their every beck and call.

The library was permeated with stillness, and this was duly noted in the titles that were never rotated, its tech-nologies never updated. Poetry was still in the back, prose in the front and textbooks were off to the right. Time stood still down here, plain and simple.

But the books were special; this place not open to the public—not for decades—now privately owned, with no upkeep to be had. Each shelf seemed a mile long and several miles high, and Tyria found herself sometimes staring so hard that the books seemed to glow with age and wisdom, sway to the music of the stories that lived within them.

"Why haven't you been returning my calls?"

Tyria nearly jumped out of her skin, swinging at the sound that came out of the darkness. Her fist caught a corner shelf, knocking down several books and unleashing clouds of dust and cobwebs. Tyria listened for the voice again, taking two steps back before something warm and fuzzy came over her, like being drunk, an embrace she knew all too well.

"How the fuck did you know I was here?" Tyria snorted.

Dorian let her go, stepping back so that she could fully see him. "You're not too hard to find when you only like being at one of two places."

His clothes were worn down, his wingtip boots ripped at the toes. Black ink was smudged across his chin, which made his teeth appear way too bright. He looked like he hadn't gotten sleep in years; Tyria could see the fear and apprehension in his eyes. How bad had the job worn him down? How much more would he be able to take? The blue-collar life was not for him.

"Are you okay, Dorian?"

Nails in his mouth, red slime on his lower lip. "I'm fine . . . I just need to talk . . . is all."

"I'm sorry I haven't called you back," Tyria's guilt now showing. "It's just been a weird time for me."

"What could be so weird that you can't tell me?"

Tyria lit a hand-rolled cigarette. "It's got nothing to do with you. It's all me. Just need to be alone."

"You'll really want to be alone when I tell you what I've seen, things your nightmares can't even create."

"Don't flower it up, Dorian. Just out with it."

And so he went into bitter detail of the encounters. How the warehouse changed when viewed from the inside or out, how it seemed to be its own little world. It had a sky, a shoreline; it made sounds like it was digesting bad food, and it had its own gravitational pull. Tyria took a seat in the closest chair she could find, losing Dorian in the dim light.

"Sounds?" Tyria said, shaking her head.

And then he pulled a book down from the shelf, proof in his hands that something was following him, trying to tell him something. A queer title, something about a great white whale, and when Dorian opened the first page the book misted Tyria's face. She smacked it out of Dorian's hand, but upon landing on the floor it begun to vomit water. She bent down and shut it.

But Dorian wasn't finished. He pulled more books off the shelves. Carter's wolves bayed and Grimm's Fairy Tales smelled like that of a forest. Butterflies and will o' the wisps were let loose from the imprisoning pages of another book. A grotesque hand reached up, grabbed Tyria's hair and tried to pull her in.

"The phone rang," Dorian said. "And I'd already pulled out the chord."

Tyria's eyes widened. "What the fuck was that?"

"Adventure," Dorian said. "I want to go back . . . *with you.*"

"Don't you work there?"

Dorian moved his hair away from his face. "I do, but you're not understanding me. Those things . . . those forgotten pieces of history . . . they don't want to be lost, or forgotten. They want to go on and they're trying to tell me why."

The rain started with no warning, settling on the old roof loudly. A heavy whistling cut through the broken window, bringing with it pelts of warm summer water. Lightning spread pale veins in the sky, its luminescence crawling across the floor and through the grate of the metal staircase so that Dorian could see the entire warehouse as if it was during the day, even if for a moment.

"That's not where it should be." Dorian picked a rotary phone up from off the floor and put it back on a shelf.

Something feathery crawled across his scrawny body, and it made him suddenly understand how insignificant he was. Might it be that the visible world was only the size of a single subatomic particle stitched into a vast quilt made up of a billion atoms, a cosmic spider web where dimensions and physical law did not hold sway? This made Dorian take a step back, look deeply into the warehouse's contents to see nothing but a big dark blanket, a blanket he wanted, and needed; one that he would certainly unravel.

"You gunna move or what?" Tyria said.

He trotted across the metal staircase, using the wall as his fulcrum and the light from his cell phone as an assistant so that he wouldn't bust his ass. Upon landing on the ground floor the phone was immediately drained of battery; he tried his Zippo but the flint was no longer functioning. Tyria silently descended, puerile in her beliefs, so said her resting bitch face.

"The fuck is that horrible stench?" Tyria said. "Did something die?"

Dorian could not have dismissed the odor if he tried. It was a smell that was born and bred in mystery, one that had been living in his olfactory sense for quite some time, though he had failed to realize it until now. The mingled scents rocketed up to his brain, spreading fire between his ears. He knew them as well as he did his reflection in the mirror: old things, dead dreams and settled nightmares; something fecund while at the same time rotting.

"Feels like I'm in a bad movie."

Tyria her own light, pale hair and neon Converse sneakers, bright tattoos to lead them on the road to nowhere. But her glow did not stretch far enough into the warehouse, for as much as its spidery fingers could illuminate, there was just as much darkness to swallow it. Dorian could see that this made her uncomfortable, and he almost felt sorry for bringing her even though she had caused just as much mischief for him in the past. When he let that thought settle, all feelings and remorse had simply vanished.

Dorian attempted to light a cigarette. "Fucking thing isn't working. The flint is . . . gone."

Tyria turned sharply. "What do you mean *gone*?"

Dorian shrugged his shoulders. "It doesn't work."

"I just bought that for you, there's no way it could have—"

Sudden noise, not a bang or a knock on the metal door, not anything coming down the stairs: the rotary phone was turning. Dorian heard the dial spin, the receiver ring. Tyria grabbed Dorian's arm, immediate signal that she was going no further, that she would not feed into any of his games no matter how true they were. And then the phone hit the floor with a sound like bottled thunder, while thunder itself bashed the sky bloody.

"You never said why you wanted to be here," Tyria said. "Is there a purpose?"

"Must everything we do have a purpose?" Dorian stepped inside, tapped the rotary phone with his wingtip boot. "It's dead as dead can be."

"Our minds are playing tricks."

"No. They're talking to us."

"Bullshit, Dorian."

"Step in further with me."

Dancing through the accumulated dark, as if to tease Tyria that this archaic sanctuary was completely safe, that nothing in here could hurt her, but certainly they could try her tolerance. She continuously rolled a cigarette between her lips, so dry that Dorian could see blood on the filter. But his wayward movements guided him now, brushing against cornerstones and clay pots, kicking up dust bunnies and soot, sailing deeper into the labyrinth of pipes and rocks.

"Don't get lost," Tyria said.

Dorian's boot smashed through a canvas that was dry as a sepulcher, then through the whorled intricacies of stained glass windows. Tyria bent down and picked up some of the glass, a wild spiral in her hands, looking deeply into a piece the color of an open ocean. Dorian saw Tyria's eyes change colors, and so he pressed his finger gently against the glass and drew a shape into the dust, a mouth of some sort, an orifice with teeth. The second he removed his finger he heard something growl.

The glass shattered as it hit the floor.

And now his hands, those gifted hands, searching for something else, falling against something warm, a hole in the wall too big to comprehend, too alive to make sense. He pulled himself further into the warehouse, giving up his own will for something he didn't quite understand. He stepped onto wooden paneling that had certainly been ripped from the floor of an old Victorian Flatbush mansion, then balanced himself on freighter crates so that he would not fall atop the pieces of metal waiting for him as if a bed of nails.

From up here the rain was insignificant. The universe was crushing in on him. Tyria looked small but fierce in her stance, pale eyes watching Dorian, bright shoes kicking glass away from her warpath. Behind her, he saw the outline of a rising Baphomet, and just as he was going to scream he realized that it was just a stone bull, half of its face lathered in soot from some fire in the past.

Dorian's hands gleamed as the sky exploded again, dripping light into the warehouse's window. The stained glass sparkled and the floor looked like it was steaming. For a brief, holy moment he glimpsed the space where he had felt that alien warmth, to confirm now that it had come from no hole, but a statue of Mother Mary with a vulgar red orifice graffitied between her genuflecting hips.

There was blood on his hands.

"That's just vile," Tyria said.

"Now you see what I mean?" Dorian smirked.

"Get down here and do it again . . . draw something—"

The stone bull snorted, dragging cloven hooves across the linoleum. Tyria braced herself as it darted, barely managing to jump to the side before it bashed into the wall, forcing itself to crumble into pieces. Dorian made his way down and picked Tyria up, nose bleeding and tears in her eyes. But there was no fear in her, there was only absolute clarity. She wiped her nose, then scrawled poetry on the floor.

"This is how I make my mark," Tyria said.

Behind them, a blighted grandfather clock began to chime, the handles frozen at midnight or noon, depending on the light, the sound reverberating throughout the warehouse. It slid beneath Dorian's feet with a strange force, ran up every wall until the sounds coalesced in the air. Dorian held his ears as Tyria continued to write, digging her nails into the floor, engraving her reality into this unstable one.

"I can't take this shit," Dorian said. "It's driving me nuts."

Tyria looked right up at him. "Then you know what to do."

"What?"

"Draw, you fuck. Draw something so they stop."

Dorian had nearly forgotten that he had his backpack on, but it was what was inside that mattered. The pad was fresh, smelled as if it had just been cut from the tree. The pencil was beaten up, but it would do the trick even with the intermittent lightning. With the sound of the clock and of Tyria's screams, Dorian unleashed something inside of him that he never knew was there.

His hands had taken him deep in the center of the page. Spirals into circles into an endless vortex. The paper gave way; his hand went in, losing the pencil. Pain found Dorian near his elbow, to which he saw that shards of stained glass ringed edges of the paper like teeth, digging into him; maybe trying to keep him. At the sound of his scream Tyria was up on her feet, pulling Dorian's arm, tattoos peeling back.

"Don't touch me!" Dorian pleaded. "Let it take me."

The burning ran all the way up his arm, pain swirling into his head. And Tyria took a step back, but this time moving into territory that also did not want her to leave. A spired gate unfurled, pulling free from concrete, pinning her down no matter how much she cursed, no matter how much she fought. The metal kept her in place.

Now Dorian's arm inside the paper mouth, but a familiar pain was rising through him, forcing his fingertips to tingle. Then he heard the tattoo needle, saw the electric socket implode with sparks as the pain reached its white-hot threshold. It all made perfect sense. They were becoming part of him.

When he pulled himself free there was no blood and no more pain, as if what had just happened was a bad dream. The rain stopped and the lights of the warehouse buzzed to life, throwing out the shadows and echoes so that Dorian now saw that the entire space was empty, except for Tyria who was sprawled across the linoleum with a bleeding lip, red stained teeth in her pseudo-smile.

"It's all gone," Tyria mumbled.

Dorian looked at his right arm, which was now taken over by a miraculous new tattoo, one that would continue to tell the story of history past, of a city taken over by new administrations and a populace that do not appreciate what had brought them to the greatest city in the world, that the change they bring, though rooted in New York's history, should not pride itself on erasing everything that people built.

Dorian, with this new smorgasbord, would now be able to keep it in his heart.

2015

"Devil Made of Crystal" was written in 2013 after a maddened night of drinking wine with a friend and discussing polytheism. In Queens, where I grew up, there is an Indian neighborhood where once you step onto its streets you are overtaken by the smells of curry, spice and herbs, the lovely sight of swirling saris, and lots and lots of gold. I love the country of India, and decided with this story that I needed to write my own love letter, with a horrific slant.

DEVIL MADE OF CRYSTAL

The heavy-metal kid called himself Shrike. He spoke in tongues of prophecy, black glitter and the dark arts. With nothing but a black quill pen, he wrote loudly about complacency and unease, and how there was nothing we could do about it. Though I loathed Shrike's poetry, he was my best friend.

My hate is a certain love.

Shrike could not gather the public following he craved, but in private he could convince any old soul, especially one as timid and curious as I. And so one August night we reflected upon our lives in hopes to find a balance between the responsibility we rejected and the spontaneity we desired.

It was our usual Friday night gimmick—we were dangerously bored, craving adventure and decadence—and what resulted was not as random as picking a number out of a hat. This time we fell into a more calculated adventure: a fevered walking tour of Little India. I could hardly refuse, for Shrike had already assuaged me with the scents of rose water, with the sights of saris hitting the wind like flags and hot black tea brewed in big iron cauldrons.

"But why night?" I asked him

"Day is when people trample you like rotten fruit. At night it's all about play. The sun sets and the claws come out."

We suffered the grumbling of the subway, metal upon metal, the dark tawdry music of the underground. We studied the train's pitiful patrons with angst and clarity: a girl juggling too much laundry, a screaming crack-head and scared families who turned their faces away to the terrible reality of poverty and drug abuse. To be so frightened of the real world was a way of life we did not crave.

Above ground, we shook off the frost of the subway and fell headlong into the jungles of Nepal and Sri Lanka. As soon as my painfully sensitive eyes adjusted, I thought I might've been dropped into a lucid neon painting. The nighttime sky was hazy with color like an erratic circuit board; a lime-green house of worship was marked HINDU TEMPLE; a royal mosque glowed an icertine blue.

A city made of brick, mortar and precious stone.

I quickly lost my sense of place. The colors of the holy land glowed dark and slow as if reflecting off the Sagar River. The streets were full of mud and the air was thick with grease vapors. A hallucinatory fist of odors curled into my nose: the spicy-sweetness of mughal, the yellow scent of biryani and the antique-brewed smell of liquor like ghosts of another time.

"The Hindus, Bengals and Pakis drink whiskey like wine, but they don't talk about it openly. It's seen as an American temptation," Shrike said, sipping his own minty brew.

"Let me taste that," I said. " I'm not drunk."

No less putrid than battery acid, the liquor swarmed my taste buds, my palate; burned all the way down. I felt the delicate sphincter instinctively tighten so not to let the liquid agony meet my stomach, to poison my bloodstream.

But it was too late. One sip and I was already hot in the face and ready to rule the world. I became deviously horny.

"Indian brewed scotch whiskey," Shrike said.

Shrike wanted to film our adventure, and he showed me his graffiti-scarred camcorder, awaiting the lunacy that blossoms within a sweltering Indian midnight. It was very hot, balmy. My skin took on a wonderful pale glow and Shrike himself seemed to sparkle like those cheesy movie vampires.

That or I was still hopelessly infatuated, secretly waiting for the fairytale day when Shrike and I would become lovers. No need to get into the dramatics because it's quite simple: I wanted him, but he wasn't like me. He was into girls.

"A bleeding queer," he called me in the gutter-punk English accent he often mocked.

"But a man can please another man in ways a woman can't. They don't have the same parts a man has, they don't—"

Shrike interrupted me. "Not interested."

"What about all of those felatio tune-ups you've been receiving?"

"Lucian, I don't believe in gay or straight. If you want to label me, you should at least loathe and love me at the same time."

"I can't loathe you . . . but you do drive me to . . . well, you know."

"I really wish you'd make a move."

And so it seemed the night streets of urban neon and deathly fluorescence would never end. Everything throbbed and wavered before my eyes, to the beat of my very heart. We entered a small greasy bakery named SHAHEEN where the windows were marked up by various fingerprints and the floor thinly dusted with powdered sugar.

Behind the counter shoeless immigrant women with gold studs in their noses worked like indentured servants. Far down the Caste they were. Everyone here was dark and quiet; it made me wonder if our gaudy pale skin—accented with the dark blots of makeup around our eyes—bothered these people.

A slew of Pakis slurped scotch from teacups and voraciously dug into bowls filled with crusted deserts that appalled my American taste buds. I'd been trained to crave high-fructose corn syrup and aspartame, but in this place I could choose a glazed cake made from congealed butter cream, or spongy cottage cheese balls called rasgulla, fermented in cooled syrup. They reminded me of jellied eyeballs.

Shrike ate a dozen rasgulla and I just watched. His tongue swiped away excess sugar from his lips. Then I heard some of the men complaining, and I didn't even know the language, but utter disgust is universal. Soon enough they went back to their sweet feast like it was their last meal. It's well known that Indian people eat with their left hand and wipe their ass with their right, but these people were maddened and grabbing food with both hands. The laws of etiquette had no place here.

"We're not wanted," I said.

"It's because we do no follow their code of dress."

Shrike's wayward language and low levels of personal hygiene—the disintegrating Doc Marten boots scrawled with pen ink, the ripped t-shirt, blonde hair in knots—wasn't what the Indians respected. I imagined bodiless hands clawing at Shrike to touch his yellow locks, and him managing to dodge them, the city boy always ready for fight or flight.

We chivied back into the black sauna. Indian hookers called out to us, craving the taste of paleness. A chilling shower of stars shattered across their breasts, their knife-like nipples. They covered their bony faces in scarlet saris, puffing their lips. Their voices skirled, small black eyes needy as much as ferocious, and the damp weather made their almond skin gleam.

Spice and sandalwood whirled as they fanned their arms in a wavering dance. I wanted to dive between their legs, curl my tongue around sweet wrinkled amaranth lips. But I knew if I would have grabbed one and kissed her that she'd bite my lips off; the burn of cayenne pepper would swell over my tongue.

"Don't pay attention to them," Shrike said.

"But they're so pretty."

"But you don't know something important."

"And what is that?"

"Oral sex is taboo in Indian culture. But look at that!"

It was a wonder I didn't see it first. A slick wind forced us down onto our knees in front of a huge crystal statue of Lord Shiva: god of destruction and transformation. He sat cross-legged upon a tiger skin, his feral face glinting even though night draped like swamp trees over his body. A large cobra garnished his neck, its tail pointed like that of Poseidon's' trident. I could swear he was alive. All it would take was the right amount of light, or a bowl full of tulsi leaves and bone dust to have him step off his plateau and destroy . . . or save us.

"A devil made of crystal," Shrike said.

Then he tugged my arm, but I was too transfixed to move. The god was now a twisted pretzel, beckoning for me to come to him. His eyes glowed maniacally with the fervor of his millions of worshippers, with the temptation of mysticism; his thighs fairy-winged like a woman giving birth. I imagined the lush and delicious smells that would cradle my senses if I were between his legs: peppery cooking oil, jasmine and rosewater, the sultry reasoning for sex.

I'd always had a naughty imagination. I dreamed of his delicate scrotal sag and a shriveled penis hardening at the sight of me. But would there be more than one? Four appendages seemed natural; Shiva was the husband of Kali—skull-necklace, eater of souls—and oh, how large those phalluses must be to satiate the Goddess' thirst for fire and catastrophe. I thought how easy they could rip into my earthly rectum. I'd always had an affinity for the larger male anatomy, and the phallic violations of India certainly lived within Shiva's soul.

"Imagine the how good a man of that size must be in bed," I said.

"Lucian . . . no man can ever be the size you want him to be." Shrike's green eyes closed, dismissing me. "And Indians find oral sex to be unhygienic . . . against the order of nature because it carries no potential for procreation."

"There are over a billion of them, right?"

"A billion bodies who believe in nothing more than to make another billion bodies. A culture that finds oral sex pornographic, but which reveres phallic symbols such as Lord Shiva. An incongruent bunch."

"His dick must be as long and gracious as his arms. Maybe he has four penises."

Then we were in the forbidden backstreets, away from the loud thoroughfare of the main boulevard. The sky was as carnal and desirous as the pagan beliefs in this part of town. We were in hell now. There was no electricity, not even a flashlight. The buildings were timeworn and ravaged by nightfall. Bodies lay like stumps of deciduous trees; the people who were not passed out on brandy wine were horrendously masturbating.

I read once that in Calcutta the dead rise at night and stink the place up, but in turn are cleansed by daylight.

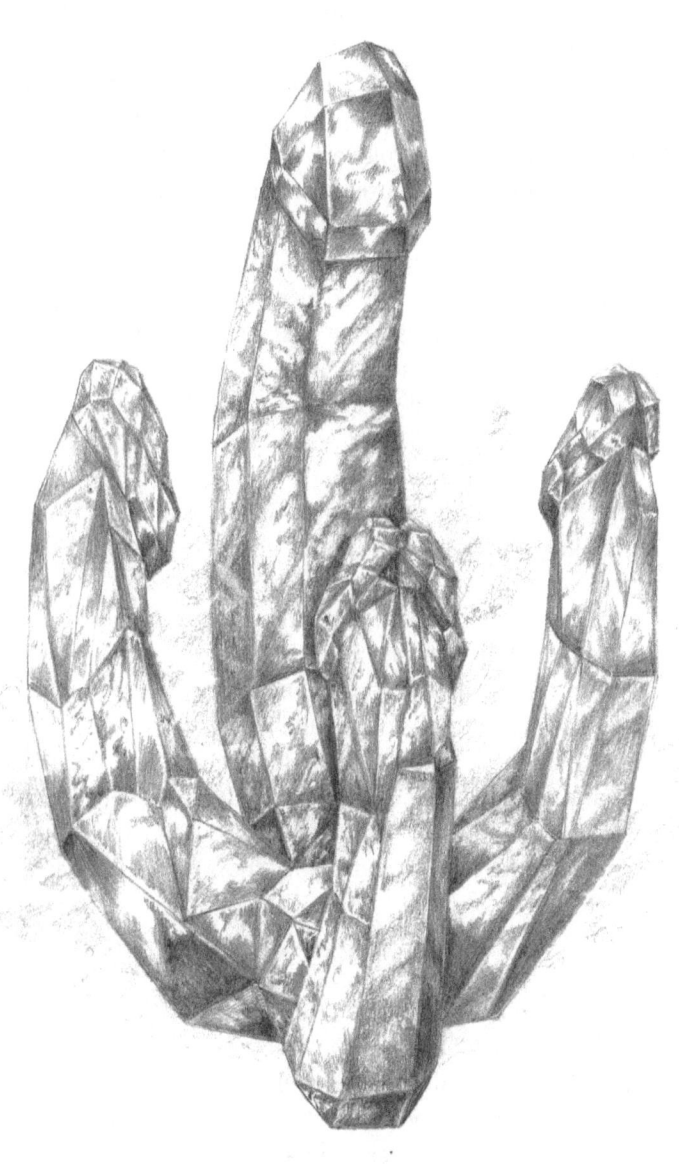

Here in the city there is no sense of time, no sun rising and falling: the people here don't have to be dead to be vicious.

Then, appearing like a trick of the eye, as if boiling moonshine had hit a tender spot in the earth, it materialized: antediluvian structure, a palace in shambles and marked with Bengali scrollwork. I didn't understand it, but Shrike certainly did, and the meanings turned him madly horny.

Once inside we quickly realized that the dimensions of the inside of the building were bigger than the outside. Before we could enter the next chamber I saw an iron gate, topped with arrowheads. I imagined lifting Shrike and letting the sharp metal slide into his intestine, coloring the gates with his blood and shit. An apex phallus.

What was wrong with me?

As we walked in a barrage of mop-haired men gave us toothy grins, sticking their hands down their pants. Their fingers were the gnarled limbs of banyan trees; their dicks were lowly ginger roots. They either wanted to fuck or eat us, I couldn't tell. They all looked ravenous.

Then Shrike grabbed my hand as we moved into a maze-like shroud of chrysanthemums. I began to see things glowing by the light of the low white moon and a billion iridescent stars; I saw swamp gas erupt, phosphorescent desert insects and bonfires. We ducked beneath a small opening clothed in gold, and slipped into Wonka's delicious factory.

The room was filled with the smell of dreamy sheesha. Filthy mirrors boarded every corner, haunted by the ghost of Hindi and Bengali poetry in terrible lipstick. Shrike took an immediate left and was soon a chameleon amongst the swarm of people. I saw him order a bitter beer and smoke his usual stale cigarette down to the filter, then fill his mouth with an unlawful amount of cough drops.

I followed the chaotic rhythm of Hindi music, horns and cryptic strings, an agonizing synthesizer. Pitchy, but effervescent; each sound was a crescendo of exotica, each vocal melody the secret pain of a country's war against its women. This all echoed into my brain, tickled like white noise down to my very balls. Brown bony hands spidered from depthless corners, ridden with human waste, looking for a chance at life as mouths begged for coins in the best English they knew. I was in no Kalighat or Holy Temple: I was in the Eastern Sodom and Gomorra.

Young girls twisted their bodies upon multiple stages garnished with incense ash, rose petals and sopping dhotis; their washboard torsos concaved and twisted impossibly as they performed belly dances of a thousand generations born into sweltering Indian midnights. Tumescent nipples and pubic hair were exposed beneath the traditional Ghagra choli in exquisite colors of lavender, salmon and gold.

Men in squalid cliques waved crumpled singles. Their eyes were hungry and deviant; hookah tobacco fell freely from their pockets as they called over young server boys with stilted arms and no sense of respect. The boys passed around hookah pipes shaped like serpent phalluses and poured liquor down hungry throats, wearing nothing but langota loincloths that barely covered the prepubescent scraps of flesh between their legs.

At the bar I found Shrike once again, drunk on Indian whiskey. He waved his arms in unison to the music and opened his hands like a horny carrion plant. He was bright with DayGlo paint; scales and petals juxtaposed on the palms of his hands, thorny stems on his twiggy arms. I contemplated the meanings of each: an ambigram prophesying the end of the world, a demigod clothed by the moon, a sexual pandemic of biblical proportions. It was nothing of the sort, for Shrike had already written the books on such subjects in quill ink by the light of candles.

"We're going to witness the Dance of Death," he said drunkenly.

I didn't know what he meant, what archaic spirits of deities we were going to encounter. Indians are so over-polygamous it becomes confusing. Each god is the shadow of another, resurrected in a new form and then killed off to be reincarnated into something eviler or purer. With that thought I indulged in Shrike's offerings of a joint, as well as a tiny pill labeled X. The pill turned blue when it hit Shrike's sharp tongue, turning his teeth neon. Soon my mind settled into the leaky dream that follows brain-altering substances, a hand of doom cradling my very soul.

The music halted; the colored lights haphazardly slowed their gyrating rhythm and a new cacophonic mix of Indian music hit the air. The stage insidiously glowed. I heard a snake-hiss and the moaning of a billion worshippers. I saw the brittle color of bones scrunched in a corner, the shadow of a full skeleton clothed in a sari. Four arms parted the velvet curtain four maddening ways and a slew of men fell to their knees with bone dust and smelly green leaves in their hands.

Not leaves, but money!

Lord Shiva took the stage.

His blue arms were melodiously knotted between dazzling crowns of fire; the cobra upon his neck waved its thin tongue in the air. Shiva took a few steps out of shadow, eyeing the silent crowd. I saw that his ankles were lined with gold charm bracelets and his toenails were painted black. I wanted to kiss those holy shining feet. A Devil Made of Crystal indeed.

Shiva's eyes filled me with terror. They glowered with craven lust, with the need for reverence. His tongue was forked and the color of ice as he projected it from his wet lips. But it was the sight of his pelvis that electrified me with despair. I needed to see what was beneath his lavish silk kilt, needed to feel those four appendages wrap coolly around my body.

But soon the crown of fire was no longer just for show. Lord Shiva's foot came around and kicked a ball of flame at a dirty man's hands that had touched the stage: his right hand! The flames caught onto the man's dhoti and quickly devoured him. Women grabbed their nipples; young boys masturbated until explosion. As the fire grew so did the howling, the screeching and the sound of snapping chords. Heavy spotlights ripped from the rotted ceiling and exploded upon the floor; glass spread like diamonds.

Lord Shiva was at the edge of the stage now, hovering, dancing blindly and his legs fanning open for me. The sight of hanging flesh engulfed and controlled me. How many phalluses? One, two, I counted, maybe three, but had to immediately stop. I became suddenly lost within the fucked-up throes of booze, THC and bad pills. My pupils refused to dilate before the darkness of the Lord's pelvis.

Balance betrayed me.

I blacked out.

... I really wish these snakes were your arms ...

I woke up in a palace, my body snarled within silk sheets. I caught the scents of liquid curry and warm bodies. I felt as if I was stuck somewhere between dream and nightmare. A hundred crystal phalluses surrounded me, and a hand came out of the darkness to feed me Indian delicacies—a sip of the milky lassi and a bite of the donut-like balushahi—until I became bloated and felt faintly sick. My tongue could crave no more.

To my dismay Shrike was passed out on the same bed, his tongue a tiny pink thing lying limp out the side of his mouth and a jug of whiskey death-gripped in his left hand. I tapped the jug; it was empty, sad to say because I was due for a mean drink. Shrike's REM eyes rolled with pleasure and pain and his right hand was artfully moving deeper and deeper into his crotch; he had a huge boner.

I wondered if he wanted me to finally touch him, perhaps because I was trapped in my own jealous nightmare, because it was time to let him go. In my hand was a blade fashioned from a hot Indian midnight, and I cut Shrike's filthy button up to expose his smooth pallor and rickety-looking bones. I cut wit no mercy, unzipping him from groin to sternum.

Lord Shiva was all that mattered.

But did I want my friend to die? My affinity for Shrike, I admit, was dangerous. He was the kid who I wanted to share my life with. But I had no more time to think. Hindi music swung into my ears; I felt the walls vibrate. A calling, an attraction, a betrayal.

Bright jade light shone upon Lord Shiva. His lips became lively, his face mounted in jewels, his hand laced with tiny bits of flesh that could have only been the dark sweet-delights between a horny man's legs. Four shadows beamed from between Shiva's legs that spread like forever. I was ready to be taken into eternity.

"I want it," I said.

But it was not I the shadows chose. It was Shrike they mounted. I asked myself the why and how. Perhaps it was Shrike's natural curiosity for the world that attracted them, perhaps his innate boredom and cravings for exotica. All I knew was that they didn't want me, as the only thing I truly wanted in life was to get laid. I failed myself miserably.

So I decided to understand it, that I was no longer in the reality I was trained to live in, that the countries of Hindu polygamy, Pakistani imprisonment and Bengali spice was my new world. The next set of actions would either have driven a kid to question life or force him to indulge in the sodomy that has plagued the world since the beginning of time.

All I could do was sing myself into a frenzy, wash myself in lyrical abandon as I learned how to loathe and love.

Shiva's four crystal phalluses elongated, dripping thick blood at the tips, and latched onto Shrike's sleeping body. I thought maybe it was that Shrike had no soul, and this made him attractive to the gods. His soul would be at some party, unable to feel death take over his body. I caught the odor of semen and spit as the phalluses began to pull Shrike into the chasm of Shiva's universe.

I also remembered something else. That strange man had had touched the holy stage with his right hand—the one he wipes his own ass with—and he paid a price for that. It was disrespect, and since Shrike was the least pure thing on the face of the earth, all of this began to make sense.

The glassy shadows forced Shrike's lips apart and ripped his teeth out with a glittery crunch, then slid down the tunnel of Shrike's liquor-stained throat. All at once my world became a gory explosion of hair and bone as the serpents cleared a red-raw hole through the back of Shrike's head.

Loathe and Love must become one, I remembered Shrike's words, *because those two words exist in a certain symbiosis*. And in order for a man to first understand what he loathes, he must first discover what he loves . . .

2013

I've always been obsessed with the train tunnels of New York City, and not just the ones accessible by passengers. There are *other* tunnels, ones that have been left neglected for decades. Rumors of mole people, rats the size of cats . . . plagues. I just love it. It's the mystery I guess, and to this day I spend a stupid amount of time looking deeply into the train tunnels hoping to see something. There's an awesome book called *The Mole People* that did a much better job than I ever could have with this subject matter. Even though the book was debunked, it's a fascinating read.

This story is another adjunct to *The Absence of Light*, and my favorite of the stories that live outside of the novel.

THE TUNNEL RECORD

Night.

Dark green night beneath the velvet shower of city stars, and Delilah was the only girl left on the rooftop. Ghost-girl spilling liquid shadow as a cold slice of moonlight ravaged her swaying body. The clove cigarette was down to the filter, but she took the last pull anyway, tasting vanilla, spice, and everything not-so-nice as the smoke twined tendrils around her calm drunk-face and through the tangle of her blue-black dreadlocks.

There were cans beneath her ragged Grinders, PBRs, BOMB craft beer, and she kicked them over the side of the tenement, peering down to look upon Avenue A, Oval Park, and the crazed night-drivers along the FDR Drive. The cans clattered to the concrete, but she wished for the crash of glass. It would liven the night so.

"You'll fall if you look any farther," a voice said.

Rez stood firm and handsome, choppy black hair pushed aside, the usual William S. Burroughs book clenched like a pistol; quill pen wagging free as a bird in flight. Sapphire eyes marked the night, the most beautiful color Delilah had ever seen. Then again, those were her eyes too because Rez was her twin brother.

"They're down there," Delilah said, pointing to the black below her. "I heard them in the pipes."

Rez nodded, lit a cigarette, then peered over the edge. He looked much younger than his twenty-two years tonight. It seemed the stressors of life did not scar time across his soft face, but simply reflected upon his attire. If one looked hard enough they'd see a glimmer of pinstriped sock through the left sole of his Converse sneakers; reflected upon his fingernails too, bitten down to bleeding nubs. He wiped some red goo on Delilah's King Crimson t-shirt, the psychedelic print resembling a Chinese fan.

"I heard them too," Rez said.

A story begins and ends. A story is formed. But no story, big or small, could encompass the adventure of two siblings looking to catch up on a lifetime.

A tricky side of the borough. Yawning streets and people hovering like will o' the wisps. Nervous fingers balance cigarettes and bottles of rotgut. You can meet your best friend here or encounter a stolid rock star as your mind is ciphered out of reality and pulled into another dimension. Rez and Delilah found themselves traversing these streets looking for something to do.

Take into account a girl who just moved to New York in search of a dream long forgotten: a promised career in music. Take into account her twin brother who could hear things that others could not; consider the two of them put together after being separated the first two decades of their life. There was much adventure to catch up on.

The Bowery at midnight glimmered with an air of gentrification and gloaming. New money brought in posh retail, sandblasted brick and the sweet smell of expensive perfume, but old traditions still said that struggle was the norm. Beat poets polluted every corner complaining about the best minds of their generation destroyed by madness and thrown into poverty looking for an angry fix.

"They're everywhere," Delilah said.

Squatters, bums, transients and stragglers. The streets were teeming with signs that said they they'd do anything to make a quick buck. *For my family*, one smelly man whispered; *WILL TELL JOKES FOR A DOLLAR!* written in scrappy magic marker across his cardboard box. Delilah bypassed a line of them digging into sloppy plates of street-meat, pulling Rez forward so he would stop staring.

"I wanna party," she said.

A sickly blue-veined hand reached out and gripped Delilah's leg with a strange force. She looked down to see eyes white and glazed as lychee fruit.

Help me. Haven't eaten in two weeks, its mouth croaked. *HUNGRY!*

She remembered one time Rez had given a homeless person a falafel sandwich, only to have it thrown in his face, the bum insulted that neither Rez nor Delilah, young like him, didn't want to join his sad party of poverty.

"Off me!" Delilah said.

"... hungry ..."

The bum's mouth was opening wide, showing off a row of brown teeth rotted to fine apex points. *They're underground too*, it whispered, and then those teeth were coming for Delilah's flesh; fingers were breaking the skin of her ankles. Delilah kicked the spidery hand away and kneed the bitch in her piranha mouth. Snot and blood smeared across her knee, black jeans ripping. But those long thin fingers were back again, so her boot came down like she was squashing an insect. The sound of crackling bones left horrible music in her ears.

SO WRONG! the bum screamed. *YOU'D HURT A HUNGRY OLD WOMAN!*

Hungry for flesh? Delilah thought.

"Fuck was that?" Rez asked.

"Squatters," Delilah said.

The block they turned onto was narrow and dark, lit only by the passing of the occasional car and the red-webbed glimmer that spoke of a stumbling drunk's eyes. There came the cool sizzle of neon lights and girls ready to play for pay. Kids huddled in front of tenements that seemed to be built from charcoal; carnal desires glimmered from the windows; lace and leather, glass dildos, whips and butt plugs. Tendrils of smoke smudged the air like streaks in a window you just can't clean as Delilah pointed to the club called *CHUDS*.

"This is it?" Rez asked.

"Music. All night."

As they slipped through the door, the ground seemed to shiver and beat along with the heavy metal music thumping inside. The smell of whiskey and wine crept into Delilah's nose. They moved so deep and so fast that Delilah was certain she'd run out of oxygen. *Down into the basement of the city.*

"How deep we going?"

"As far as it takes us," Delilah said.

The glow of spiral light bulbs reflected Delilah's hair spidery white; made her skin so translucent one could see the row of teeth beneath her lips as if it were some kind of X-ray. On the ground floor ears popped to the sound of glass breaking and virulent laughter. Drugs were passed around like candy, blotter acid stamped with languid skulls, GHB in tiny vials and a new drug called Bath Salts. *The Zombie Effect.*

"That's the one I like."

Rez made the exchange, swallowing the pill as Delilah took hers in a shot of Jäger. The drug hit Delilah in an instant. At first the club lilted in a shattering juxtaposition; there was a separation of reality like tearing paper in half, then a wave of colors mixed before her eyes and burst like a supernova as the music came to life.

The bar area was in full swing. Kids hounded for alcohol, their dyed hair stiff and filled with static electricity; faces marked by steel piercings, skin scrawled with flamboyant tattoos. The artistically inclined, the hipsters and the metal heads. They sat around in packs or cliques ordering beer and paid attention to nothing but the band on stage, knuckle-deep in the brain of the most irrelevant gossip Delilah ever had the curse of hearing.

Like life matters anymore? she heard. *Can we still smoke cigarettes down here?*

"So thirsty," Rez said.

His eyes fixed upon the vast selection of craft beer on tap. Weyerbacher, Dogfish Head, Dragon Slayer, Ommegang, and Brooklyn. Delilah ordered a Dragon Slayer IPA and Rez a Weyerbacher Sour Black. Beer in hand, Rez ventured away and touched everything he could: the obscene grime built upon dust, the insignias of magick, delirium, and the swirly band patches stapled to the lone billboard. It was then that Delilah saw the screaming graffiti: *LiVe FoReVeR! and THE TUNNELS TaKe YOUR LiFe!*

The tunnels, Delilah thought.

Living in the big city, rumors were bound to make waves. She'd already heard the stories encircling the Cannibalistic Human Underground Dwellers; how they lived below the streets, how they made the train tunnels their home of party and decadence. New York City is a puzzle on the outside as much it is on the inside. To imagine the life that thrived beneath her feet enthralled

Delilah. To experience that life with Rez was all she could ask for.

"Party time," Rez said.

They were on the dance floor now, sycophants twisting in sweaty unison, the strobe lights blending them into one knot of flesh. Mosh pits and violent dancing. The music jangled and raged, filling the room with a fear and loathing that rose above the horrible laughter of the crowd. And then Delilah saw why.

"No fucking way."

They shuffled in packs, albino forms that looked as if they'd grown up in basements. Bodies were plucked off the dance floor like flower petals and pulled into dark spaces until Delilah saw puddles of blood. Fish-gill eyes shimmered, webbed hands outstretched and grins of sharp decayed teeth brought the smell of rot to the dance floor. But it seemed nobody paid any attention, too preoccupied with music and drugs.

"Get behind me."

Delilah grabbed Rez, but soon they were upon them—ravenous forms in black and silver. Something tugged her dreads, and a hand came up between them like a tongue from hell and separated Delilah from Rez. Delilah let out a heartbreaking cry. With her mouth open and voice wailing, a wobbling assailant affixed rubbery lips to Delilah like suction cups; a slug-tongue dug so deep into her throat she felt her gag reflex take charge.

Another one came upon her left side and assaulted the maddened patterns of her tattoos, the fine points of her bones with blood-slimed lips. Delilah pushed it down, but its sharp fingernails dug into Delilah's arm, bringing bright beads of blood to the surface. Its nose crinkled in delight, smearing red down her belly into the hairless cleft between her legs. Time slowed to a crawl; the neon became as bright as the sun as the Bath Salts took charge. It made her feel strangely hungry; that is until she saw her brother scared out of his wits.

They formed a circle around him, writhing to the crunch of the metal band like a ritualistic dance that sent shockwaves of bodies to the floor. Hands groped Rez's beautiful black hair, sweet face, and exposed chest, sliming his xylophone ribs. They were drawing blood: a bite mark resembling a hemp leaf could be seen. *Cannibals.* Delilah immediately elbowed one of the mole people in the face, its soft gummy features spattering green goo onto her arm. That's when they began to scamper away, dragging Rez in the direction of a hole in the wall she hadn't noticed before.

"Let him go!"

She lifted a bottle of Old Number 7 from the bar and swung without looking, connecting it to the head of a bum. But the bottle didn't break, rather, it sunk into its skull like Jell-O and formed a crater that quickly filled with swampy blood. Somehow they received her angry message and let Rez go. Off they went, slithering into the hole behind the poster board of cryptic advertisements, gone as quick as they came.

"You okay?"

"Only in fucking New York," Rez said, looking dazed.

"I'm going after them."

Rez reached for his sister, but before he could stop her she was already diving into the deep dark chasm, holding her breath, ready to swim the murky waters of the city beneath the city and kick some mutant ass.

It all started when Delilah saw the news report: thriving homeless communities discovered *beneath* the streets of New York City. Pulled out of their dank caves by angry police, lugubrious forms with talons for fingers and rat teeth, others strung-out and blinded by the sun. Their lizard eyes were glossed over and they did not speak like that of the world above them. Sadly, this was a glimpse of how a city could degrade an entire population so badly that they were forced to seek life in the tunnels below the black top. It was a sight straight out of a Rob Zombie film.

Some of them lived so deep they became blinded by sunlight, an officer said.

Some live only in the train tracks . . . others live deep as deep can get. We needed gas masks so we could stand the stench.

Delilah was still living in Pennsylvania and hoping that Electric Orchid would be her one-way ticket out of the boondocks. After the band had traveled to New York City and won a battle of the bands contest for the contract of a lifetime, the thought of the mole people came right back into Delilah's head.

She came, she conquered, and she thought she saw it all in New York. But there were still the mole people. Alphabet City is where Rez resided, where the ghosts of beatniks partied around huge garbage can fires, drinking and pissing in the same clothes day in and day out. Alphabet City is where she first heard the sounds from the bathroom pipes. So many fucking sounds, yet not ones like you'd think.

Deeper than the clatter of resting drainage, not the flush of a toilet two floors above you; it wasn't the dark glittery tap-tap-tap of insects invading various apartments, or the sound of a leaking drain patting against rusted metal. She heard voices that belonged at the bottom of the sea. It was the secret tongue of muck and grime. Fish gossip, zombie-stomp, *mole people.*

"I hear them down there," Delilah said as she took her head away from the shower drain.

That night she found Rez resting upon the couch, jotting things down in his moleskin notebook, trailing the pen along his raven quill tattoo, swirling the black ink in the same pattern that twilight was descending upon his window. Blood orange light crept over everything; it illuminated the array of posters tacked to the ceiling and the magazine cutouts he'd saved since he was a teenager. He wore glasses now that he could afford a pair, tortoise print Converse frames, and they sat upon his aquiline nose like a maddened librarian as he flipped through a book called *The Mole People*, which was written by a journalist accused of fabricating the entire manuscript.

Life in the Tunnels beneath New York City.

But with every story, falsified or not, comes some truth. Delilah thought about Manhattan in the days when it was a growing baby, its shape still being kneaded out around the edges. She thought about the story of the pirate ship buried beneath Front Street; she thought about how Wall Street got its name, a literal wall that was used to block the Indians from invading the Quakers. She thought about the families who escaped to the underground to get away from the poison of modern society. There was so much to discover.

A city beneath the city.

The tunnel was a whorled oblivion that branched into endless directions. You couldn't tell time here, couldn't tell which way was north, south, east or west. Could you even go more south once you'd landed yourself skyscraper-deep into the city's underground?

"Anything?"

Rez waited for something to mark his sensitive brain, but nothing came to him. There was only the snap of electric lines, the humdrum rush of water in pipes, the hissing of toxic chemicals eating away the asphalt. He looked up and saw a dazzle of darkness, and to the left of that a pile of what seemed to be the skulls of rats.

"Smells like shit down here," Delilah said.

Each step they took brought a new stench, a spiral of sounds. To Rez, this echoing catacomb was like living in-real-time that pivotal moment he'd read about a hundred times in *House of Leaves*: Navidson uncovering the secret to his dreamy Virginia home, that the internal measurements were slightly bigger than the external ones . . . and then all hell breaks loose. Random doors appear across blank walls, the house growls, and the honeycombed darkness begins its ascent until Navidson becomes controlled by it, led willingly into the never ending world of nothingness.

This is what happens when you hurry through a maze: the faster you go, the worse you are entangled.

"Move it."

Rez's mind rode the tunnels. It was a jungle of darkness; within lay cadaverous hands and thorny teeth. Down here the ghost of trains still puttered, BMT and the Lexington line that formed the veins and arteries of the boroughs. Sporadic light bulbs lured them, which now Rez could see the source of the sweet smell of garbage and the angry state of mind in the tunnel art.

MoDeRn   SoCiEtY   Is   GUILTY   of   INTELLECTUAL TerRoRiSm.

ThE FaBuLoUs FiVe FoReVeR!!!

"They seem angry," Rez said. "I can feel it."

"Bitter is a better word," Delilah said, lighting a cigarette.

Get out! said a snake voice. *WE DON'T NEED ANY HELP!*

Rez saw reptile eyes, Delilah tensed in a protective stance, and then charged ahead. She swung her fists, hitting nothing but the thick darkness, the reluctant ghost. But what followed were the noises. Weird whistling like a phantom train, like a rat's throat being ripped out. Rez thought about the rats, how big they were above ground, and could not imagine the size they would grow to down here. If the squatters had webbed feet and bathed in the sewer water, then the rats would be big as dogs and hungry as lions.

"It's a labyrinth," Rez said.

"But a labyrinth *leads* to something," Delilah's eyes flushed the color of inquisition.

"To the mole people."

A homeless man snatched Delilah's cigarette out from her mouth and showed off his meaty smile. His clothes were shredded and Rez could see his penis, the color of overripe fruit; his arms were marked up from the needle still plunged into a bleeding vein. Rez and Delilah stepped over him and held their nose to his carrion comforts. But their cautions superseded them. Another whistle-like sound panged into their ears and the man's eyes shot open; his bony hand reached up like the arcade claw and latched onto Rez's pant leg.

"Haven't eaten in weeks," he said.

"Eat this!"

Delilah's boot found the man's nose with a wet crunch. A freshet of blood sprayed, slicking Rez's hand coolly as he bent to supply the man with a warm touch. They ran, but in what direction they didn't know. Rez imagined the streets above him, the smell of roasting Halal meat, dirty water dogs, fumes and charred pretzels, forging a map in his mind. He thought about Tompkins Square Park and the families of lost youth in full regalia, the beatniks leading the pack, the bums who beat tin garbage cans for change, the leftover Occupy Wall Street kids with instruments on their backs putting on a show for free; the skaters scratching off paint on the hand rails with their boards, the punks in leather who still rocked out with boom boxes on their shoulders.

But it was of no use trying to think about all of this. The avenues and walkways were clouded; the numbers and figures were incalculable. The streets of Delancey, Bowery, Orchard, and Hester were all useless down here. The tunnels didn't abide by traffic laws or governmentally placed pathways.

No single blueprint of New York City can truly exist! Every day something changes, something is vastly skewed. One who spends his days dreaming of a concrete map only finds himself lost in his own dream-version of the city, the old Dutch colony that never truly was.

"Down here man, becomes an animal. Evolves," Rez said.

"Yeah . . . well animals work in teams and have means of communication."

Like families of maggots vomiting their brethren . . .

Like peace in the dark?

A string of rats scampered over their feet. Rez saw huge black eyes, mutated legs, and razor teeth; he, smelled their fetid drool. *Track rabbits*, he thought. *They're prey as much as they're predators.* But the rats did not look for the attention of the two pale shadows in the tunnels; rather, they began nibbling the corpse of a woman still clutching her malnourished child. Her breasts were leathery, her nipples dried and dead as the stems of funeral flowers. One of the rats had already dug its way into the eye socket of the infant, suckling on a jellied mass of flesh.

"This is just sick," Delilah said.

Rez nearly cried. There would be no funeral for this woman, no one to mourn her existence like so many people above ground took for granted. Not even her child had survived. *The tunnels take your life*, he thought. Rez could tell this woman would not even be useful to medical science if she was excavated and studied for her abilities to live so long down here. Her body was too decomposed to determine the cause of death; too much of her meat had been stolen by the rats. But one could say her death had to do with the array of broken whiskey bottles and hypodermics lying by her side.

"The Dark Angel must be down here," Delilah said. "Like we read in the book."

"Matted feet, long hair . . . the ruler of the drippy underworld. Delilah—"

"Truth is stranger than fiction, is it not?" Delilah's eyes were wide sparkling sapphires.

"Yes, it is. But once you get your mind wrapped around something you don't stop even if it will kill you!"

It will kill you.

The sound of another whistle commenced and Rez instinctively ran toward it. If the people turn to animals down here, then these sounds warranted a warning, a signal . . . something. They stumbled over more drunken bodies with flippers for hands and gills for lips. One could hear the slither of worms returning to their chemical holes it was so quiet, and the slush of water mixed with exhaust dripping upon their heads.

No strangers in here, a voice said. *No one from above!*

"We mean no harm," Rez said.

I can't hurt you, but I can hurt the ones you care about.

"No."

You've a fascination with the darkness of my tunnels. The evil within. And it is evil!

The voice skidded into Rez's head. A schism ripped through his brain and poured out his ears hot and thick as plasma. He fell to his knees and allowed the voice to take him. A nightmare of loneliness, a fountain of pain. There were the sights of desperate clawing youth running from the society that deemed them wastes of life and useless to their cause; the homeless that were asked to leave the shelters that clothed and fed them.

Down into the burrows to create families bred by darkness, riots and blood. People who avoided daylight for the comfort of the bottle and the sweet alien warmth of it. They were like anyone else: people with opinions and feelings. But down here they were free from the strict perversions of the world upstairs, from the sickness that wept stale tears through the streets of Manhattan.

Rez saw all of them huddling away from sunlight, from wind, from warmth. He saw them cutting up junk, melting it in spoons, saw the needles filling with diaphanous swirls of blood. He saw mothers eating their children out of desperation. The angel-headed hipsters clung to the starry dynamo of dream and false hope. He breathed their sadness, tasted their shame.

He felt their anger.

OUT!

The hands were many. The faces were peaked like bird beaks and their tongues were sluggish. Their fingers kissed Rez's face like octopus tentacles, tugging his hair and biting his neck. Delilah tackled a whole pack of them into the near wall and she became lost within a sea of gummy appendages. Rez ran to her aide and pulled four gooey bodies off of Delilah. As she rose from the frenzy, Rez heard another one of them whistle.

"We're outnumbered."

They came from all directions now. Though he had never felt more peace than when he was in his sister's presence—and wasn't a violent person to begin with—he couldn't bear the thought of anymore of *them* getting in the way, especially if they were going to hurt Delilah. So with all his might, Rez completed a roundhouse kick and knocked the whistling sewage squatter to the ground. He felt the snap of its brittle bones and the wail of its pain radiate up his leg.

"Out now!" Rez yelled.

"Fuck the Dark Angel and fuck this place!"

But the walls were caving in somehow; the air was rising in temperature, choking them. Behind them were the hungry mole people; in front, a wall of blackness. *Could this be the end?* thought Rez. *All my life I've fought to get out of danger, and this is how I'm repaid?* Just like in that tormented Virginia home, there was no certain way to piece their way back up into the city. They hadn't left a trail of breadcrumbs, and so they might be trapped here and become one of them. But it was a destiny Rez refused to accept.

Their eyes . . . their eyes can't take the light! Rez remembered.

He lit his green butane lighter, found a dry walking stick a brown paper bag and crumbled cigarettes. He crushed everything together and lit it like a torch. The squatters squealed.

NOOOOO LIGHTS! NO LIGHTSSSSS!

When he found his sense of direction, Rez noticed that they had barely moved five feet from where they initially dropped through the hole in the club. The burrows had played a trick on them. Delilah backed into the wall, looked up into Rez's eyes, and nodded. He read them clearly: *step on my shoulders and get up there.*

Rez reached for the small door, swinging his homemade torch like a crazy person, and pushed it open. The sound of music and the saccharine smell of craft beer was like home, and it gave him a quick burst of energy so that he could climb up. He threw the flaming stick at the hobbling squatters, grey hair shielding their eyes, hands clawing for Delilah's knees as he pulled her up.

"I'm never trusting you again," Rez said.

Two days later, a few bruises and a new nightmare to worry about—but everything was fine. Electric Orchid was due to play a show; the club was bloated with gossip. Their fans were growing in numbers—it was only a matter of time before Electric Orchid was going to make it even further than New York City. But she didn't want to think about that tonight; how the band's music promised disaster and hope, how her sibilant melodies sounded like demons pissing on Heaven's gates.

Tonight she wanted to spread a message.

Delilah had written a few new songs and wanted to try them out. Songs about the Dark Angel, the squatters, and the infamous underground. Her first solo set, opening for her own band, a new rock n' roll riot within this new day of rage.

"It was a nice change of scenery."

"Yeah, a nice way to rot in hell . . ."

Delilah hit the stage. The kids didn't make any noise for her at first, not like she cared anyway. Delilah didn't need anyone's confirmation to judge the quality of her songs. The music cued and Delilah began to hum behind the keyboard's spiking rhythm that bordered on the insane, the drums that beat in time with her, slow and mischievous.

The guitarist crept up to the chorus pressing various pedals, mixing wah-wah, distortion and overdrive. When Delilah opened her mouth, the crowd seemed to sober up and stood attention; their graceless hands moved into the air and began to clap. Her voice was ripping but soft, like that of a goddess, and she told her story through the lyrics, wondering if they were listening.

There is a city beneath the streets, and with it comes peace in the dark.

2013

"Ecdysis" was born out of my fascination for the movie *Silence of the Lambs* and my natural fear of non-avian things with wings . . . and things with more than four legs. I'd never known what a death's-head hawkmoth was before the movie, and maybe that makes me sound ignorant, but it's the truth. Somehow the image of a moth grew into a trans story . . . a story of horror and dark fantasy.

In a part of Queens that I will not name, I once decided it was a smart idea to break into building that had burned down. On my way in there were two choices, kind of like a fork in the road: stairs leading to the basement, or the long hallway where parts of the floorboards had holes big enough to fall through. I chose the basement, and was introduced to so many insects and rodents it's a wonder I didn't lose my voice. That little adventure of mine helped shape an important part of this story.

This is my favorite story in the collection, hands down. It's also a story that made the shortlist of so many professional horror anthologies I lost count, but never made it in. Funny how an author's favorite is never an editor's favorite. Maybe one day they'll regret it.

ECDYSIS

"I can't be in this body forever," Daryl said to me. "It's a shell that's holding me back."

Tie-dye hair done up scream-queen style, red lips stretching away from little teeth. The costume he wore laved his bones in black, iridescent wings against the Zippo's flame-light. We stared at one another, moonpale makeup and Daryl's exotic cigarette half-chewed; me biting my fingernails to bleed.

"What do you want me to say?" I asked.

"Tell me that one day I'll leave this body behind," hateful little voice.

"A promise I can't keep."

We stepped off the A train at West 4th, the blocks springing to life like a picture book of the weird. I felt the cold gloom of ghosts still haunting these dark streets, a time capsule within the new fashions of the city. Smoke shop shelves gleamed with trippy glass instruments; liquor stores sizzled with neon temptation. Boys kissed boys and whores fanned their legs. A drug deal was made in front of my face.

"This is the place," Daryl said.

The building greeted us with a tongue of smoke and the freaky ambient sound of runaways, hipsters and street poets. Upon entry a family of rats ran over my boot; to my left a mattress was weighted with a body too drunk to move, lopsided mouth decorated with a necrotic tongue.

"Where's the alcohol?" I said.

From the top floor I watched fireworks explode illegally in the sky. Daryl turned his head towards the luminescence, let it drizzle down his sharp features. He blinked once, twice, and then grabbed my hand, knife-like fingers and nails black as beetles. I tried not to react, but as if he'd sensed my weariness, his sugar-venom tongue went right into my mouth.

"Let's move," Daryl said.

The party was a Gatsby-esque affair. On the dance floor the lights were dizzying and streamers glistened like dragon wings. I saw a languid Dracula, a clumpy Werewolf and a barely breathing Frankenstein. Victorian mourning jewelry was worn like shriveled organs; thrift shop scrims hung ugly as meat. A monster grabbed his wayward princess in freaky abandon. Salvia smoke clouded everyone's judgment.

But I didn't want to dance, not at least until I was too drunk to care. At a nearby table there was a punch bowl that stunk of Pinnacle Vodka the color of blood. But so long as it killed the guilt of loving someone who would never reciprocate, I would happily imbibe. I poured myself a cup and then drew my inebriated mind back to the bass and thrash of the dance floor.

Daryl threw his wispy arms around my shoulders. I smelled his fancy cigarette breath and fell deeper in love. His smile was loose and infectious; it made my dick hard. We gyrated, melded, molted . . . shed a unanimous skin.

"You adore me," Daryl said.

"Maybe."

I dipped my girl down, stared into her eyes for what seemed like a millennia, then looked away. I did not want to give into temptation. Daryl turned me on in the worst way. Boy or girl it didn't matter, it was the essence—the meat of his soul—that kept me interested. When I removed my body from his it was like trying to pull a cobweb off my face: some parts of him I could never wipe completely clean.

"Imagine that," I said. "A room full of people like us."

"Nobody is like us," Daryl hissed. "Now hold me tight."

He craned his neck to meet my mouth, then smiled.

"Am I not the prettiest girl in the room?" Transitioning voice like a woman gone muscular. "I want to be the prettiest girl in the room."

"You are," I said.

Daryl stopped dancing. "Even though *you're* not the best looking guy in the room, I still adore you."

One comes to expect backhanded compliments from a person who feels that they are trapped inside a skin that does not match the bones inside. Pronouns become the enemy and gender a blur. It's why Daryl grew his hair down to the middle of his back and took hormone pills that made his tits look like golf balls no matter the bra he wore. But I'd never tell him such; it would crush him.

"I'm tired," I said.

We took a seat at the back of the party. Daryl rested his insect legs upon my lap and let his hair come undone so that it covered his face. I knew he was dissatisfied and uncomfortable, even though Halloween is the only night of the year when a person doesn't have to cover up the demon that they are forced to hide the other 364 days. Living in a world where we are told that boys can never be girls—no matter if they were born that way, no matter the public shame—can scar a person forever.

It could *change* them for worse.

"Look at these," Daryl said. "What if I just flew away?" Bad little wing flap.

"What's stopping you?"

"This!"

Hand raking across his skin, nail polish streaking. *When will it give way?* he cried. Such a pretty little thing to be so self-loathing. Tonight the insect queen and tomorrow the androgynous boy I love. *I have reason to be this way*, Daryl whispered.

Turned my head back to the party, I could dance until my feet bled. But now Daryl's tongue at my throat, my dick rising. A thought came to me. If he cut it off would I still want him? Did I enjoy this cat and mouse chase? Was I the perpetual puppy lurking for its mother's tit? But then a few wandering eyes caught us. A guy who looked like Trent Reznor circa 1994 opened his stupid mouth to ruin the night.

"Are you a boy?" Crow-hair asked Daryl.

"No. *Are you*?" Daryl retorted.

They stared one another down. Daryl's black eyes resembled that of a giant fly, or spider. After two grueling minutes the kid's ears bent inward, bad little doggy, and he scurried away. Daryl turned back to me, pleased to have spread his hate.

"You think they'd find better pick up lines."

"He had reason to ask. It's Halloween."

"He was as stupid as your costume." Daryl assessing me harshly. "What the hell are you trying to be anyway?"

Black on black, death-head imprint on my leather jacket; two dark holes slathered over my eyes. I am you, I wanted to say, the nastiest insect of all; I am the grin that follows death. But I said nothing, removed my body from his heated grip and got myself a beer that was as warm as the disgusting October night. Daryl drank a cup of the blood punch but spit it out ferociously, showing off his newly red teeth.

"This party sucks."

He didn't ask if I was going to come with him or not. Too selfish to care, eyes moving in metronomic insanity. You could almost hear his fragile thoughts: screw the universe, screw the human mind and how it loves to inherently judge.

Screw me.

Screw you too. *You're no fucking good for me.*

Daryl would be the first to admit it.

But I need you.

Daryl had something important to show me. Serious bug eyes casting shadows about his face, chitinous legs jutting beneath the spooky skirt. Down abdominal stairs to the storage room of his tenement, fading twilight dappled through dust-painted windows, and the boxes piled like morgue bodies.

"We've been descending for a half hour," I said.

"It's only a little bit further," Daryl's fingers were in his mouth, white spider legs.

No light but the uncommon occurrence of orbs and what seemed to be fireflies. *FREE BLOWJOBS* and *SEX NOW* said the graffiti, but no number for me to call. Bastards. Just when my head began to spin we halted at a heavy metal door. Daryl had to hit it a few times to get it open, and when it did I knew that we had landed somewhere that wasn't meant to be seen by the world above.

The slow dark smell of things brooding.

"My best kept secret." Something like a smile squeezed Daryl's face.

An organic luminescence slithered across my skin; the floor was sticky with rheum. There were flies everywhere, big black ghost-clouds pricked by the colored light of lava lamps and the bubbling red glow of a puffer fish tearing apart its dinner. On the ceiling I saw a thumping colony of nymphs, eggs and larvae. An entomological nightmare.

"I can't breathe," I said.

"Sissy Crissy."

Wings, legs and feelers assaulted me. I heard glass break and saw a cephalopod squirming to bloody freedom. On the wall stretched a glass maze fit for the king of all hamsters, but upon closer inspection I saw that it was filled with the warmest, wettest exotica imaginable. Down at my feet mason jars toppled over, alive with house centipedes craving mad escape. Then I saw something straight out of *The Twilight Zone*: a chrysalis with a death-head skull insignia.

Things were evolving down here, leaving the past behind.

Daryl was too.

"What the hell is this?" I asked with my hand covering my mouth, afraid of a swallowing a flying beast.

"You scared?"

"No." Liar, liar pants on fire! Bug phobia since I was a kid. "How do you keep them all down here . . . *alive*?"

"The morphogenesis of insects," Daryl quoted from a book. "Apolysis to ecdysis."

"Meaning what?"

"They adapt to any environmental circumstance and still successfully *change*. I envy that."

"Never knew you had such a fascination."

"Pay attention sometimes. You wonder why I have no patience."

I sat down on a moldy couch, subsequently tipping over a suture removal kit. A needle and black nylon thread landed in my lap; a scalpel nicked my middle finger. I found a book about insects and the process of molting, enzymes and increased blood pressure to shed the old skin. I thought of the many cicada shells I had crushed as a kid, and now that I was aware of the biology behind their survival I rendered myself ignorant.

I thought about Daryl's transition.

My harlot already nine months into the process, voice softening and his little tits tumescent as grapes. The pills had halted all the growth of his facial hair, subsequently widening his hips. That gave him *power*, sustenance. It took away all heartache in trying to escape his original gender.

"Won't even have to change my name," he once said to me. "Daryl Hannah, Daryl Palumbo. Singer, actress. I'm blessed," hectic grin.

When he broke the news that night it tore me up inside. Daryl had just turned twenty-four, and I admit I saw no signs of gender issues other than the long hair and sometimes throwing on a pair of heels. Throughout our relationship I was timid and he was assertive; I followed and he led, as things like morals or law never restricted Daryl. I was blinded by love and he with hate.

The only time I ever felt in charge was when we fucked. Daryl would only allow it doggy style, rough and without lubrication; feral, as if to degrade my need for an old-fashioned romance. I would always want to cuddle after, but he'd push me away, not allowing me to inquire about his internal struggle.

Then he told me what he wanted to do.

I closed out the world and drank for three days straight, dreaming the silent dreams of a normal relationship, the stereo in my head turned up so loud that there was no temptation to listen to all the voicemails—*where the fuck are you, I need you, call me!* Thirty-six hours freed me of Daryl's negativity and of my regret for falling in love with him . . . now *her*. But then came the pang of loneliness, reflecting how judgmental I had become. And then I simply got over it. Love can overcome any hurtle.

"They don't have to worry about having a pussy or a cock," Daryl broke my daydream, grabbing my crotch.

"I don't want to," I said.

Oh, but I did.

"Don't resist me!"

Going in for the kill, not me, but *her*. Buggy hand crawling into my tight underwear, pulling my pants down. I thought of the bad boy he once was, the smelly hair and evil laugh, but all that was left was the molted skin of him, a little girl budding to the music of her new puberty.

Cold fingers walked up the beads of my spine. It was the most feral display of her I'd ever witnessed. I could feel the fading five o' clock shadow upon my face but I daren't say a word. I missed the feeling of being wanted too much to ruin the moment. And then her wet hand groped all of my cock—I almost came, I couldn't hold it—and her shirt off now for me to see those little, little tits, concave stomach and sharp hips spreading like birth. She turned around and propped up those two snowy globes, tie-dye hair loose against her back, and when I moved it out of the way I saw a dark, protruding outline of wings.

"What is this?" I said.

"New ink. You like?"

"No."

I closed my eyes and wished for a man as I spit into my hand, cupped his tits and slid myself into the wild heat of Daryl's intestine. Her moaning was the mad ticker of many cicadas, a billion moths bashing themselves to dust. I came so hard that I felt the foundation shiver. After, I fell to the floor and pulled my knees up to my chest.

In my dream I heard the stretch and snap of skin. Daryl crawled toward me like an insect, his tongue black and furry, eyes wider than I'd ever seen. Arms in Benediction but not so much arms as they were appendages; the markings I had seen on his back were now a filmy pair of wings.

Mothra.

Death-head Grin.

I woke to the taste of thunder in my mouth. Stale electric smoke.

Daryl was gone, and I had no recollection how I'd made it home. There was a note on my nightstand but I couldn't make out the handwriting. I rolled over on the bed, pulled the covers up to my face, until I heard the clicking on the floorboards.

Rising, my lips sealed but something wriggling against my tongue. I realized that my face was covered in a cobweb, and when I opened my mouth to scream a death-head moth took to the air. I wiped my face clean and saw that my apartment had changed. There were bugs every-where, biting, mating . . . slithering.

A pale brown smell filled the room, followed by the music of Armageddon. But nothing made sense. I remem-bered fucking Daryl, venomous kiss and his tongue leaving a trail of flame on my skin; my crotch was slightly burned. Fake pussy between Daryl's legs, secret sphincter alluding to some magical delta.

Why are you doing this to me?

A memory opened up in my head.

White chrysalis hanging pale as my dick. I thought of Daryl inside that pouch, slimed in strange fluids, grinning wide as death for the transformation. As I put my hand against the slick surface it moved slightly away from me, bold stretching sound, and I thought how rude of it to not like me because I should not be liking *it*. I wondered what really was growing inside of that thing: a creature reborn, a new breed of disease.

Daryl: the insect virtuoso.

Stepping outside, cold as fuck for October, light snow bejeweling the dark rising buildings like a fur coat. Icicle claws edged the balconies and fire escapes, frozen cocoons shedding skin drop by drop. It got me thinking that if we can change the things that bring us grief then why feel grief at all? Why not tear away the soft exoskeleton from the start? We are all the same when we remove the outer layer.

With nowhere to go and no reason to give a fuck, I walked shivering and guilty, waiting for Daryl to contact me with trenchant patience. I kept my head on the lookout for bugs and weird trappings, for mire or muck. I heard no vertiginous buzz of cicadas, found no jungle like that in the storage room, nothing like knowing all of those things humming and thumping and thriving. It was the basis of Daryl's transformation: the uncontrollable effects of nature, the food chain . . . a desire to keep living.

My cell phone blew up with countless text messages and scathing voicemails. I happily ignored them while eating a peanut butter sandwich on expired rye. Fungi slid between my teeth, mossy new smile of mine, and the food crashed into my empty stomach so that I immediately farted. I chugged a warm Natty Ice and threw the paper plate into the over-flowing garbage can.

My living room welcomed me into its dirty slumber. For now, sleep would do me best to get Daryl out of my head, and so I stripped off my clothes to meet the clumpy sheets on my bed. I ran my fingers down my body, through the swirl of bone and hair, my rib cage and scalp. My penis rose in defiance to my mental state; I slapped it down, would not allow it to enjoy Daryl's abandonment.

Sleep was not even an iota of my reality as there, in a smelly clump beside my own, was some of Daryl's hair. Leaving pieces of himself behind was his idea of a bad romance: he knew I'd miss him terribly, and that I'd come crawling back. I decided to chug down another warm beer, found a pair of jeans and searched the pockets for money I didn't have. To do what with it?

Moths flew out of my wallet.

Literal moths.

Fuck.

They were everywhere. Above, below, wings and eyes. One of them perched on my shoulder; I could feel its little claws as if Daryl's nails digging into the most sensitive parts of my body. I swiped it away and saw it bash itself into powder against the kitchen window, failing to find a light that didn't quite exist. The rest of them plummeted into a meaty mist.

Fuck this.

I slid my clothes back on and was about to call Daryl so he could get his friends under control, until I saw the text messages. Half of them were drunken mumbo-jumbo; the ones that I could decipher all revolved around the same rhyme and senseless reasoning. The only one that caught my attention was about missing me.

I knew that she'd stopped taking the estrogen since starting her research on insects, and maybe that caused her to not think straight. *Wanna do this naturally*, she had said. *From the inside out . . . like they do*. So came the night sweats and thin yellow vomit; her body was *resisting* the transition back to utter maleness. My hands cradled her face because I could not watch her be in pain, teeth marking me up because she said I deserved it.

But how could stopping the hormone cocktail cause such nasty side effects? His reaction ironically mocked that of an insect's growth into a new skin. So I made it my business to study the science, realizing that it was a process most intricate and extremely sensitive to any and all environmental change.

An insect cannot survive without its outer shell, and so to grow a new one it must start growing it internally. I imagined a new skeleton growing inside my body, the skin ripping, osseous matter crackling as the old bones are replaced by new; imagined the pressure in my head as my brain was crushed and the former skull pushed itself to the surface like sandglass on a beach.

Ametabolous insects undergo little structural change from egg to adult; hemimetabolous undergo gradual changes from the immature nymph to the adult; holometabolous are the most unique as the immature eggs mature into winged adults via the pupal stage (cocoon or chrysalis). I imagined Daryl only as the holometabolous creature, full of the determination to become something so different from the way he was born.

Sometime after midnight I fell asleep and dreamed of insecticide.

The sound of fists pounding against hollow wood, but I am paralyzed by nightmare. Rain of fire on my skin, Daryl's eyes rising chunks of onyx, his hair swaying and his mouth a proboscis unfurling. We were fucking madly, butterfly squat, seated scissor and missionary.

Can't do this without you.

And Daryl's skin melts away; I caress the slick surface of his back to find wings.

Now the doorknob turning angrily to wake me from my haunting slumber. *Where the fuck is he*? Daryl's insect hiss. *You sure he's home*? said another voice I was not familiar with. I didn't want to move but my heart was leaping. Then the knocking changed into frustrated kicking, me cursing because I knew it was only a matter of moments before one of my nosey neighbors began to complain. I opened the door in my birthday suit to see Daryl's pissed-off face.

"Why aren't you answering your phone?"

No salutation. Just rage. Typical.

Dressed in hellish rags, Salvation Army demise and her make up will-o'-the-wisp fabulous. A ghoul if I ever met one. A death-head moth. And at her side two sycophants jetting past to inspect my apartment, *Black Swan* poster and sticky notes of whatever goes through my head.

"This him?" the girl said. "Not all he's cracked up to be."

"Smells in here," her counterpart said, a boy of small stature.

"You two losers would say that," Daryl yelled.

Daryl's funzies were not what I'd call friends. Obsessed art geeks whose lives were dedicated to unleashing the strange unto the world, as if to claim the fringe for themselves . . . then gloat about how they survived it. Anything to make them more appealing than they truly were, as even the people in their own psychedelic circle couldn't stand them.

Through hazy memory I remembered that I'd seen them before at a gallery, but they were too cool to remember someone as sad as me. Daryl half-managed to gargle their names, something that sounded like Jack and Jill, artists drenched in the seed of their own rebirth: colored hair, tattoos and piercings. Walking string beans. No brains.

"Show us," they demanded.

"What are you talking about?" I licked my dry lips.

"The *metamorphosis*."

I felt like I was on some television show of the strange.

"I don't know what you mean," I said.

"What about these?" Jill pointed to the dead moths.

"Warfare."

Jill smiled deeply and Jack swiped his finger through gooey remains. Daryl stepped into the kitchen and I followed suit, wanted so badly to yell, to scream, but could not find the courage to do such. The cold spill of moonlight made his eyes so black they shined, his skin almost silver. I noticed then that a moth had cracked the windowpane, spilling light in spider-web patterns across my kitchen floor.

"They're all dead," Jill said. "And the others will die soon."

"Why are you here?" I managed to finally say.

"Because Daryl says you're the only one who understands."

"He would never say that," new spurt of anger coming to its crescendo.

"Chill out, dude," Jack said. "She can't do her trick without you."

"What trick?"

Now my anger spilling. I was out for blood. Fists clenched so tight I imagined they were bricks as I began swinging. I hit the wall, then the floor, managing to clock Jack in the side of the head and see the bright spill of blood, feel it hot and wet in my hands.

Jill began to scream. Not because we were fighting, and not because my dick was flopping around, but because Daryl's dark eyes were focused on something greater than us, scream-queen hair rising like static and her skin shivering, until there came a choking explosion of bugs and black smoke.

Follow the leader.

Perhaps I'd never really known the way to the storage room, because this time we were in a stairwell burrowed a million miles into the earth. It was pitch black, and all I could see around me were the crooked smiles of the two mouth-breathers and Daryl's glowing hair from the recent dye job. But something else was in this long dark hallway, something alive and pulsing.

Pupae. Cocoons. Larvae.

"She eats them whole," Jill said. "But only when Cris is with her."

I gagged at the thought. Not the one of the bugs.

"Will you stop talking about Daryl as if he isn't here?"

Sudden halt, sharp elbow thudding against my jaw. Smell so familiar.

"You all are fucking stupid. Stop calling me *he* or a *she.* No labels, ever."

Then we carried on, sticking close to one another, both mouth-breathers holding onto my leather coat, led by Daryl's smell and the gleam of his teeth. Loved both. So did he. They talked about transposition, hideousness and beauty. *It's about growing into the flower you never knew was you!* Daryl said. *I will not remain stagnant.*

Finally a sound. A click like a coqui frog. Sonorous song of the death-head moths. I felt a great wind come upon me, listened to the slide and stretch of them breaking from the chrysalis. I remembered what I had read, that they liked to hang upside down to let their wings dry before taking flight to feast on potatoes and flowers.

The storage room was rank as I remembered it, the light still guided by bubbling lava lamps that made neon shapes twist upon the walls. Families of pupae glittered and throbbed like a living blanket; billions of larvae crawled over my shoe; cocoons webbed in dust and decay swayed upon the ceiling.

I thought it queer that it was not cold down here, where the sun never shines; how is this place humid as a rainforest? But then my concentration was jarred by laughter, and Daryl lighting a fancy black cigarette.

"Did I say you two can talk?"

Ah, there's that serpent temper I'm used to.

"You're in withdrawal," the girl said. "Take something to feel better."

"I don't need those pills anymore," Daryl said. "I'm one of them now," pale sash of smoke wrapping around her.

"Show us," the twins said together.

Daryl's black eyes scanned the room. I knew within them that she was saying something as hollow as a good-bye. We would fight no more, fuck no more, be friends no more. But I needed him. Boy or girl or insect it didn't matter. There was no life I considered worth living without her.

Hands on the green-furred wall, pale as the pupae that she began to pluck and swallow whole. Daryl's skin lost all of its color, x-ray dark so that I could clearly see the grin of death beneath the parchment layer on her face.

"It's starting."

Jack took out a camera. I remained fixated on the acid trip of imagery unraveling. What else could I have done? If I stopped her she would have beat the shit out of me.

Daryl was slick with sweat; pain changed her face as something bubbled and roared beneath her skin. At the sound of her scream there came a blinding cloud of slime until the cocoon was complete.

Daryl, the only person I ever loved, was gone.

I kept a holy vigil at the site.

I dreamed nothing because I did not sleep. I envisioned delirious consequences of the transformation. I never heard from the twins again, last I remember was them kicking and screaming to get out of the storage room. For all the insanity they craved, once they claimed it, the reality was too scary for them to bear. Their existence is moot.

But one night I did sleep.

Everything was wet with milky insect placenta, my hands, my lips, my tongue. I did not know what time it was, but for some reason I knew it was night by the great pressure in my head. Above me Daryl still pale, a meaty cocoon, but then she started to come to life.

I saw her new leg poke through the center, leg more like a hand, and then the sharp antennae feeling for sweet dank air. She ripped herself from the shell. Alive, hanging upside down to dry her new filmy wings, using her huge black eyes to see me in a new light.

Beauty in transformation?

Death to the old soul.

And so what does one do when their dreams come true, forcing life to become ordinary? They keep growing and going, or they fall right back down.

2013

Afterword

Every time you pick up a book by J. Daniel Stone, you are at risk of transformation. Stone uses the subtle devices of horror and finely cleaved words to draw us into the thoughts, indeed the very juices, of others and we find ourselves intimate, engaged in strange and separate couplings.

Oh, but this book, these tales, are fiction, aren't they? Surely, no one has ever starved in mourning or taken drugs to journey to the edge of death in pursuit of the object of an obsession. The desire inside a chrysalis would never flare so bright as to sear the wings set to lift it. No one would piece together a temporary lover and kill their only friend to feed it, would they? Surely not.

Did Stone chronicle a dark underworld filled with artists who need a bump, [a drug, a drink, a cut] to get the magic flowing, wild creatives who aren't quite like you and I, or did he touch on the truth of a brief period of feral youth each of us must pass through? A time when the world's great books appear, as if freshly inked for you alone to discover. When music electrifies your skin and throbs through your solar plexus, pulsing your libido into overdrive. When drugs and sex are dark, forbidden and free to you, for you are special. When other people die [old people] but never you. And only love hurts.

Has Stone evoked nights you'd forgotten, has he re-constituted images erased from your conscious mind, or did he imprint you with another's psyche separated from you by only time or distance? Whatever witchery he has performed, now his tales are indelible memories. Believe me; I am afflicted.

As Tyria, I watched New York engrave its history on Dorian's arm. I've been Dorian. I've spent time too much time inside his head to ever forget him. As Jason, I flew down Tenth Avenue on my Mongoose bike seeking a con-nection to the dead. In yet another life, I hung suspended, inverted, wondering at the sight of Peter's tears as they flowed up toward the floor . . . and the quickening inside me stilled.

I was lustful Lucian, stupidly jealous of a god's atten-tion. I have been Rez, hearing things no one else can hear. As Delilah, butterfly blade in hand, I jumped the third rail, in search of the answer to life after death.

In harsh San Francisco, I feared for Joey, in all his cruel innocence, a lump in my throat . . . oh, but this book; these tales are fiction, aren't they? Please. Yes? No. Not really.

I've caught his characters' eyes, met them in quick startled glimpses as if through a broken glass. When I have been forced to set this book aside, I've looked into my mirror and been surprised to see myself, I was not Tyria, not Dorian; I did not have dreadlocks, dark snaky hair, black tattoos, or even the faintest of visible razor scars.

The sweat of Stone's characters is on you, you'll ache for the heat of their sex, thirst to taste the Jägermeister from their mouths on your tongue, and the sulfuric smell of the East River will haunt you like a primal pull toward hell. You'll long to feel the crush of strange bodies swaying in the dark as Delilah pours her dangerous songs into air so thick breathing becomes a transcendent experience.

J Daniel Stone has filled your head with his rich voice, gentled your uneasiness with beautiful words, and slid you through his dreamcatcher's rough lattice into a personal collection of nightmares. If you felt your skin abrading, relax, it was merely the opening of your mind.

Dona Fox

Sacramento
August 2017

Did you enjoy the book?

We welcome all feedback and queries.
Villipede.com

J. Daniel Stone writes from NYC, where he was born and raised. He is the author of the urban horror novels *The Absence of Light* and *Blood Kiss*, and the collaborative, stand-alone novella *I Can Taste The Blood*. In 2016 he was selected by readers to be included in *DREAD (The Best Horror of Grey Matter Press)*. He writes under a pseudonym to keep the wolves at bay.

www.ingramcontent.com/pod-product-compliance
Lightning Source LLC
Chambersburg PA
CBHW022153170626
46807CB00005B/2189

9780692980774